Listening to Jamal as he drove, Noelle found herself drawn to him. For a hot minute, she thought about reaching across the seat and drawing him into her arms to deliver the kiss she felt etched upon her lips. Silently, she chided herself. *You've got an entire evening to get through.*

Jamal parked carefully, and swung out of the car to open Noelle's door. She rose easily to stand near him. Her perfume drew him again. You've been lucky so far but don't rush it, he warned himself.

"Noelle!"

Noelle's head jerked in response to her name, and Jamal bent forward to catch the jacket she almost dropped. At his slight movement, Noelle turned her head. When their lips met with sweetly shocking brevity, they both tried to think of an immediate way to prolong the contact, but couldn't. Jamal moved away first, surprised by her gentle response. His lips burned desperately, branded by the accident.

Noelle stepped back, her eyes following Jamal. Her tongue lightly traced the trail of his kiss. Her upper lip still tingled from the brush of his mustache.

Noelle remembered her jacket and turned to take it from Jamal. Her fingers met his with an electrical jolt that rocked them both. She folded the jacket over her arm and carefully put her hand in his. A bold move for her, but he liked it. The evening was looking more promising by the minute.

# The Best
# For Last

## Gail McFarland

Pinnacle Books
Kensington Publishing Corp.
http://www.arabesquebooks.com

For my mother, who taught me how to dream,
and my proud father who shares the dreams.
For Shanika who always believed I could, and
Abbo who always knew I would.

PINNACLE BOOKS are published by

Kensington Publishing Corp.
850 Third Avenue
New York, NY 10022

First Printing: September, 1998
10 9 8 7 6 5 4 3 2

Printed in the United States of America

# One

"That does it," the round-faced woman said, looking over at her friend's still covered desk. "I'm done and God knows it's time to go. What've you got left that I can help you with?" Her fingers reached efficiently to the left side of Noelle's desk.

"Pat, go home!" Noelle didn't look up, but her hand found the pile of case records easily. Smiling, she looked up at her friend. "You've got enough to do without finishing up for me. Go home. The kids are waiting, you've got a cookout planned. . . ."

"Speaking of which," Pat backed into a chair and crossed her short legs at the knee, smoothing her cotton shirt as she spoke, "you never did let me know your plans." Both women looked around at the now-empty office. "The kids want to know if you're coming or not."

" 'The kids.' Right." Noelle got up from the desk, collecting files. Pulling open the drawer, she shoved the manila folders in one by one. "Thanks Pat, but I'll pass. Tell the kids I'll see them soon."

"Soon. That's what you always say." Pat tugged the strap of her shoulder bag from her desk drawer. "We've got plenty. Girl, I'm gonna make a red velvet cake. I've got ribs and chicken and some . . ."

"Potato salad, and anything else you can think of to seduce a hungry woman," Noelle laughed, "but, no." Alert dark brown eyes appraised her friend and coworker. "You feedin' the whole neighborhood again?" she drawled.

Pat ran her fingers through her short black hair. Tugging gently at the curls framing her face, she made her eyes big. "It needs to be done."

"I don't know how you do it. Two growing kids, house and car notes, and a paycheck barely larger than mine."

"You know how it is, bills have got to get paid, but you don't stop living. And sometimes you've gotta do it even if you have nothing to do it with."

Noelle nodded and laughed again. "Don't I know it."

Eyeing her friend, she knew they were thinking the same thing. Five years with the Department of Family and Children Services had shown them a lot about living. They had both seen enough at DFACS to know that they fared better than most, even with hard times behind them.

"Are you ready to go?" Pat broke into her reverie. She had keys in hand, purse on shoulder, and a bag under each arm. "I have to get my kids from my neighbor, feed them, put them to bed, then it'll be me in the kitchen 'til sometime after midnight."

They both listened to the *thunk* and then the following silence that meant the building air conditioning had shut down.

"Girl, I know you're coming out of here now. The air is off." Pat hummed to herself, "and in this heat!"

"You're right," Noelle stuffed the last of the folders into the cabinet. Pat watched her work.

"I'm not fooled, you know." Pat was doing her mother hen imitation. "You'll hang around that hot little apartment, eat things out of cans, and finish off a dozen paperbacks."

"No. I won't. Really. I'll buy a flag, watch the parade and fireworks on TV, and everything. Now, that's a proper celebration for Independence Day—right?"

Pat shifted her bags and rolled her eyes. "I'm gonna fix you a plate anyway. . . ." Still talking, she switched off the overhead fluorescent lights.

"Keep dinner. Just bring me dessert!" Noelle countered. "I'm right behind you—two minutes at most." She pulled her sweater off the back of her chair. "See you Tuesday."

"Two minutes? Yeah, I believe that! I'll talk to you before the weekend is out. You know I will." Pat warned, pushing the door open with her foot.

"You really ought to come over." Snakelike, Pat's head wove sassily, "it's not like you'll meet anybody you don't already know in your apartment!"

Trying to cover growing irritation, Noelle faked a whine. "I'm not going to do it. I already told you, I'm going to stay in, read, get some rest. I'll be fine. Okay?"

Pat's full lips tightened. "Maybe." Turning with quick, determined footsteps, she walked quickly back to Noelle's desk. "You stubborn cow. Give yourself a little credit."

Noelle could make anybody mad sometimes. Not that she was unduly mulish, but once she made up her mind, it was hard to get her to budge. Tucking one foot beneath her, Pat slid into the chair at the side of the desk. "You're scared."

"Thank you for wanting to protect me, but I don't need it. I'm a big girl, and I promise you, I'll be fine. Not lonely. Not scared. Fine."

"Scared. Noelle," Pat puffed in frustration, "the world is full of people who need to forget things in their lives, and can't. If you go over and over the same things, you wind up in a permanent funk, and what good does that do you or anybody else?"

"You've got a lot of nerve! In all the time we've been friends, you've never thrown my past up in my face, and to start now . . . it's cruel, mean . . . reprehensible! In fact, it's . . ."

Pat's hand on her shoulder halted the outburst. The touch, full of love and good intent, was both warm and calming. Looking at her friend, she paused wondering how to soften her next words.

Soft tendrils of dark, permed, shoulder-length hair had pulled loose in the Atlanta humidity and curled about Noelle's head. Cocoa skin, flushed with a dainty rose in the growing heat of the closed office. She looked soft, tenderly romantic, almost ethereally delicate.

"Look at you. I mean, all that's happened with you, your family, not to mention this job." Pat's eyes widened. "A lot of folks would be suicidal by now, or on drugs, but you've just gotten stronger—even if you are still afraid of that strength."

Looking away, not yet fully ready to forgive, Noelle collected another stack of folders for filing. "You know what they say, 'what doesn't kill you makes you stronger.' "

"And none of what you went through killed you. You survived growing up with your mother and stepdad, Wayne, and the mess that ran you to Atlanta. It's a choice you've made. Just like being alone. I mean," Pat shrugged, bullying her way past obvious frustration. "You took the blows. You got past the hard part. That makes you a survivor, but now you've got to learn that living is more than just surviving.

"Like you know? You were hiding behind your pregnant belly when I met you. Your son was just a little tyke, and things weren't exactly . . ."

"Yeah, like I do know." Pat tried to hold onto her relentlessly cheerful, professional caseworker smile, but the gentle curves of her cheeks and brow were shadowed with remembered pain, determination, and urgency.

Five years ago, then twenty-seven-year-old Pat had been reeling from the recent horrible death of James, Sr. Her fireman husband had been called a hero for rushing into the burning warehouse, pulling out the homeless men. A hero for dying on what should have been his day off.

As she and her young son stood at the mayor's side accepting the posthumous award for bravery and service, Pat had been angry with James for deserting her. Even now, sitting tensely in Noelle's worn wooden chair, she remembered wanting to fling that bit of silver and ribbon into the brave smiling faces of the fire's survivors.

Unconsciously, her fingers curled then flexed with the memories. James was still gone. Leaving her with his babies. She'd almost hated him, and had awakened screaming from fiery nightmares for months after his death. Losing the father of her children, the bedrock of her life, was hard. Losing the man she had grown to womanhood loving, was harder. Making peace with the cold side of her bed, and the loss of his touch had taken every minute of the last five years.

Reminiscing with the children had been easier than she'd thought. James, Jr., proudly accepted the fact that they shared a name, and that his daddy was a hero—the medal and photos of the funeral proved it. Kelly, who would never know him as more than mythical Daddy, accepted him as more than a mere mortal: He was Superman, Batman, and all of the X-Men rolled into one.

And on cold nights, Pat's hand still swept the cold, empty spot her husband's warmth had once filled.

James wanted her to find someone else—not be alone if something should happen to him. He had told her so, over and over before the fire. She could almost hear his strong, laughing voice scolding her.

"If anything happens to me," he would say, "find someone else. I love you too much to see you alone, wasting your life. You need people."

She had leaned closer to kiss him, her full stomach pressing against his firm chest. "I hate it when you talk like that," she had whispered.

"But, the possibility is a fact of life in my line of work. You can't ignore it, Sweetface." His arms had been comforting and safe. She had felt secure in knowing nothing bad would ever touch her there. "So," James had continued, "promise me. If anything ever happens, promise me you'll go on. Promise me!"

And she had softly given her promise, every time he asked her to. Now, mostly because of her promise, she found herself occasionally dating and joining church and community groups. Nobody she'd met had come up to her standards—yet. But James was right, life did go on, and the only way to live it was as an active participant. Maybe that was one of the reasons she and Noelle had become such good friends, and now was the time to share the lesson.

"But, I did survive it," Pat continued. Her body seemed to vibrate with her fervor, "I learned, I healed."

"And you did it alone."

"Not all alone Noelle. Nobody ever does."

Remembrance of her year-old son and the fullness of her then-pregnant belly, Pat's hand now strayed to her still rounded, slack-muscled stomach. James, Jr., had been so little then, barely walking. Her family down in Grier, Georgia had urged her to come home, bring the kids and rest in the smothering bosom of its collective love.

Tempting as it was, she'd remembered her promise, and instinctively known that going home was the wrong move. Instead, she'd waited for Kelly's birth, then held her children closer, and clung to her job. DFACS, and all its related tragedies and melodramas had become her life raft to independence, with a towline to sanity.

Noelle heaved a sigh, and sat deliberately straighter in her chair. Her arms crossed tightly under her breasts. "I need some quiet time. I'm not coming to your house."

Pat fanned a denying hand. "Don't round off on me, girl. I knew the day I met you, that you were special, and I couldn't have been more right. When they called me from the shelter you were staying at, they told me you were attractive and well groomed. They never said that you were intelligent, and capable. Hell, nobody had to tell me that. I could see it. It was written all over you.

"I could tell by the way you handled James, little as he was, that you had more love and tenderness in you than the law allows. Girl, you need a family, children, a dog! You need to share all that love with somebody—something else."

"I'm very satisfied with my life and my job. I've made a place for myself here."

Pat's arms, unconsciously echoing her friend's, crossed her full breasts in tight, silent denial.

"I am satisfied," Noelle tried to sound convincing.

"You need a child in your life—and a man. Someone to love and devote some of that love to."

"We've talked about that Pat."

"Wrong! I've talked about it, and you haven't listened—at least not so I could tell."

Noelle dropped the files and leaned against the wall. "I've told you before, I never saw myself as a single parent. Besides, I've always heard that it was difficult . . ."

"You're blowing smoke. You're a caseworker, and you know better. Single people adopt all the time, and you're a great candidate. Maybe not for an infant, but there's a child out there who needs you."

"No. I don't even want to talk about this. It's just not meant to be."

"Shoot," Pat drew the word out derisively. "You need to get over that anger. Put it behind you."

"I am not angry!"

"Right!"

"I am not!"

"Are too! You're still trying to get over things that did or didn't happen when you were a kid. Stuff that still pisses you off—you're angry. If you're still wishing you could have had some kind of major revenge against your ex—you're angry."

"I told you, I'm not angry!"

"Have it your way then, just come out to the house."

"Go home and leave me alone!"

Raising her hands in surrender, Pat shifted for comfort. "If you still feel that badly about it, you shoulda stuck the bastard up for alimony," she muttered.

"Wayne? Don't talk foolish, I'm lucky I didn't get stuck paying him."

"Okay," Pat shifted again, easing her now tingling foot to the floor. Standing gingerly, leaning on the desk, she looked down at Noelle. "I'm still your friend, and the kids and I still love you. We'll be there whenever you need us, but you need more than just us, Noelle. You really do."

"I feel sorry for your kids. They have to put up with maternal overkill on a daily basis." Noelle shook her head in mock dismay. "Go on home and get your kids together."

Pat smiled, the woman was incorrigible—as usual. Obviously, there was no way to save her from herself. "I'm gonna call you. You know I will." She let the threat carry her out the door.

As her friend left, Noelle felt her smile slowly fade, kind of like a Cheshire cat. She couldn't help herself, even as she changed her shoes and collected her purse. Truth was, Pat and the kids were all the family she had left.

"For all her nagging, it's good to have a friend like Pat. Someone who cares."

# Two

"This is pitiful." Bringing her thumb and forefinger together, Noelle looked at her right hand and thought of the old joke she'd learned in school. *Know what this is?* Watching, she rubbed the fingers together, *it's the world's smallest violin, and it's playing for you.* "For me and my wasted self-pity."

Maybe, Noelle thought, she only did this to remind herself of how far she'd come and how much things had changed. She'd had friends before. Casual friends, but never anyone she could count on. Pat was different, one-of-a-kind and completely loyal.

Pat's holiday plans triggered memories of summers past. Swimming, cookouts, family parties, family things—except Noelle no longer had a family. Pat was right. It would be nice to have someone else in her life.

"I've got to admit it," she whispered softly, "one is an awfully lonely number."

It was her own choice, and her own doing. Leaving had been the only thing to do. At least she was free, and you couldn't miss what you'd never had.

Or, so they said. She felt betrayed for a moment, then thought better of it. Self-pity was a waste of time.

The still air was growing warmer by the minute. The silence of the empty office seemed to bounce off cheaply plastered, institutional green walls. Dust collected in narrow corners, and around stacked cardboard boxes of case records. Filtered, late afternoon sunlight crawled lazily along the far wall, picking out fingerprints and scuff marks from chairbacks. Noelle turned back to her desk in the dim office.

Sitting, she drew a blank piece of paper from the pile in the corner and began a letter. She tried to write regularly, and had written the last one just before Easter. Sometimes it didn't make sense to keep writing. It wasn't as though she would get an answer, nor did she expect one. Intentionally, she never included a return address.

Besides, they had never been interested in what she had had to say—before. Maybe it was just the protocol of politeness. Maybe, deep inside, she still wanted to care, wanted them to care. A reminder of childhood.

" 'Scuse me. Ma'am?" Startled, Noelle looked up as the office door pushed open.

" 'Scuse me?" Mr. Jackson, the maintenance man, peeked around the corner. "Sorry to bother you, but before you leave," he stepped around the door. "There's somebody needs to see you."

"Uh, see me?" Noelle ventured. The child stood slightly behind him, round-eyed and silent.

"Nobody else around," Mr. Jackson looked around for effect.

"Who is she?"

"She won't say." Mr. Jackson scratched his closely shaven head.

Feeling like the straight person in a bad vaudeville act, Noelle watched him smile down at the little girl as he urged her forward.

"Where did she come from?" Noelle asked, coming closer.

"Don't know," he replied.

"Where'd you get her?" Noelle was getting tired of the game.

"Yonder. Sitting in the lobby." Before Noelle could ask, he added, "she was by herself and she won't say nothing. Ain't it funny? Little thing like this, all alone?"

"I'm sure she can't be all alone. Her mother or someone must be nearby. Maybe, in the rest room?"

"No ma'am. I already checked."

The little girl, an obviously patient child, was thin, probably small for her age. She had haunted dark eyes, and thick shoulder-length braids. Standing, quietly observing her surroundings, she didn't seem to be waiting for anyone. As Noelle came closer, the child's eyes became wary, but she said nothing and made no move to escape.

"Are you lost?" Short lashes swept down, then up, but not a word passed her lips.

Kneeling, Noelle looked at her more closely. Maybe, she thought, English is not her native language. She tried halting, mostly forgotten high school Spanish, and the child's brow furrowed. Still, she didn't speak.

Three, maybe four years old, she was wearing a well-laundered floral cotton short set, anklets, and high topped tennis shoes. All of her clothes seemed just a little too large for such a small girl. Her braided hair sported a variety of colorful barrettes. Noelle's hand strayed to the child's hair and then her soft brown cheek, she visibly relaxed at the touch.

"She took a likin' to you," Mr. Jackson announced. "Guess you'll take it from here." He scraped a hand over stubble on his cheek and flashed tobacco-stained teeth. "Y'all 'scuse me, I got to get back to work."

Noelle watched him hurry off. She smiled at the child, "Hi, I'm Noelle. What's your name?"

No answer. Instead, the child stood still and passive. She continued to stand, waiting, as Noelle checked her clothing for identification—nothing.

"Where's Mommy? Daddy?" she tried hopefully—nothing. "You're very pretty," Noelle tried.

The child's rosebud mouth trembled then quirked in a small smile. She spread her hands and smoothed her shorts, smiling, trusting. Heartened by the response, Noelle guessed the child's hearing was fine.

"Well honey, we've got to do something with you," she returned to her desk. The little girl followed her example and climbed onto the chair beside Noelle's desk. Noelle grinned broadly. "You're cooperative if nothing else." Big eyes watched her carefully.

"You're really pretty brave. I think I'd be scared if I were left alone. . . ." God, she hoped the child wouldn't cry. Everything probably seemed awfully big and scary to her.

Noelle folded her letter, stuffed it, and addressed the envelope as she talked. She'd drive out to Bremen or Newnan over the weekend to mail it. The child was almost unnaturally poised and quiet.

"Most kids your age would be screaming bloody murder," Noelle said as much to herself as to the girl. "I guess you were taught otherwise." *Like me.*

The wall clock ticked loudly. A quick glance showed they'd waited nearly an hour.

"If I had somebody like you, I'd know where you were," she murmured, tenderly touching the child's smooth arm. Alert, the child's dark eyes flashed to meet Noelle's.

Abruptly, there was a new sound in the room—tiny, irregular rumbling. It caught Noelle off guard. "You're hungry!" Fine, softly fuzzy eyebrows lifted.

Rummaging through her purse and desk drawer, Noelle scrounged up an orange, a dollar and seventy-eight cents in coins, three Lifesavers, and a battered packet of hot cocoa mix. The little girl watched the growing assortment with interest.

"Not great, huh?" No answer. Standing, Noelle offered her hand, "Why don't we see what's over here in the machines . . . maybe we'll find something good to go with this orange."

Still silent, the child hesitated briefly, then scooted and wiggled her way out of the chair to stand next to the tall, slender woman. Noelle held her breath, hoping the child would trust her. Another vague hesitation, and the tiny hand rested moistly in hers. To calm them both, Noelle continued to talk, her voice light and pleasant.

Passing the wall switch, Noelle turned on the bright overhead lights and they made their way to the vending machines.

"Okay girlfriend, what'll it be?"

The little girl looked up at Noelle, the light highlighting her rounded baby cheeks and the dark fuzziness of her eyebrows. Noelle pointed to the machine and squinted against the glare, trying to find semi-neat, child-size cookies or chips.

"How about these," she pointed. She really hadn't expected an answer, but was surprised to find she was talking to herself.

"Oh great!" She looked at the rows of wooden chairs lined across the center of the office lobby. "I've lost a lost child."

Walking to the counter that usually separated secretaries from clients, she was aware of how quiet it was. Her heels tapped loudly against the tile floor.

"Where are you?" Her voice was a raspy stage-whisper. It seemed wrong to speak too loudly in the empty space. Peeking over the counter, she hoped to see the top of a tiny head—no such luck.

"Girlfriend, where did you go?" She turned to go back to her desk. Maybe the child had returned to sit there; she hoped. A whispery brush of cloth caught her attention before she could move. The sound repeated, drawing her attention to the play area set up in the waiting room.

Kneeling on the floor, amid an array of dolls and other toys, the little girl curiously handled each toy. After a few moments, she pulled out a lanky green figure. Noelle smiled quietly, watching as she recognized it. Patiently, the child unfolded and smoothed the stuffed felt body. Her fingers traced the wide grinning red mouth and touched the huge eyes. A satisfied sigh preceded the gentle smile on her face as she folded Kermit into the crook of her small arms.

Finally remembering the child was hungry, Noelle fed coins into the machine. She thought about the child's simple needs. Food and affection—she was even willing to accept the love of a stuffed animal in the absence of her parents.

What the girl needed was her real mother or father. The thought was a natural reflex. She needed someone who cared enough not to abandon her.

Noelle collected the cookies she'd selected and punched a button for milk. Maybe this brave, silent little girl lived with her grandmother or an aunt. So where was the missing grandmother or aunt? Surely they'd missed the child by now. *Until somebody showed up, she has me,* Noelle told herself.

The thought was pleasant—oddly warming. At the agency, she'd seen her share of women, with unwanted children. You couldn't take them all home—no matter how much you might want to. If she had the money though, Noelle knew she'd work with those children. Show them how very wanted they really were. Maybe even help those parents learn how to want their children. She shook her head, canceling the thoughts.

Pat had been right, even though Noelle knew she would deny it to her grave. Noelle was so ready to love that it hurt.

She'd planned her imaginary future family for years. Even now, just thinking about them, her arms ached to hold her babies. At night, in her lonely bed, she craved the companionship of a man who would be more than a transient lover. She craved someone who would be with her for both good and bad times.

"Fifty years of happily ever after," she prayed softly. "Is that so much to ask?"

She risked thinking about things that had been denied her by twists of fate. With Wayne, she had hoped to build a family and do all the things she'd never done with her mother and stepfather.

Pat kept telling her the right man was going to "just come along," and if he did, Noelle wanted to grow old with him, have babies with him, and make at least fifty years of good, loving memories with him.

So far, she wasn't even close. Holding the cookies and milk at her breast, Noelle watched her child playing. Funny, how easily and comfortably that thought had slipped through her defenses. She'd begun automatically thinking of this beautiful, silent child as *her* baby.

It was silly. She didn't even know this kid's name, but that didn't stop her from feeling maternal and protective. Maybe, she mused, that just goes to prove that you don't have to have a baby to be a mother.

*Like my mom,* Noelle thought with a twinge of bitterness. Mattie was married too young, to a boy in the Air Force, who'd died in cold Korean mud, for a country that found him too dark.

She'd had a baby too soon, at a time when miniskirts were all the rage, and pregnancy was not considered kinky, kicky, or cute. Not, of course, that she didn't care. She just wasn't interested. She'd given her daughter a cute name, and dressed her well, figuring those were all the tools any girl needed to get along in the world.

Young, pretty, and hot for excitement, Mattie Parker had found more interesting company in wealthy Louis Perry. The moment she met him, she knew he would protect and care for her in all the ways she needed and deserved.

From earliest childhood, Mattie had known she possessed the skill to bind men to her. She knew that the curve of her hip and the lilt in her voice drew men to her like iron filings to a magnet. After marriage, she'd learned other skills that kept Louis loyally by her side.

Twenty years older, Louis Perry saw mother and daughter as toys. He adored and pampered his spoiled wife, but Noelle wasn't *his* child. He was good to her, never unkind. Materially supportive, fatherhood only nicked his surface. Generously, mother and stepfather allowed Noelle the privilege of visiting *their* real life.

From childhood, Noelle never fully escaped the feeling of having been tacked on to form *the family;* making Louis and Mattie look good in public was her prime function. Mattie Parker Perry—her mother, Louis's wife. Noelle supposed she should be grateful Mattie at least acknowledged her first husband, even if she only did it to be socially acceptable. It proved her accessory-child was a legitimate trinket, not a bastard.

Shrugging off mournful abstraction, Noelle found a handful of paper napkins on the receptionist's desk. The child was still on the floor, dolls waiting patiently before her.

"I think we can have a snack now," Noelle smiled and extended her hand. Bright eyes, still keen with caution traveled from Noelle's hand to her face and back again.

Trust won. The tiny, warm, baby hand slipped into hers. Noelle stepped toward her desk, and the girl refused to move, looking longingly over her little shoulder. Noelle followed her gaze.

"Of course, if you think Kermit will miss you, you must bring him along." The smile was still spreading as the child swooped on the toy.

# Three

"Is it good?"

She blinked in answer.

Using both hands to hold the milk carton, the child sucked happily at the straw, occasionally nodding at nothing in particular. She was so content, she even offered some to Kermit. Apparently he refused, so she finished it while Noelle peeled the orange. Coaxing her child to eat the cookies was only a little more difficult. She kept offering them to Noelle.

"Thank you, but you should eat them," she told the child. Charmed with the child's manners, Noelle tried to figure out what to do with this lovely baby.

"Can you tell me your name? Do you know where you live?" She asked patiently and was rewarded by raised eyebrows. "Do you have sisters or brothers?" earned her a large, clear-eyed stare.

Still trying, Noelle lifted the doll from the child's lap. "This is Kermit," she wiggled the doll to hold the child's attention. "My name," she pointed to her chest, "is Noelle. Noelle Parker." Pointing to the child, "you?" The child yawned and squirmed in her seat.

"Yeah, I know." The clock said seven-fifty. "It's been a long day." Noelle kicked off her shoes and sat forward in her chair. "Girlfriend, we've got to figure out what to do and you're not helping me much." The girl rubbed her eyes and swallowed a yawn.

"Everybody in Child Protective Services is probably gone, but let's take a walk and see." The child waited quietly as Noëlle collected her sweater, shoes, and purse. "I hope somebody's there. I don't know what else to do if they're not . . ."

"Come on." She collected the child's hand. "If anyone is looking for you, they'll find us there."

She flicked the wall switch as they walked out of the office. The heavy click of the locking door felt a lot like the sealing of fate. The woman, the child, and Kermit climbed the stairs.

Child Protective Services. Three flights up, and light-years away from the reason anybody worked in social service.

Noelle didn't like taking these stairs. Ever. She'd heard rumors of illicit sex and more in the stairwell, just upstairs from the satellite police office on the first floor. A caseworker had been roughed up on this flight about a month ago. The client had been angry about changes in food-stamp regulations.

Air conditioners had been off for a while and the hot stairwell stank of urine and ammonia. Noelle looked down. The child's nose wrinkled distastefully, but if Noelle went, she was following.

As they slowly climbed the stairs, Noelle realized that she was one of the lucky ones. This stairwell was only a path from one floor to the next for her. It wasn't a place she had to go just to make ends meet. She was managing to make a life for herself in one of the most vivacious, and controversial cities in the country; in spite of the easily accessible squalor.

Atlanta had always appealed to her, in spite of its contradictions. Noelle liked the seductively balmy weather, and the expansive feel of growth and unlimited potential she felt driving down Peachtree Street, or lunching in Buckhead.

She liked that the city was homey too. Walks along Auburn Avenue, or through the historical Atlanta University campus, saying "hey" to friendly strangers, made her appreciate her ethnicity. It made her feel she had roots. Yes, Noelle loved Atlanta with an earned passion. It often felt like the biggest small town in the world, to her.

But, for all its diametric oppositions, Atlanta was a city—a big modern city—and she'd had no better reasons for coming here when she had nothing else to lose.

Noelle had fled her comfortable, gilded life in panic with scarcely a backward glance. She had hacked away her past, giving up a lot materially, but learning in the process that autonomy and self-respect were worth the effort.

Still trudging gamely beside Noelle, the little girl clutched Kermit and silently climbed the stairs, oblivious to Noelle's silent musings.

"One more flight," she told her little companion. Woman and child paused before climbing further. The child yawned hugely. She was exhausted. This must have been a long, eventful day for her.

At the third-floor landing, Noelle pulled at the heavy fire door. Locked. Now it was her turn to hesitate. She stared at the door. Two options: walk back to the first floor with a weary child, and try telephoning for help, or knock and hope somebody was on the other side. She looked at the fatigued child and chose number two.

Noelle raised her fist and vigorously pounded the metal door. The little girl responded by squeezing Noelle's hand and blinking up at her. Noelle smiled to reassure the girl and pounded again. "Somebody's coming," she promised.

Stepping back, they waited. Finally, the door creaked open.

"Oh, I thought I heard banging out here." The man peered around the edge of the door.

Noelle bit back the sharp retort teetering on the tip of her tongue. It wouldn't do to restate the obvious.

"You an' the kid wanna come on in?"

Not trusting herself to respond to this very articulate gentleman, Noelle simply nodded and pushed herself and the child past him, and through the massive door.

Disoriented by bright light after the dimness of the stairwell, Noelle stopped walking and stared around the office. A lot like her own unit, it was decorated in antique institutional. Musty, scarred beige and brown walls seemed to absorb the light struggling through watermarked, dusty windows. Worn metal desks, battered chairs, and scuffed floors showed signs of their occupants hasty departure.

She watched two uniformed police officers cross the murky, brown linoleum, leaving with a sheaf of papers. Heads close together and voices low, their expressions were intent—obviously their task would not be a pleasant one.

Tensing, the child sensed a change in Noelle, and looked up with questions written across her face. Fragile little fingers wiggled, then tightened. Noelle patted the small hand she still held, and tried to smile reassuringly.

"Well, girlfriend . . . let's see if we can get a little help here."

"Tom, look at the regulations!" Three men on the other side of the office were talking furiously.

"Jamal, we've got to take the human expense into consideration here. Tell him. Make him understand!"

"It's not me you've got to convince. Judge Miller's not going to accept some half-baked . . ."

"Half-baked!" Their posture and agitated hand motions told Noelle the conversation was a heavy one.

When the telephone rang, the men scowled at it in reflexive unison. They were so involved, they probably didn't know she was there.

Looking closely, Noelle recognized only the man perched on the edge of the gray metal desk. She didn't know his name, but he worked in the building. Regular caseworkers, like her, didn't often mix with the elite CPS workers.

One long leg dangling, he talked on the phone. Scratching notes on a yellow legal pad, he relayed information to the other two men. She watched them rake through the big black notebooks that held the Child Protective Services's regulations.

Noelle's eyes swept the room again. Though emptied of its regular staff, there was a feeling of constant motion in the sordid, open room. How could they stay so active in this heat, she wondered. A trickle of sweat rolled down the center of her back.

*Where is my mind!* Noelle could have slapped herself for forgetting. As many referrals as she'd made over the years, she should have remembered, weekends and holidays, all the CPS calls were referred through the police department. These men were the only people who might be able to help her. Cautiously, she walked in their direction.

But the child had other ideas. Instead of following, she put on brakes and tried to wrench her hand free.

"Damn!"

One of the men slammed the thick black manual to the metal desk. The child stiffened, prepared to flee.

Noelle, belongings shifting and sliding, knelt next to the twisting child. "Honey," she coaxed, "it's okay. I'm with you. There's nothing to be afraid of . . ."

The child's fear-filled eyes looked hopefully up at her, and Noelle brushed at the droplets of perspiration beading her hairline. Pulling the still-silent little girl into the circle of her arms, Noelle continued to try to comfort her.

Another phone rang. The three men argued, flipped pages, and wrote furious notes. Obviously, they were in a world of their own making and from the look of it, there was trouble in that world.

One of the men, still unaware of Noelle and the child, shrugged impatiently out of his jacket. Though aimed at the chair, the jacket slid across lazily, landing mostly on the dusty floor. He didn't notice, and without thinking, snatched his way out of the confinement of his colorful tie.

Noelle heard random bits drifting off the buzzing conversation of the men. This sterile, hard-edged room, with three obsessed men wasn't an ideal place to leave her child. Clearly, the little girl had sensed it too. She was obviously ready to go.

Kneeling again, Noelle looked at the still fearful girl. "We're leaving now. We won't stay here, okay?"

Standing, Noelle gave a hopeful smile. *Looks like I've already made a decision. Legal or otherwise. And, it's probably against the law. Probably?* Her swift glance swept the office again. *There's no choice. I'm taking her.*

Besides, there weren't any other available choices tonight. She wasn't about to leave her baby here in this hostile place—the child was coming home with her. She'd think of something else later.

Noelle bent, scooped the child into her welcoming arms and turned to look for the nearest exit.

"Can we help you?"

Noelle froze. The voice was strong, male, and inquiring. Startled by its authority, she turned slowly to face its owner.

It was the jacket man.

His eyes narrowed darkly, holding her startled gaze and forming an opinion. Though his face held no particular expression, Noelle felt trapped—like a robber cornered with stolen goods. Her mind beat and plunged, flailing for a good plausible reason for being here. At this hour. With a child. She felt her mouth open and close.

She had to say something. There was no way to simply step around him and go on her merry way. He was too imposing for that. Noelle had the feeling that this was a man of strength and power. Possessing more than the authority of intellect, he seemed to absorb his surroundings. He filled her field of vision.

Tall and broad shouldered, his body suggested fitness was a way of life for him. Beneath his well-cut shirt and slacks, she could see that his body was sturdy and well-muscled. His ease of movement suggested athletic activity. Black hair, cut stylishly close, coiled furiously about his head with a dusting of silver at his temples. It was so attractively placed, Noelle wondered if he had it done.

There was a cocky, unmistakably aggressive attitude to his stance that told her he was both physical and vigorous. For some odd reason, that made her nervous. She didn't like that he made her nervous.

It gave him an advantage over her. Implied, perhaps, but an advantage all the same. She didn't like that his assurance seemed to give him the right to make her nervous. She felt her skin prickle in response to his nearness, and she didn't like it. Her resentment was growing by the second.

"Do you need help?" He placed special emphasis on *need*.

Noelle shifted the child in her arms before answering. Tightening her grip at the back of Noelle's neck, the girl pressed her damp face close. She was still afraid. For better or worse, Noelle was committed now.

"No." Noelle, carefully standing well away from him, raised her head in determination. She didn't *need* anything from this man. "No," she repeated, "I work in the building." She jammed her hand into her purse to dig out and display her ID badge.

"I'm a caseworker and I just wanted to see if anyone else had stayed as late as I had." She giggled nervously, and hoped the lie would work. When he raised his eyebrows in response, her stomach lurched. He's not buying this, she worried. Just please, she prayed silently, let this story be good enough to scrape by.

"Well, as usual, we're here holding down the fort." He still looked skeptical.

His heavy-lidded eyes seemed to be riveted to the child, looking a little too closely. Unwillingly, Noelle took a step backward, giving ground. *I've got to get out of here,* she thought. *What'll I do if he asks her name? Say, I'm Noelle, and this is Jane Doe?*

"I'm calling it a night," she said. "Enjoy your holiday." Her voice was hurried but polite as she averted her eyes and moved toward the stairs again.

"Here. Let me help you. You've got your arms full." Noelle's heart sank. He was reaching for the child! She back-stepped, angling the girl away from his open hands.

"She's almost asleep. It's better if I carry her." Almost on cue, the child's breathing slowed, and her body relaxed naturally against Noelle's chest.

He accepted her statement with a sideways look. "The night elevator's over here."

He led her around the corner and pressed the button for her.

"By the way," he looked down at her, over the child's head, "I'm Jamal Harris."

He paused, waiting for her to offer her name. Instead, she dropped her eyes to the gentle rise and fall of the child's back.

Noelle almost wept with relief when the elevator finally arrived.

"Are you sure I can't carry her for you?"

"No. Really. We'll be fine." His offer to help seemed sincere, but Noelle still felt intimidated. Besides, what did she know about this Jamal Harris? She had no reason to trust him or his offer to help. She shifted the child again, watching sleepy eyes flutter.

Jamal's eyes changed slightly and he nodded to her. There was no reason to push the issue, but he followed her onto the elevator, anyway. He wasn't the kind of man to force his attentions on any woman, but this woman piqued his interest. He had a feeling that he wanted to know her and she wasn't making it easy.

"So, you work in this building." He was trying to be polite, but she walked faster. "I get assigned to this office a couple of times each month."

Noelle wished he'd just go away.

On the main floor, he matched her step for quick step. He opened the door. Passing close to him, Noelle felt her skin tingle—like passing through an electrical field. *It's the humidity,* she told herself. *Maybe a storm coming up.* Taking her keys from her hand, he opened her car door.

As she slipped into the driver's seat, he got a good, careful look at her. She was pleasing to look at. Her soft hair looked classically feminine, warm almond-shaped eyes tilted coyly at their corners, the generous, full-lipped mouth looked ripe for lush kisses and pouty smiles.

Watching, he tried to be discreet as she pulled her long, well-toned leg into the car. She checked the child again, then tugged the seat belt into place, and he realized she was getting away.

"Here's my card." It materialized in his fingers with the grace of a stage illusion. He placed it in her slender cocoa-colored hand, ". . . If you change your mind."

She slammed the car door shut, and asked through the open window, "Change my mind about what?"

"Needing help." He slipped his hands into his pockets as he watched her reaction.

Noelle's skin colored warmly, as she turned her key in the ignition. "Good night Mr. Harris."

Head turned to avoid looking at him, she pulled out of the parking lot. His card still rested in her hand and she tossed it onto the seat beside her.

Every man in Atlanta has a card, she told herself.

Jamal stood watching her taillights make their way down MLK Drive. That was one complicated lady. He was sure she had a problem, but she was a caseworker. Surely she knew how to handle any problem that might come up. He shook his head at the thought. Couldn't have been the little girl. The kid looked healthy and cared for.

He turned back to the building, walking slowly in the sultry evening. Whatever the question, he'd bet she hadn't found the answer tonight.

# Four

Safe in her car, the sleeping child at her side, Noelle took in a huge lungful of steamy summer air. Blowing out hard, she arranged green, grinning Kermit on the seat between them, while she tried to calm herself. The damp, sleeveless navy linen dress clung to every curve of her body in the heat, and the humid air rushing through the window wasn't helping. Stopped for the traffic signal, she rolled the car windows up, and turned on the air conditioner.

Cool air blowing, Noelle draped her sweater across the still-sleeping child. As the light changed, she centered raging thoughts on the man she'd just left.

Jamal Harris was the reason for a lot of the heat she was feeling. She wasn't sure what it was about him that caused it. It could have simply been his enigmatic presence—the way he seemed to absorb and reflect the light and air surrounding him.

"This makes no sense at all," she chided herself. "You might as well put him out of your mind. He's not your type."

That wasn't exactly true, and her traitorous mind was trying hard to force her to acknowledge it. Any man *that* tall and good-looking, with a voice like his . . . well, if he wasn't her type . . .

"Besides," she tried to soothe herself, "it's not like you'll ever see him again." That's not exactly true, her devious mind insisted. Didn't he say he sometimes worked in the building?

She didn't really know what kind of man Jamal was. She only knew that she wasn't going to *let* him be her type. That type of smooth, good-looking, socially schooled, urbane man was always seen in upscale magazine ads and Sunday paper society photos wearing designer suits, smiling into the heavily mascaraed eyes of slinky, sensual, drop-dead beautiful women. Not women who led day-to-day lives like hers.

That kind of man led a life of intrigue, season passes to pro ball games, and the jazzy parties she'd never be invited to. He was the kind of man who usually left her stammering and embarrassed. A man of casual, temporary suspense and charm. She really didn't care for his arrogance, either. The man was cocky, and too assured of his manhood, too absolutely in charge to be any good, she rationalized. Good for what? Does it matter?

*The man works my nerves and makes me itch,* she griped silently. She rubbed at her bare shoulder, and tried to concentrate on driving.


"Okay, we've done all we can do here." Morgan dropped the heavy CPS manual back on the desk. "Besides Jamal, man you've been out of focus ever since that lady came through here."

"Yeah, she was pretty too," Tom chimed in. "Cute little kid. I think she works here in the building."

"Smart kid," Morgan smirked.

"Smartass, I meant the woman. I've seen her around. I didn't know she had kids . . ."

"Well do you know if she's married or anything?" Jamal asked, hoping he was being subtle. He really hated to follow up with, "So . . . what's her name?"

The other two men grinned at each other, dark faces twitching as they tried not to laugh out loud.

"You followed her all the way to her car so you could come back up here to ask *us* her name?"

Tom propped his chin on a fisted hand and grinned broadly. Morgan reached for his own humidity wilted jacket from the back of Tom's chair, winking over his shoulder. "That's real clever, brother."

"So?" Morgan turned to face Tom, "You work here. The man asked you a question. Spill it!"

"Well, you know I like you both, and I'd tell you anything I know." Tom was still grinning. "What was it you wanted to know, anyway?"

"Keep your day job, man," Jamal said drily.

"You'll never make it in stand-up comedy," Morgan finished.

Tom smirked, looking from one of the men to the other. They were of equal size, although Jamal with his broad chest and back was the more muscular of the two. They also shared the predatory economy of movement typical of performance athletes. Tom paused to roll his shirtsleeves again before answering.

"I think her name is Nicole or Noelle or . . ."

"Thanks." Obviously, Tom wasn't going to be any help. Exasperated, Jamal grabbed his briefcase and jacket. "I'll see you guys next week."

He should have known better than to ask.

Morgan watched his friend walk away. He and Jamal were old pals, former roommates, and fraternity brothers. They had gone to Douglas High School together, pledged Alpha Phi Alpha during their sophomore year at Morehouse, then gone on to the Emory University Law School. They had even planned their tenure with the Department of Human Resources together.

In all those years, Jamal Harris remained the most goal-oriented, focused person Morgan Dennison had ever met. Especially where women were concerned. Jamal made it manly to say that he was waiting for the right woman to come into his life. He made it plain she was going to have to have more than a pretty face, a good body, and an agreeable personality.

"A complement . . . you know, in the mathematical sense . . . that's what I'm looking for," he'd said the night before Morgan's own wedding. "I want a woman who fills in all the empty spaces in me, and I fill in all the empty places in her."

They were drinking at Dante's, at Underground, and Morgan was trying to talk his friend into joining him by committing to marriage with whoever the girl of the week was.

" 'Til I find her, I can wait," Jamal had insisted.

He'd been waiting for a while. Morgan laughed at himself; *I'd have done better to wait too.* Thinking of Kiandra, he chuckled again. *No way was she my complement. Heck, she didn't even like being my wife.* They had divorced eight months later, and Jamal had been there to see him through that too. If this mystery woman was the right one, Morgan knew nobody deserved her more than his friend.

Lifting his warm, almost forgotten canned drink, he toasted Jamal's back. "You deserve the best my man, and I hope she's it."

Shifting gears to move away from the traffic light, Noelle thought she heard an unfamiliar sound.

*"Sip, sip, sip."* It seemed to follow her down the street. She pulled into the nearest service station—closed. Curious, she stepped from the car to find her front tire rapidly deflating.

"Don't panic. You know how to change a flat." At least, she knew how, in principle.

Turning back to the car, she checked on the child and set the emergency brake. She popped the lock on her trunk and got out her jack and her spare.

"Okay, the hardest part of this has got to be getting the hubcap off," she promised herself as she promptly broke two fingernails. The metal disk finally surrendered and clattered to the ground at her feet. She cast a baleful look at the closed service station then began to work on the lugs holding the tire in place.

She levered and pulled, and the stubborn rusted nuts held firmly. Noelle muttered under her breath as another car pulled into the station. Looking up, into the glare of headlights, she wondered who this other person could be. The city was full of all kinds of people. It could be anyone from a drug dealer or pimp to someone's kindly grandfather.

"I hope it's the grandfather," she prayed softly.

Still bent by the tire on the driver's side, she hazarded a look in the window. The child still slept peacefully. Through narrowed eyes, Noelle was able to see the man's foot and leg as they descended from the open car. She couldn't see the car clearly in the dark and the glare of the light.

He was coming closer and seemed to be saying something over the sounds of traffic. Okay, she figured, she'd be less vulnerable in a standing position. Stiff knees slowed her standing process. Finally upright, hands smoothing her humidly sagging dress, she came face to face with . . . Jamal Harris!

"I stopped at the station to top off my gas tank for the weekend and noticed the stranded car." He'd seen the woman crouched beside the still-hissing tire. As her head turned in his direction, he knew who she was. Nicole or Noelle, or whatever her name looked a little less than thrilled with her now-flat tire.

When he'd first seen the woman back at the office, looking a little heat worn, with concern etched on her face, he'd felt more than a basic curiosity about her. Seeing her now, wearing her independence like a badge, renewed that interest. Seeing her in distress, made her seem more approachable—even if she was handling the tire iron like she meant to do business with it.

"You didn't get very far." He looked down at the spare and the hubcap.

Here he was again with that attitude! Why didn't he try telling her something she didn't already know? Aggressive and forceful, his authority rankled her nerves. Who did he think he was, anyway? It was hot, she was tired, and she had a lost child sleeping in her car. She didn't need him to tell her she was stuck.

"I heard an odd sound from my tire and stopped to see what it was," she gestured impatiently to the tire.

"You look like you could use a little help." He paused, waiting for her to supply a name, maybe a few personal details. She didn't.

"It's a good thing you stopped. Do you take the highway home?" She looked away and didn't answer audibly. "Hand me that tire iron." He didn't wait for her to offer, taking it from her hand. He bent to change the tire.

Noelle backed a few steps away from him and again checked on the child—still asleep. Leaning against her car, she watched the broad muscles of his back and shoulders. The heat and humidity worked together to mold his shirt to his skin. He was strong. She knew, firsthand, how tight those lugs had been. She noted that he had large, long-fingered hands that he used quickly and well.

He finished the job by giving one final thump to the hubcap. Storing the flat tire and tools in the trunk, he stole a sideways look at her. She was a pretty woman, but he wasn't used to pursuing a pretty face. Beyond the face, and her other obvious charms, there was something else. Maybe it was a challenge, or an underlying sadness, he didn't know which.

He had a feeling about this woman. A good feeling. His sixth sense told him she was a woman of character and intelligence with a gentle aura of kindness. His instincts were seldom off the mark, and over the years he'd learned to trust his gut.

"All done," he dusted his hands off.

"Thank you," she said dryly, and stepped into the driver's seat, drawing those exquisite legs under her for the second time that evening. For the second time, Jamal felt his heart squeeze as she pulled the door closed.

*Oh no you don't, not again.* A man of action, he refused to let her drive away a second time without even knowing her name, and it was going to take more than a closed door to stop him.

"You're more than welcome. Tell me," he pressed both hands against the roof of the car as though he could hold it and her there by will, "what's your name?"

"I'm sorry," her slow smile was slight and tired. "I wasn't

thinking. I'm Noelle. Noelle Parker. You must think I'm pretty rude . . . after my tire and all."

"Nah." He liked that smile—what there was of it. He guessed that under the right circumstances, that smile could grow and shine brightly enough to blind a man at thirty paces, and brand his heart forever. "Hot, tired and in trouble with a tire would've been my best guess."

Noelle. Tom had been right. He liked the name. It suited her well. Beautiful, gentle, almost ethereal, but not frail or weak. Yep, he nodded to himself, she was very much a Noelle.

Her smile grew firmer, "Yeah, hot and tired. That's about it." She reached across the seat to pull her sweater from under the child's cheek.

"Cute kid. What's her name?"

Noelle went completely blank, the smile frozen at her lips. The pulse jumped wildly at the base of her throat. Moisture collected at her forehead and across her upper lip.

"Kid?" She echoed him as though hearing the word for the first time. "Oh," she looked over at the child who still slept like . . . like an angel. "Angel. We call her Angel."

*We who?* Noelle bit her lip at the escaped lie. She knew she could have told the truth. She probably should have told the truth; what if the child woke up and decided now was a good time to start talking?

Of course, if that happened, she would be up the creek. Why was she letting this man make her so defensive anyway? She hadn't done anything terribly wrong. Surely by Tuesday the child's parents would turn up, and they'd all have a laugh over it, and things would get back to normal.

"Well, thanks for the help. I'd better go," she looked meaningfully over at Angel on the seat beside her.

"Where do you live? I mean, is it far from here? I could follow you to make sure you're okay . . . that your other tires are alright. . . ."

"I've already inconvenienced you enough." Her voice was cold as she keyed the ignition. The engine roared to life and she pulled away from where he stood watching her leave him behind for the second time that night.

Making her turn onto the highway, Noelle tried to justify her resentment of the man she'd just met, and left behind. Who did he think he was, anyway? *Who do you think he is,* argued the deceitful gremlin in her mind.

Noelle pressed the gas harder and ignored her gremlin. Because after all, whoever he *thought* he was, he was really just a poseur, putting up a front of—actually, his helpful efforts seemed quite sincere. He was nosy and invasive—no, that wasn't really true. He was tedious and boring—if only that were true, maybe she wouldn't be sitting here trying to get him out of her mind.

She reflected on the intensity of his eyes. They had been alert and knowing, crinkling slightly at their corners. She had a feeling that Mr. Harris was a pretty worldly guy.

Not that he came across as jaded, he just looked like he'd seen a lot. He had eyes that could read secrets you didn't even know you were keeping. She reached across the seat and found his card. Under passing streetlights, she read his name again. Jamal Allen Harris. The tiny legend, "Attorney at Law" was written beneath it.

Attorney—that certainly accounted for his take-charge attitude, and the all-knowing look that said he was no easy mark—not easily fooled, nor impressed. Closer to home now, turning off the highway farther away from him, she felt more relaxed and decided that maybe her initial reactions had been for other reasons.

Atlanta, queen of "The New South" had a strong, strange influence on her people. Noelle knew that a lot of the people here were very conscious of themselves, their power, and their abilities. Imposing as he was, Jamal Harris had seemed bigger than that. He seemed to have no need of pretense, and that had been mighty unnerving.

Other things about him made her nervous too. He had a square jawline and a deeply cleft chin, like the men in the romance novels and movies she devoured on weekends and late at night. His generous, full-lipped mouth was framed by a carefully manicured mustache. It had immediately caught and held her eye, even as she was trying to think up a good lie about the child.

There had been his voice too. Low and dignified, with a mellifluous resonance that touched something deep within her. His voice, and now the vibrating memory of it touched her. She imagined he didn't have to raise that voice very often. She also imagined how well he used it to seduce throngs of women—no, she meant jurors.

Parking easily behind her apartment, she looked down at the gently snoring child. It really had been a long day. Noelle wondered at all this little one had gone through today. Slipping her arms carefully under the tiny body, Noelle maneuvered herself and the child from the car to her apartment.

Pressing through her back door with an armful of sleeping child, Noelle managed to drop her other bundles on the kitchen counter, just missing the microwave. In her living room, she paused and for the first time worried about where Angel would sleep.

"If I put her on the couch, she'll be lonely and afraid if she wakes up alone. On the other hand, would she really be happier in my bed?" Indecision stalled her.

Any other time, the one-bedroom apartment seemed fairly spacious. She even had a den. But, tonight, it seemed awfully small. Trying to trust her instincts, Noelle decided on the airy bedroom. Slipping Angel onto her bed, "I guess the next thing to do is to get you washed up and dressed for bed."

If she never did it again, Noelle would always remember how natural and pleasant a chore it was to get Angel ready for bed. Removing the sleeping child's play clothes she marveled at how small they were. Using a soapy cloth, she cleaned Angel's tiny hands and face.

The finishing touch was an old tee shirt that made a perfect though long nightgown. Angel slept through it all.

"I don't know where your mommy is, but *I* wouldn't have missed this for all the world," she whispered softly.

Smoothing hair back from the even, brown forehead, Noelle planted a tender kiss there. The naturalness of tucking the child between the clean, fresh sheets charmed Noelle. Looking around, she wished for a Donald Duck or Mickey Mouse night-light to go with Kermit—something to make the room more special for the child. She finally settled for a pink scarf draped over the bedside lamp, satisfied with the soft effect.

If things had been different . . . Noelle thought from the doorway, she'd walk through this door and into the arms of the right man. She shook her head at her own absurdity. Wishful thinking, she told herself, turning back to the living room.

On the couch, Noelle plopped onto her butt with a heavy sigh. Another sigh heaved its way out of her body as she looked around the familiar living room. People said that if you lived in one place long enough, your home would tell your whole life's story. And, perhaps the old saying was true. At least it was true of everyone's home except mine, Noelle guessed.

Here, there were no family pictures of smiling, gray-haired relatives. There were no school yearbooks, or souvenirs of proms past. She kept no trinkets of family vacations, or even of her hometown. It would only be more junk to dust, she told herself.

Her shelves were barren of used texts from high school and college days. No handicrafts, left over from her own days at summer camp, adorned the rose-colored walls she'd painted over a long, empty weekend. And there was certainly nothing left over from . . . Noelle crunched the thought in her mind. She had just made very sure that there was nothing here to remind her of her past.

The apartment was furnished simply enough with an odd assortment of furniture, assembled over her years in the city. It was a long way from modern. In fact, during her college years, she'd referred to this type of classic decor as "early Goodwill."

Her functional taste had filled the room with sturdy pieces gleaned from thrift stores and yard sales—boy, did she love those yard sales! Then there were the neat stacks of books. On the bookshelves, piled on the floor, even lining the windowsills. Looking at them now, Noelle smiled to herself, Pat had been right about one thing—she was a reader. Her tastes were varied and she indulged them liberally. The stack of romance novels caught her eye.

The books were worn and often read, with soft, curling, sometimes smudged pages. Cracked, flaking bindings testified to all the nights she'd read and fallen asleep—living someone else's love. Pat was right. There was a limit to the satisfaction you could get from one of these.

Noelle ruffled the dog-eared pages of the book on top. The creased, bent cover pictured an olive skinned, ruby-lipped, voluptuous, raven-haired seductress. The fiery beauty wore a wickedly low-cut clinging, red gown.

Her ample, no-doubt heaving bosom, was nearly exposed amid a tempting fall of lace and satin ribbons. And even more obviously from the look of surrender in her flashing eyes, her heart churned with love and lust as she rested securely, even luxuriantly in the arms of her man.

Her man. Her hero. He was also dark-haired and bare-chested, with pants fit so closely, they looked as though they had been spray-painted on his manly body.

He stood strong and arrogant. Above his woman, his security and masculinity were unassailable. His artistically perfect, parted lips showed white teeth, and bore the triumphant sneer of the victor. The brand of his woman's kisses was fresh on his mouth, and he would fight to the death to protect her, Noelle knew. She'd read the book four times.

Blazing eyes, and strong arms insured he would forever and always meet her every need. The drawn sword he held aloft would defend her honor, or even take his own life to spare hers, so deep was his devotion. His was the posture of a lover's wanton possession, accepting her surrender as his due.

Unlike real life, there was no question of emotional pain or misuse in their love. Unlike real life, caring was a given, not an option. Unlike real life, their course was one destined for passion and glory, not stupid winner-take-all games where someone had to lose everything before the game ended. Thoughtfully turning the book face down, Noelle tried to remember if the dashing hero had offered to *help* anywhere in all those hundreds of pages.

Noelle sighed. This was her real life. She ruffled the pages again, before tossing the book aside. No matter how hard she wished, or how long she read, *her* happily ever after wasn't going to be written there. Everything she needed was right here.

She looked around. Food, warmth, and shelter were here. There were plants too. Lots of healthy, green, leafy plants filled the apartment and reflected the care she lavished upon them. She had planned to spend part of the long weekend repotting the larger ones, but that was before Angel came into her life.

One wall featured several bright, framed, one-of-a-kind drawings done by Pat's children. Kelly and James put a lot of time and thought into these wonderful pictures. Noelle loved their imaginations. She especially liked the picture of the lady. She'd read them the poem about the lady riding a ". . . cockhorse to Banburry Cross . . ." and they'd done the drawing together.

Because she baby-sat for the kids on a regular basis, Noelle also had a large basket of stuffed toys and children's books tucked under the bay window. At least there was no need for Angel to be bored. The stack of videos would probably supply some entertainment for her too. Noelle was an experienced, well-prepared baby-sitter.

Standing at the refrigerator Noelle wondered again at the child's silence. "It's not natural for a child that age to be that quiet."

Trying hard to remember little things from her training, Noelle recalled, children that age are supposed to still be in awe of their arms and legs. She searched her memory for more. And talking. That little kid should be talking her merry little butt off!

Carefully removing ice from the tray, she wondered again, how in the world did that little kid come to be in that building, on the second floor? Alone? Slipping ice into her sweetened tea, she tried to recap the evening as she walked the short distance from her kitchen.

Pat always said children made things happen. Dropping wearily onto the couch, Noelle gnawed gently at the fullness of her lower lip. Pat's right. If it hadn't been for Angel, and her unplanned appearance, she might not have ever met Mr. Harris. And truthfully, she was not sure that would have been a good thing.

Jamal Allen Harris. Even his name made her uncomfortably warm. She wondered why he felt the need to use all three of his names. Southern tradition, she finally decided. Shifting in her seat Noelle admitted to herself, it's a nice enough name. My goodness though, he was a very nice looking man. Nice looks, in my experience, can be very deceiving. Still, something about the man was staying with her.

Could it have been his intense eyes, or his generous mouth that so easily caught and held her attention? Maybe it was the serious note of concern she'd heard in the rumble of his knowing voice? Or, maybe it was just the way he'd shown up when she needed him—no, she corrected quickly when she needed help.

A man like that should mean nothing to her, she warned herself. Even if he did sometimes work in the building, she'd been there five years and had never seen him before. She'd never see him again. She'd forget about him. She'd just put him out of her mind.

Sitting with her tea, the gremlins in her treacherous mind turned on her and began examining Jamal again. He really hadn't done anything wrong. He'd been considerate and helpful, even caring. She just found his presence to be so very troubling. Who told him he could care about her anyway? What was there about the man?

Leaning her head against the back of the couch, she savored the coolness of the glass in her hand almost as much as she savored the remembered image of Jamal Harris's taut, well-muscled body laboring over her tire. She hadn't meant to watch so closely as he neatly folded his long legs under him to squat closer to her car.

The long muscles in his thigh had bunched, and pressed against his formal lawyer's slacks, then tightened as they molded against his rounded buttocks. Jacket off, shirtsleeves rolled to the elbows, the muscles in his forearm and back had tightened and twisted as he'd lifted the tire. Sweat from his efforts glistened on his skin under the city streetlights. If she'd reached out, just a little, she could have touched him. Her fingers knew exactly how he would feel.

Her small laugh was touched with irony. "I wonder what our book cover would look like?" The words were barely past her lips when the gremlins in her mind went to work.

Two forms, she imagined, meeting in shadow, painted with a glaze of subtle twilight, in a room filled with draped walls and rounded cushions. Reclining perhaps, in tones of sepia and umber, like carved statues of some exotic darkly burnished wood, faces gracefully overcome with learned mutual knowledge and expectation. Long-limbed bodies with hard planes and soft fullnesses, embracing with a fluid passion she had yet, even in marriage, to experience.

In Jamal's arms, looking into a handsome face that made her heart beat faster, and encouraged moist warmth in unexpected but eternally known places, Noelle knew her eyes would shine, too, just like the woman on that other book cover. Her breasts would swell in welcome, and her skin would flush in anticipation and entreaty. And his face, it would give promise to fulfill all the dreams she could manufacture, while his body vowed the raw fulfillment of all she could demand.

Yes, she believed that was exactly what it would look like.

Bringing the tall glass with its cool melting ice to her forehead and along her cheek, Noelle squeezed her eyes shut. She needed something to cool the images blazing behind her rapidly fluttering lids.

# Five

Cramped and stiff, Noelle felt the muscles of her back and legs protest her waking movements. One leg was twisted beneath her and the other foot dangled off the edge of the sofa. She heard herself grunt, then moan as she tried to arrange her sleep-tangled body on the cushions. For a moment, as she rubbed her itchy eyes, she wondered why she was on the couch.

Sitting up, she rolled the sheet and spread into a ball. "Oh, yeah," she muttered to herself. Scratching the persistent itch at her ribs, she remembered Angel. Hair in disarray and stretching as she moved, she walked to her bedroom.

Through the partially open door, she could hear the child's soft and rhythmic breathing. The small figure stretched across the middle of the bed. Noelle smiled at the child's willing abandonment to her sleep. One small leg had been flung from beneath the covers, both arms were thrown open, her head lay gently to the side. Comfort and rest were apparent now.

Not like in the middle of the night when Noelle had awakened to soft breathy sobs, fast rolling tears, and a pitifully downturned mouth. Half awake, the child had been troubled enough to fear abandonment. Still not talking, she sobbed—mostly silently—until Noelle had come to her.

"Poor baby. I'm here. I haven't left you," she said as she held the child.

Rocking and crooning to her, Noelle felt touched again by the child's abandonment. Where were her parents? Somewhere there was someone who knew just the right way to hold her, the right way to soothe and comfort her. Whoever that someone was, Noelle was the only available substitute for the mother that Angel was so painfully missing now.

The simple words to the childish lullaby had poured from her lips. A barely remembered tune from childhood soothed the path of Noelle's tender task. She sang without thinking.

Eventually, the shaking and sobbing gave way to gentle sighs and sleepy yawns. Humming and rubbing the girl's back, Noelle stole a look downward. Eyelids had drooped and the child found sleep again, her head resting easily against Noelle's breasts. Ah, she'd missed this, Noelle thought. Even when Pat's kids visited, she never got to do this kind of loving nurturing.

"I guess it must be pure instinct," she breathed. That maternal instinct Pat kept telling her was natural to all women. *Except my mom,* she thought as she quietly tucked the child between the muslin sheets.

In the morning light, Noelle admired the child again. Walking over to the bed, she carefully pulled the rose-printed sheets free, straightening them, then covering her again. Annoyed by the movement, Angel tossed her head and fanned her arms and legs, settling just as quickly back into sleep. When she was sure Angel remained soundly asleep, Noelle grabbed her own shorts and a top, and headed for the kitchen.

The clock said seven-thirty as Noelle poured coffee. Was it only twelve hours ago? Things were so different, she told herself. During the night, she hadn't come up with any brilliant insights.

She still had no idea what to do about Angel. It was too bad there was no place to go except Protective Services. She shivered remembering the bleak office where she'd almost left the little girl.

The options, as Noelle saw them, were pretty limited. The police or herself.

Using a finger to trace the line across the list she kept on the refrigerator, Noelle finally located the telephone number. Lifting the phone, she weighed the options, then dialed. It was the right thing to do for the right reasons, whether she really wanted to do it or not. She counted six rings.

"Yeah, fit' precinct, Off'cer Hopper speakin'."

"I was wondering about missing children, umm . . ." Noelle's voice faltered.

"You find one or lose one?" The man chuckled thickly into her ear.

"Found. I mean, umm . . ."

"Can you hold?" Dead air took over before she could respond. Noelle waited five minutes, then hung up the phone.

She mentally crossed out the police. The best they would be able to offer would be temporary foster care—that meant warehousing the child in a shelter where she'd just sit and maybe not even have anyone to help her through the frightening nights.

"No, in the meantime, I'm her best alternative. I can't keep her forever, as much as I'd like to, but . . ." Noelle left the thought unfinished. "I'm not prepared to think beyond this weekend or break the law, but Angel needs me. And as quiet as it's kept, I need her."

Turning on the radio over the sink, she wondered if there might be any news of the missing child and her missing parents. Twenty minutes later, she had breakfast ready and had heard no news. But, she reminded herself, that doesn't mean somebody's not looking for her.

Unbidden, and unexpectedly, the image of Jamal Harris reared its handsome head. She might need a good lawyer before all of this was over. "I wonder if he's any good. . . ."

He *had* offered to help. She found his crumpled card on the counter where she'd dropped it last night. Flattening it out with her hand, she rejected the idea even before it was fully formed.

"It's not going to come to that," she tried to assure herself. "It's not like I'm planning on stealing her or anything. Besides, Jamal Harris doesn't owe me a thing, and I certainly gave him no real reason to help me out of the mess I seem to be creating for myself." She cringed mentally as she remembered leaving him after he'd changed her tire.

"No," she pushed the card away. "This will work itself out—somehow."

"I've got her, for the weekend anyway. I tried contacting Child Protective Services—and it didn't work out. I'll just have to get back to them on Tuesday."

Combing her fingers through her soft hair, Noelle twisted it into a braid. "Okay," she told the mirror, "I've made a decision. The next thing to do is to figure out what we're going to do today."

What would a little girl like to do on a hot Georgia day? Pat would know. She hated to drag her into it, but who else could she ask?

Before she could answer her own question, the phone rang and she raced to answer it before the second ring hoping it wouldn't wake Angel. Fear danced lightly in her stomach. What if it was the police? What if they traced her number? Now, fear was wearing combat boots.

"Hello?" She held her breath.

"Hello yourself. I'm still trying to lure you over here. I could use some help with the grill and stuff . . ."

Noelle grinned in spite of herself. The woman had to be psychic. "Pat. Honey. It's not even nine o'clock and you're working on a grill?"

"Lots of folks to feed. I figured if I couldn't get you here as a guest, I'd try appealing to your service-oriented side."

Noelle could hear the children in the background. "Sounds like you've got all the help you can handle."

"Child! They're better than any alarm clock, but they leave a lot to be desired as cook's helpers. They've been up since . . . No, James. Noelle hold on." Muffled sounds of Pat's mediation came across the line.

"If you're sure I can't get you over here," Pat finally continued, "I could use a favor."

"Just ask." Noelle knew she would do it if she could.

"Could I talk you into adoption? On a temporary basis, of course."

Noelle's heart jerked with unexpected anxiety. "Umm," Noelle waffled. "Yeah. Sure. A couple more won't matter." And she could have bitten her tongue out.

"The parade is today," she rushed on, hoping Pat hadn't heard her clearly. "I'll pick them up and take them to Mickey D's for lunch. We'll get that kid's meal they love and make an afternoon of it."

"Thanks. I still have to run to the store to pick up some things, and I want to . . . wait a minute. A couple *more?* That means you already have at least one." Pat's voice slowed and became inquiring. "Whose child have you borrowed?"

"I was going to call you about it later," Noelle ventured.

"But, I'm on the phone now. Can you talk?" Her experienced caseworker voice came over the line.

"Now?"

"Now." Pat was firm.

"Maybe that's not such a good idea. If things get sticky later on, well . . . I wouldn't want you to be an accessory."

"Noelle, we'll talk shoes, hats, gloves, and any other accessories you can think of all you want, later. Right now, consider me thoroughly involved. What's going on?"

"Pat, I don't . . ."

"Honey, please—don't give me that mess. Talk to me, girl."

Noelle took a deep breath. Pat was a good friend. She was also a good caseworker. She knew her job—regulations and all. There was no real way to put a good face on this, and Pat was the closest thing she had to an alternative. Noelle jumped in.

"Someone left a child at the office yesterday—after you left."

Pat's gasp nearly froze the words in her throat.

"The janitor, you know—Mr. Jackson, brought her in. No one, adult or child showed up to claim her. She looks about three, maybe four, and she's healthy. I think she hears fine, but the whole time we were together, she never said a word."

Pausing Noelle caught her breath, then rushed on, "I'm

guessing that the loss of speech or the refusal to speak is a temporary aberration. I have no idea what kind of trauma or shock could cause this behavior in such a young child."

"Noelle, don't you dare go clinical on me."

"It's the strangest thing Pat . . . I waited for a couple of hours and no one ever came to claim her."

"You checked the waiting room, and the bathrooms?"

"Mr. Jackson did, and like I said, I waited for hours—past seven. Then, when nobody showed up, I brought her home with me . . ."

"You did what? For real, though? What?"

"Yep," Noelle chewed her lip and waited.

"So, now wait a minute . . ." Noelle heard the scrape of a chair as Pat sat down, trying to absorb the situation. "You're telling me that an abandoned child was brought to you and you brought her home with you?" She waited, digesting the facts. "Girl? Have . . . you . . . lost . . . your . . . mind? Why didn't you take her to CPS or call the police?"

"I tried. Pat, it was awful up there. I just couldn't leave her with a group of strange men—not over a long weekend like this one. And she would have been in a shelter over a holiday, and—oh, Pat, you should see her!"

"Noelle . . ." Pat sounded dubious.

"Pat, it was hard enough trying to convince that Mr. Harris to let us out of there, then I had a flat tire, and Angel fell asleep . . ."

"Whoa! Girl, slow down. You've lost me. Who's Mr. Harris? And who's Angel?"

"Mr. Harris is a lawyer who was working on something in the CPS office. He started talking to me, and I thought he'd never let me go. And after I had the flat, he found me and fixed it, and then he asked me what her name was and I told him it was Angel because she was asleep, and I had to tell him something, and . . ."

"Okay. Okay, I think I kind of understand, but back up."

Pat was trying hard to follow the tone and tempo of Noelle's story. She listened dutifully while Noelle related the entire story of the previous evening.

"Honey, I hope you at least let him have your phone number after all the help he gave you."

"No way!"

The outburst didn't surprise Pat. Over the years, she and Noelle had talked a lot and she knew better than anyone, Noelle had her own reasons for avoiding entanglements. She'd been in love once and it had cost her—a lot.

She listened now to the sigh pushing through the phone line. Pat understood that while Noelle had once wanted love more than anything in the world, experience had taught her that its cost was high. She was afraid to risk the price again.

"Well . . . I think *I* understand your decision not to leave her in a shelter, but I gotta say, you *do* have custody of a child someone is probably looking for. Legally it's a fine line."

"So, I'm back to square one." Noelle was thoughtful.

"No. You're not even on a square. Could she have been abandoned?" Pat was trying.

"Nope. Too well-cared for. Except for refusing to speak, there's no sign of abuse. Maybe on Tuesday somebody will just show up, be glad to get her back safe and sound, and nobody will ask any other questions." Pat heard the hopefulness in Noelle's voice.

"Noelle, I still think you need to call someone."

"I already tried calling the police. They put me on hold and never came back."

Noelle could almost see the look Pat was giving her. The image of raised eyebrows accused her boldly across the phone lines. "Something wrong with your phone, you couldn't call them back?"

"Pat . . ."

"Don't whine." The sound of swiftly turning pages interrupted her. "You know I hate it when you whine. Here it is . . . I want you to call Caren Whittaker. She's with CPS, and she's good. She was planning to visit relatives in Tennessee, but maybe you can catch her before she leaves."

"Great." Noelle grabbed for a pen and copied the numbers Pat rattled off. "I'll call until I get her."

"So, in the meantime, between now and Tuesday . . . what time are you going to be here to pick the kids up?"

# Six

Grady Hospital had never been one of Jamal's favorite places. But today made it one of his least favorite places of all time. It sat, dingy and dull, squatting in the midst of a beautiful and glorious historic city. He'd had to go in today to visit with an abused child.

When he saw that term in the newspaper, it never made him think of girls like Andrea Pierce—until this morning. Thirteen, and badly beaten by a drunken mother and her boyfriend, the girl had lain in the hospital bed all night, swathed in bandages and raving through a drug-induced haze.

The neighbors had found the girl lying by a Dumpster behind the apartment building where she lived. A woman said she'd heard Andrea moaning when she went to take her trash out late last night. She'd gotten her husband and teenaged son to help her get the battered, nearly comatose girl to the hospital. They'd waited until the call had been relayed by his office. They wanted to tell him what they knew. The good churchgoing lady kept saying she wanted to testify. Jamal wasn't sure whether she meant prayer or legal statements. Either way though, he understood that she wanted her words heard by a higher power.

Andrea was the third of five Pierce children. She was also the third one to wind up, critically injured, in the pediatric ward at Grady.

"Seems like the wrong trash was being taken out," Jamal muttered to himself as he left the building. "If I get my way, and I intend to, that neighbor lady and her family are going to get their chance to testify."

Without really thinking about it, he found himself in his car driving down Butler and across Decatur, through the tangle of old streets surrounding the hospital.

He kept thinking about the time he'd spent with the girl. Thirteen really was very young. She'd been so small and defenseless lying there, with her straight dark hair flattened against her thin face. Every time she'd moved, she'd moaned.

How could anybody do that to a child? Too bad people didn't have to be licensed, somehow checked for suitability, before they could become parents.

Bending over the rail of the bed where Andrea lay, he'd promised her that this torture was about to come to an end. He had already collected statements from the neighbors. Her summer school teachers were next on his list of people to talk to, and then . . .

"What the hell!"

The blue uniformed Atlanta Police Department officer was waving him down. "You gotta pull over. Parade today. Can't let you through the barricade." He swung his arm in a wide arc, indicating a parking lot to his left.

Jamal checked his rearview mirror. There was a line of cars behind him. People either lost like him, or going to the parade were lined up behind him. No chance of backing up.

"Looks like you're going to a parade," the officer smiled. He followed the APD officer's arm and pulled into the lot.

Hands shoved into his jeans, Jamal wandered down the crowded street amid the noise of parade preparations. He'd read that it would start at noon. A quick glance at his watch showed the participants had about thirty minutes to bring order to this noisy chaos.

Walking, he smiled as some mothers adjusted sequined uniforms on tiny majorettes, and others tried to tone down makeup on complaining teenaged float riders. Wincing, he passed a few hundred high school band members practicing their steps and tuning their instruments.

A native Atlantan, he'd never been this close to a parade before—especially not one of these fabulous Fourth of July extravaganzas. He crossed the street to avoid "the Briefcase Brigade" in their dark suits and ties. Their precise steps were measured to coincide with their militarily executed briefcase maneuvers, not wandering pedestrians. Rounding the corner, his eyes scanned the crowd, almost as though he was expecting to see someone he knew.

On Courtland, he saw a man station himself near the curb, looking down. When the man reached an exact point, he bent and lifted a small boy to his shoulder. The child screamed with glee, and wiggled himself into position.

A father and son. Jamal sighed. He wouldn't mind trading places with that man. No, he amended the thought, He'd like to be that man. Just for this afternoon.

Fatherhood and the comforts of family life seemed like a rosy, elusive, far off dream to him. Seemed like some folks realized that dream with ease and then spent the rest of their lives throwing it away with both hands instead of cherishing it for what it really was.

He'd almost married ten years ago. He wondered what ever became of Marie Campbell? The last time he'd heard from her, she was working for the World Health Organization in some third-world country he couldn't pronounce. He seemed to remember that she organized a lot of embassy parties, or something like that.

Remembering Marie made him wonder what life would have been like if he'd married her. He wondered if they'd still be together, if they'd have kids. He looked over his shoulder at the happy father with his excited son. What would their kids have looked like?

If he'd married Marie, would he be standing there like that with—their son? Their daughter? Or would they have become a life casualty—victims of health, economics, or divorce?

A wistful sigh escaped Jamal as he walked up International Boulevard toward Peachtree Street. No point in belaboring what-ifs. He'd never been to an Independence Day parade, and by George, he was going to enjoy this one. He'd see the parade and get some lunch at Underground—make a day of it. He kept walking.

"Jamal!"

He turned to see Tom running toward him and towing his eight-year-old son by the hand.

"Yo, man. What're you doing here? I figured you'd be relaxing instead of plowing through this crowd on a Saturday."

Jamal grinned down at the little boy in the backward Braves cap. "Your son?" Tom grinned and patted the child's head, nodding.

Lucky guy, Jamal thought. "Well," he decided to pick up the first question, "I was over at Grady. Got a call on the Pierce case. I think we've got 'em this time." He noted Tom's raised eyebrows.

Trying to avoid telling too much in front of the little boy, Jamal abbreviated the story. "Neighbors found the thirteen-year-old last night and brought her to Grady. She's conscious now and able to talk about what happened to her. She's scared. And again, we've got the neighbors' account. For a change we've got witnesses who aren't afraid to come forward and I want to get them in court as soon as we can."

"Have you touched base with Morgan on this? I'll bet he's as hot on this one as you are. . . ." He smiled down at his impatient son. The boy was jumping from foot to foot on the summer hot sidewalk.

"Not yet. I'm going to give him a call a little later. I got tangled up in all this traffic and so I figured this parade was a good way to kill a little time."

"Why don't you join us?" Tom's son was hanging on to his dad's hand and leaning perilously toward the crowd.

"I think I'll just walk. . . ." The bands were coming toward them. Jamal could see flags raised and waving. ". . . but hey,

I'll see you in the office next week and we can finish pulling this together."

"Sounds like a winner. See you then." Tom hurried off to follow his son, recklessly plunging through the crowd.

Hands still in pockets, Jamal's eyes followed the sight of another father and son. Some guys had all the luck.


Angel looked really cute in the little yellow sundress Pat dug out of a box of things too small for her own daughter. She seemed to even like the tiny white sandals they'd buckled on her little feet. Pat's children seemed to have taken her under their collective wing.

Kelly stood close to Angel holding her hand. Like her mother, she tended to care easily and quickly. James was asserting his almost six-year-old independence—being the man of the group. Noelle had to laugh as the girls humored his bossiness, standing where and as he told them to.

After digging her purse and Kermit from under the car seat, Noelle ushered the children up Baker Street and toward the noisy crowd. The closer they got to Peachtree, the louder the crowd became. Angel, still silent, looked anxiously at Noelle clutching her hand with trembling fingers.

Conversely, James and his four-year-old sister were dancing with excitement. They developed a little song that began, "Oooh! I see . . ." and they were singing it for all they were worth.

"Oooh! Balloons, I see balloons . . ." They were thrilled. Noelle, weak woman that she was, couldn't resist.

"Would you like a balloon?" she asked. In response they nearly knocked her over with their abundant enthusiasm. Even Angel was nodding, smiling shyly up at the opportunistic vendor standing at Noelle's elbow. Kneeling, Noelle tied string knots at each child's wrist: even as James declared, "But I'm big! Big kids don't need this stuff!"

Occupied with the balloons, Noelle didn't see the man staggering toward her. She felt his approach and looked up as his shadow fell across her. Standing quickly, she brushed her hands over her khaki shorts and began gathering the children.

"Them's your chirren?" The man was staggering closer, his dirty flannel shirt and oily gray pants fluttering and stinking on the breeze.

Noelle offered a nod and a half smile. She hoped it would appease the man and he'd move on. No such luck.

"You goin' to the parade?"

Not willing to answer again, Noelle herded the children down the street toward the waiting throng on Peachtree Street. Undaunted, her new fan followed closely, talking all the while.

"So, what? You ain't gonna talk to me?"

*Hell no!* she thought to herself. *And if the Lord is with me, I'm going to out-walk you too.* She picked up the pace. The kids, balloons trailing, were running now.

"You think you better'n me cause you goin' to a parade?" He was puffing from the exertion, but chasing her anyway. "Well, you ain't," he continued to argue. "You ain't. Gimme a dollar!"

Flying around the corner onto Peachtree, Noelle managed to grab the hands of all three children and prepared to dive into the crowd. Across her chest came the sharp snap and bite of the thin leather strap of her purse. She stumbled from the force of the man's pull. Too startled to cry out, she continued to grip the now frightened and confused children.

"Gimme it!"

The man was growling, showing decayed and rotting teeth. He pulled hard and the slender strap popped free. Over-balanced, Noelle fell into a stranger's suntanned arms. The children screamed.

In slow motion, Noelle saw a tall, jean-clad man step out of the crowd. He shot one long arm out to snag the raggedy man. His large, long-fingered hand neatly plucked Noelle's small purse out of the robber's grasp.

"I don't think you want to do this," his quiet voice rumbled, and he let the would-be robber go. The man moved away quickly, his flapping clothes melting into the crowd.

"I believe this is yours." He offered her purse. Moving swiftly and economically, the man helped Noelle right herself and corral the three kids. Numb from the close call, and grateful for the rescue, Noelle looked up into the heavy lidded, darkly, intense eyes of Jamal Harris.

She dropped her eyes immediately, as though just looking at him would burn her. She was having trouble breathing; his closeness pressed in on her. The air seemed redolent with the clean, soap-washed, man-scent of him. The smell drew her and she found herself sagging weakly against the waiting hardness of his chest.

"Are you okay?"

She nodded absently.

"She needs air," he announced to the world at-large as she leaned against him. Jamal kind of liked that she seemed to need him—even if that need was temporary.

A camp chair materialized beneath her, and sympathetic bystanders produced cool water and made soothing sounds.

"You need some help," he stated flatly, reaching for Angel's hand.

"I'm fine, thank you." Noelle's chest tightened.

"No, you're not. You're still a little shaky," he looked down at the wide-eyed children, "and you've got these little folks to contend with. I think I'll tag along for a while." He grinned knowingly.

What did he mean, "tag along"? How long was "a while"? And who invited him anyway? Noelle wanted to get angry, and stay that way. Jamal was way out of line, taking charge of things—again. But his proximity had the hairs on her arms standing at attention.

In the warm afternoon sun, she felt him sweeping her along. It wasn't that she couldn't resist—she found she just didn't want to. The man was too close, and his nearness made it hard to breathe. She felt rushed and pressured—immediately resenting his ability to make her feel so vulnerable.

What was he doing here anyway? There was no way this meeting had been planned. He'd honestly only made a kind offer to help her with the children after her near-disaster.

This has to be fate, she tried to tell herself. Okay, she assuaged her nervous stomach, this is fate. Kismet. She looked at him again, refusing to admire the strength of his chiseled jawline. Aggressive kismet.

The small group made its way down Peachtree. Noelle risked another sidelong look at Jamal. A look that spoke of her growing attraction. Her eyes widened in surprise when she caught him looking at her the same way. A shy smile crept across her lips.

"What're you doing here," she finally ventured.

"I told you last night. I'm here to help." He smiled innocently, then maneuvered them to a spot where the children could see the passing floats and colorful clowns.

"You're really going to help me whether I need you to or not, aren't you?"

She got an arched eyebrow and a broad grin in response. This man was determined to work her one good nerve! She could already tell. . . .


"You know," Noelle clawed buttery popcorn from the bottom of the shared box, "you're really going to make these kids rotten. In one afternoon, they've had enough cotton candy and junk to feed a family of six. Now, you've gone and found them a carnival. Angel's going to be sick all night. I just know it. And James and Kelly, their mother will never . . ."

"You worry too much."

Jamal stood calmly beside her managing to make his soft, worn jeans look elegantly tailored as they traveled smoothly against his well-muscled thighs. He even looked good with Kermit as an accessory. The green puppet was draped across his arm, smiling dizzily as he waved to the three happy children on the carousel.

"When you don't have kids or family, you learn to appreciate them. You and your husband surely learned that with Angel." He didn't look in her face, and he didn't seem to expect an answer.

"I, uh," how to explain this? ". . . uh, I'm not married . . . anymore." She kept her eyes straight ahead.

He looked at her more seriously then, hoping his happiness didn't show on his face. Widowed, divorced, it couldn't have mattered less to him. She was available! He wasn't about to take the edge off his thrill by worrying about other guys and their losses right now.

Noelle held her breath. She didn't want to add anymore. She didn't want to tell him about the dismal blot on her life that marriage had been—didn't want to tell him about the useless sacrifice she'd made. Then there was Angel. Even as she hesitated, she knew instinctively that if she did try to tell, he would listen.

"Well, if you don't have any plans for tomorrow . . ." Something told him to start slow and carefully with her. She was very cautious. Better to give her time to get used to him. "If you're not busy, would you like to have dinner?"

The ride had ended and the children were dragging them toward a kid-size Ferris wheel. Jamal, sucker that he was, had already handed over tickets for the ride. They stood back to watch.

"Dinner?" Noelle hated the way her voice quivered and almost stuttered as she rephrased his invitation.

Bending slightly, he looked at Noelle, nodding pleasantly.

"No." She could have, should have, kicked herself. She couldn't believe she'd said that! It was just so automatic. After all these years, she guessed she'd just refused and rejected so many men, it was just a reflex.

"I mean, tomorrow's not good." She tried to repair the damage. He looked crestfallen. It was no act, she noted, he really looked disappointed.

"I mean, would you like to go to a cookout?" She looked away from him. His radiant change of expression stunned her.

"The kids' mother," she extended her hands toward the cheering children, "is having a lot of people over, and I promised to help." Pat would forgive her fib.

"Yeah. I'd like that. Sounds like fun."

The ride was over and the laughing children were stumbling toward them. Jamal reached out, catching Angel in his large hands. She screamed aloud, thrilled when he swung her through the air into the bend of his arm. James clung to one of his legs, while Kelly teased around the other.

"I just have to tell you," both Noelle and Jamal started at the sound of the new adult voice, ". . . how good it is to see a strong black family unit. You two look so good with your happy, healthy children. Anybody can see . . ." the woman looked directly at Jamal as she tossed braids over her shoulder, "that they are loved. And that little one," she pointed at Angel, "looks like her mama spit her out."

"Uh-huh," her cornrowed friend agreed volubly, looking from the child to Noelle and back, "ain't no way you could deny that one."

With as much dignity as they could muster, Noelle and Jamal murmured thanks, and beat a hasty retreat from the carnival midway.

"Wait 'til I tell Morgan," Jamal chuckled to himself.

Glancing around at his temporarily adopted family, trying not to shout out loud, he cherished the warmth he felt from the children. *Damn,* he thought, *this is sweet.* Giving in to an irresistible urge, he reached down to move his hand across the top of James' head and along the side of his childishly smooth sunwarmed face. James grinned up at him, showing all of his front and back teeth. It was hard to believe that some men ran away from this: responsibility repaid in full with love.

He was tickled again by the way Angel's warm arm curved about his neck and the confidence James put in his hand. Kelly's smile and shining eyes, even as she gazed up at him from the other side of Noelle's leg, said that she would willingly follow him to the ends of the earth. It felt good and right. Better than right, it felt natural.

Noelle felt panic. First it seeped slowly through her skin. Then it grew, covering her body. She felt something akin to anger, but it was more adrenal driven. She was scared.

All she wanted to do now was throw the kids in the car and hit the gas, she thought. She wanted desperately to be on I-285. She wanted desperately to be anywhere away from Jamal Harris. He was sucking up her air again.

Scanning the parking lot, she headed toward her car, towing Kelly by the hand. *I could have lived a long time without those two women,* she thought angrily. Who asked them anything, anyway? Why couldn't some people keep their thoughts to themselves?

"Well, here we are." She tried to sound festive, but her despair came through as she pulled the car door open.

"Okay. Last stop." An obviously disappointed silent Angel was lowered to the ground.

James launched himself into the backseat followed by Kelly. Angel clambered into the front seat and sat looking expectant as Noelle fastened her into the seat belt.

"So, about the cookout?" Jamal was embarrassed. He didn't want to force himself on her and he certainly didn't intend to beg. He would if he had to, he just didn't intend to.

"Would you like me to pick you up?"

"Oh no!" Noelle almost screamed. She'd only been trying to be polite, wanting to repay him for his kindness throughout the day, when she'd extended the invitation. She tried to think of a graceful way to uninvite him now.

"Alright." He was calm, refusing to react to her panic. "If you'll give me the address, I'll meet you there." He pulled a small notebook from a back pocket of the snug jeans.

"Well . . ." She hesitated for a moment.

"To my house? We live at 723 Erin Avenue Southwest." James piped from the backseat. "It's a white an' green house. We got a big yard too. It's got three big trees in the front. Pecan trees. You comin' tomorrow? For the cookout? In the afternoon . . . you know, after lunchtime . . . okay?"

James had obviously found a new hero and he wasn't going to let Noelle chase him away without a fight.

"Sure will. I wouldn't miss it." Scribbling rapidly in his notebook, Jamal caught the address, then moved quickly.

Noelle rushed around the car, snatched her door open and dropped into the seat. She clicked the seat belt into place and reached for the door. She was moving fast but Jamal was faster. He was there as her hand touched the door handle.

*I will not let this man intimidate me,* she promised herself silently, *I just won't.*

Reaching, he pressed the lock down and looked into Noelle's eyes. Annoyingly, she felt her breath catch—again. Those heavy-lidded, bedroom eyes were scanning her, as though they could see secrets she'd never planned to keep.

His fingers rested scant inches away from her, but she could have sworn she felt the heat from his hand sizzling right through the metal and padding of the door. The man was no longer just intimidating her. He was drawing her. He was attracting her just like a bee was drawn to honey. That was dangerous. In the past, it had almost been fatal. Better not to try again.

He looked at her—hard. She felt both promise and threat in his dark glance as it pierced something deep within her. The feeling was of something warm and primal flooding her body. She wondered if he could see or sense her combined, warring fear and attraction.

With difficulty, she wrenched her gaze from his. Could he feel her need for flight?

"I'll be there." His voice was husky and as intoxicating as aged Scotch. She drank it in as he closed her door. Stepping away from the car, he waved at the kids.

"Tomorrow," he promised as she drove away.

# *Seven*

"No-well! Angel!"

James and Kelly careened around the corner of the house toward their newest guests. Hugs were exchanged as though they hadn't spent yesterday together. The children claimed Angel and swung off around the side of the house to pursue important games Noelle couldn't possibly understand.

Angel tossed a quick look over her shoulder, to make sure it was okay, and—clutching Kermit under one arm—silently followed her hosts at a run.

So much energy. It seemed like they did everything at a run—double-time. Obviously it's a kid thing, Noelle smiled to herself. It was good that Angel had taken so quickly to James and Kelly. She was so serious, she seemed to need the emotional outlet of play. She was so quiet, she seemed to need the childish excitement of play.

Noelle knocked at the doorframe and stepped into the house. "Pat! Where are you?"

"Out here! Come on through the house."

Noelle followed her friend's voice to the back door. The yard was crowded with Pat's usual restless, cheerful collection of neighbors and friends. Music played across the heavy summer air from a sound system set up near the front of her two-car garage.

Teenagers in oversized shorts and high-top tennis shoes were chanting song lyrics and trying out new dance steps to the delight of a group of senior citizens, sitting in the shade of the garage. Old Mrs. Bolton from across the street stood, rotated her heavy hips beneath her flowered housedress, and swore she "used to move just like that."

"Back in the day!" the teenagers laughed.

Noelle could barely make out Pat's round face and big white apron through the smoke coming off the grill. Standing next to a tall, smoke-shrouded man, fanning, and squinting through smoke, Pat used her big fork to test the tenderness of sizzling meat. She looked right at home.

"I brought some stuff," Noelle called, backing into the kitchen.

"Okay, let me get this man to watch the meat and I'll come see." Pat came through the back door wiping her hands on a coarse dish towel. Her face was streaked with sweat and she smelled like smoke, as she accepted Noelle's welcoming hug.

"So tell me about all the excitement yesterday. You left here flying and I didn't get the whole story. Give me details. Details, girl. I want all the news. : . ." She turned to check the beans baking in the oven. "James said a man chased you?"

Noelle laughed. "You know James and his imagination. He made it sound worse than it really was . . ." she rolled her eyes. "There was a wino or something and he was trying to get me to give him some change. He followed us around for a while. He was real persistent, that's all."

"And . . ." Pat urged.

"And he finally left us alone." Pat's cocked head and raised eyebrows showed she knew there was more to the story.

"What?" Come on Pat. For a change, let this go, Noelle begged in her heart.

"Tell me about how you ran into Jamal. . . ."

The woman was like a dog with a bone: tenacious to the bitter end. She wasn't going to give up until she'd wrung every last word out of Noelle. Obviously, there was no way out. Resigned, Noelle gave a blow-by-blow description of the previous afternoon, ending with an opinion.

"I think I could like him—as a friend—but I don't think that's what he wants." She looked down at the hands folded in front of her. "I'm not sure I'm ready for what he might want from me. I'm afraid to chance it."

"Girl, you know I didn't ask you that."

"I know you didn't, but it's the next logical question—for you, anyway." Noelle couldn't meet her friend's eyes.

"What do you think he wants," Pat probed.

"I don't know. Me. Sex. Control . . . I don't know! He just . . . just . . ." Frustrated hands batted the air as words failed her.

"I heard it was dinner."

Noelle giggled nervously. "James strikes again. You know you need to get a license for that boy. He gave the man your address, so . . ."

The screen door slammed and the man with the meat stepped into the kitchen. "Where do you want this?"

The shiver that raced up her spine at the sound of his voice was unstoppable.

Noelle turned, starting her gaze at his feet allowing it to travel up the long, powerfully muscled legs, past the neat runner's hips, and strong torso, to the broad grin he pleasantly displayed upon seeing her. Jamal Harris had tracked her down again . . . with a little help from James.

"Hi," she said shyly, "I see you made it."

*Damn,* she thought, *he's good-looking!* Knowing he would be at the cookout hadn't helped to prepare her for the powerful reality of him and his all too easy charm. The warmth of his smile didn't make him any easier to take.

"Yeah. James gave me great directions."

She couldn't even make small talk with this man, Noelle argued to herself. She sounded socially retarded. Blindly, she bumped her way out of her chair grabbing her purse and keys as she went.

"Tell Angel," she blurted, like the silent child might ask, "I'll be right back. I'm going to the store." She was through the door before they could stop her.

"Store?" Pat was catching on slowly. Noelle was escaping again.

Jamal and Pat heard the crunch of Noelle's tires as she drove away.

"Damn, she's good." Jamal's voice was barely audible.

"That's just it, she really is," Pat answered.

A short snort of sardonic laughter and Jamal shook his head in confusion.

"No." Pat gamely defended her friend. "There are a lot of things you don't know and don't understand. Remember, most behavior is learned . . ."

"Thanks teacher." He grinned at her. "What you're telling me is that she's been hurt and that entitles her to hang some other man's guilt on anyone who gets too close—or wants to."

"Nice try Counselor, but it's not that simple. I suggest you stick to law. You're not doing so hot as a psychologist."

Jamal pulled one long leg across the yellow vinyl-covered chair and sat next to Pat at the kitchen table. Without asking, she went to the refrigerator and returned with two cold beers. He accepted one gratefully, popping the top. He took a long sip straight from the can, watching her over the rim.

"So what's a fella to do?"

"Depends on how serious a fella is . . ." Pat poured her can into a plastic cup and watched it foam.

"Well, I'm a pretty serious fella. I'm ready to settle down and make a real commitment to the right woman. I like family and I'm pretty normal."

"Let's see," he rolled his eyes in exaggerated thought. "I had a great childhood, supportive parents, a big brother I loved, who loved me. No horror stories there. We lost my brother in Vietnam . . . that was while I was still in high school."

He sipped thoughtfully at his beer, giving himself a few seconds to think. "I always believed the loss may have been what killed my mother." He sipped again. "I miss her a lot."

"After she died, my dad grieved himself to death two years later. They had been married twenty-six years when she died." He paused, then shook his head before continuing, "I miss my family. I miss being a part of a family. I guess you can tell how important they were to me. . . ."

"I'm beginning to understand," Pat murmured quietly.

"You really want to hear this? I get pretty maudlin." He waited for her nod.

"My family was a good one. Not large, but real solid. None of that dysfunctional stuff for us—we were close and sensitive before it was fashionable. Growing up like that means that if you like it, and I did, you want to continue it into your adult life." He turned dreamy eyes to Pat. "Know what I mean?"

"Sounds like you might know what you want."

"Oh, yeah!" He leaned heavily forward on the elbows he propped on the table. "Pat, I'm thirty-six years old. I've had some time to think about what I want to do in and with my life."

"I was engaged to a woman who couldn't imagine life without cocktail parties, and a featured place on the society pages. She didn't like the idea of my working with the state or with poor people. Charity work, she called it. A salaried spouse didn't fit in with her image of the future."

Pat pursed her lips and nodded wisely, *we all know someone like that,* she thought.

"Don't look like that. I'm a big boy, and I'm not carrying a torch here. She's part of the long distant past. Marie. Her name was Marie, and she dreamed of money and class . . . power. She was a smart woman, though. She knew that you have to sleep to dream, and she was no sleeper. No dreamer . . . like me."

Pat could see the professional attorney in him, despite the casual shirt and shorts. Presenting his case calmly with just enough emotion to convince, he leaned forward, both hands clasped tightly around the can he still held.

"I always hoped the woman I'd love and spend my life with

would be like me. A dreamer. But what I really want you to understand is that I've waited for a long time to love a woman with heart—I mean integrity and intellect. Good looks and sex appeal are just fringe benefits. If she'd stand still long enough, I have the feeling Noelle could be the woman I've waited for. All I want is a chance."

His earnestness was convincing. Pat fought her conscience, but it never had a chance.

"You sound like your life may have been the flip side of Noelle's. I mean, she comes from a really good family and all that, and like you, she also treasures the ideas of family and long-term commitment, but . . . well . . . things happen."

Pat paused, unsure of how much more she could tell without compromising her friend. "Things happen, and to tell you more I'd have to tell the girl's business, and that would be wrong. But, let's just say she hasn't had a really good record with men and trusting is hard for her. She has a good heart. She is a good person. She is worth salvaging."

Jamal grinned broadly, and crunched the empty beer can in his large hand. "I get the feeling she's not the only good person around here. What you're telling me is to persevere. Right?"

"Yeah, I guess I am. Want another beer?"


Oh, this was really good. Now she was hiding in a locked car, in ninety-seven degree heat. This was not the mature way to handle the problem of Jamal Harris. He was not nearly as irritating as she kept pretending he was, Noelle scolded herself. She admitted that the anxiety she felt each time she encountered Jamal was a smoke screen. Easily, he was the most seductively enigmatic and attractive man she'd ever met.

Jamal looked so natural carrying the ribs and chicken into the kitchen. The truth was, even carrying a platter of semiburned, smoky meat, everything in her reached out for him. No matter where she'd seen him, he never seemed out of place.

He seemed natural in a suit and tie, arguing the merits of

child placement. He certainly was at ease in those wonderful, soft jeans from yesterday. And today, those shorts . . . she shifted in her seat, stirred by the tempting memory. No doubt about it, the man was good-looking and he truly moved her.

So, what was the problem?

She just didn't know enough about him. She didn't know if she could trust him. She was not even sure she'd know how to trust him. Trust. In the past, that had been a problem. Noelle thought she knew Wayne too. Apparently knowing and trusting were two different things, she noted.

Meeting Wayne Sterling during her senior year at Case-Western Reserve University, had been a major point in her life. For the first time in her life, she had felt connected to another person. When he said "I love you," she believed him. When he asked her to marry him, she accepted thinking they had a lot in common, that she would grow to love him the way he claimed to love her. That, she sneered at herself, is what she got for thinking.

Wayne had been easy on the eyes—looking good was a life skill for him. Good-looking and no good. He'd certainly done her no good.

She looked down at her hands, noting the third finger of her left hand. It was bare. A constant reminder that she'd left good-looking, scheming Wayne for a reason.

Rolling down the car window, she looked around the busy parking lot marveling at the number of holiday shoppers rolling carts and loading groceries. Dropping her head back against the headrest, Noelle squinted through the harsh glare of the afternoon sun. A breeze stirred the hot, muggy air outside, while heat settled more snugly in her car.

Good old Wayne.

Noelle hadn't thought about him in a long time, but she'd never forget Wayne. He promised he would cherish her in ways her mother and stepdad never had. He capitalized on her loneliness and her ingrained desire and need for love. She had been so hungry for the love and support he offered, she'd followed him like a horse followed a carrot on a stick.

Eager to have Louis Perry all to herself, Mattie rushed her daughter into marriage. Actually, Noelle thought, they practically sold me off to Wayne.

He really did get a good value. Wayne had taken her off her parents' hands for a two-bedroom condo full of furniture, a new convertible, a seven-day honeymoon cruise, and full payment of his student loans. On top of it all, he got a slave.

And after all those years, she'd become bitter, Noelle noted with some surprise. She'd always believed she was a better person than that.

With the omniscience of hindsight, Noelle thought of all the things she could have said, should have said to avoid Wayne. She could have just opened her eyes and seen him for the user he really was, but she had said nothing. She'd allowed herself to be groomed and dressed and partied right down the aisle, and that part wasn't really anyone else's fault. She wished she could have been less needy, or maybe if she'd had the self sufficiency she'd learned over the years, she brooded. Maybe then, things would have been different.

It had taken a lot in a short time to finally drive her away from Wayne. She'd hated the idea of failing at the marriage she'd wanted so desperately. His ego-driven rages, the money, and the emotional pain he was so readily able to inflict upon her had been the catalyst.

Man, that last time—she shivered in spite of the shimmery, engulfing heat. The last time Wayne turned on her taught her a lot about life, love, parental support, and about men. Noelle could still hear her mother's voice.

"Oh, Noelle what happened this time?" Disgust and anger fought for control of Mattie's face and voice.

"Mom. Help me please," Noelle had begged.

She'd wanted to say more, but her head seemed to sag with pain. The migraine was predictable and debilitating. She'd been having them since her honeymoon.

From the hospital bed, the pain convinced Noelle that running away from her ten-month-old marriage was a good idea. Her mother hadn't seen it quite that way.

"What happened this time?" Mattie was determined to know.

Noelle bit her tongue. She'd wanted to give a rude, crazy answer like, "Wayne just loves me so much, he ignores me, does what he wants, and leaves me to clean up his mess, and this time it's a big one." Instead, she answered her mother with silence, hoping she'd think it was the medication and just go away. It didn't work.

"Noelle, what happened?" Now both Louis and Mattie were demanding her attention and response.

"I walked in on Wayne and some woman," Noelle finally answered through the haze of medication. "It wasn't the first time, but this is the last time," Noelle promised herself. "I can't take his doing just anything with anybody. When I complain, I'm wrong." She didn't mention the other thing. She didn't dare.

"What!" Her stepfather exploded. "I just don't believe it! Wayne loves you. He's a good man. He'd never do anything— Mattie, I told you the girl was unstable! I don't believe it! You're making this up. . . ."

Mattie instantly, and instinctively moved to silence and protect her outraged husband, finally sending him into the waiting room. Returning to her daughter's bedside, she'd turned on Noelle with unexpected venom.

"Exactly what was that little act supposed to accomplish?" Her eyes narrowed suspiciously. "Your little bid for sympathy is not going to work this time. You had no right to disturb *my* husband like that. You're an adult and you'd better damn well start acting like it."

"Wayne is your husband, for God's sake. Why can't you overlook a little indiscretion? Why did you have to act so childishly? Every man does things like that. It's part of being a man and you need to just understand it.

"I don't want to hear any more of this noise about you leaving him, either. Where do you plan to go if you do leave him? You cannot come crying home to us if things don't work out. I have my own husband, and my own life to take care of. As it is, I'm missing my club meeting tonight. You'll have to go back to Wayne. I won't hear of you doing anything else." She fanned a hand in dismissal.

Adjusting her jacket, Mattie had pressed her hands to her carefully dyed and styled hair. She was trying, visibly, to calm herself. "I'll see you tomorrow . . . you need to talk to Wayne . . . decide what you're going to do." And she left.

Noelle spent an indeterminate amount of time staring down at her hands. She thought about her mother's words. Obviously, in Mattie and Louis's eyes, Noelle was wrong—the culprit, not the victim.

Wayne never loved her, and at the time Noelle thought his abandonment would kill her. Six years later, she still had trouble with the idea that her mother and stepfather believed that was Wayne's right. Noelle passed a hand across her eyes, still looking at the past.

And then there was the night she'd left. Across the shadow of years past, Noelle still felt the anger and pain of that night. She wondered how Wayne had taken her leaving. Of course, he would see it as her abandoning him in his time of need, but that was Wayne.

She brushed the back of her hand across the bridge of her nose, sweeping tears away. Getting out of the car, she walked toward the store. Maybe the movement would make her feel better. She moved quickly through the parking lot, sun-warmed asphalt burned through her sandals and she actively appreciated the air-conditioned coolness of the grocery store. Brushing hair back from her face, Noelle meandered up and down the aisles. Thinking.

She could still remember her late-night departure from St. Vincent's Charity Hospital.

Broken-spirited and crying after her mother's departure, Noelle's options were loveless and limited. No job, no money, no love. Then the phone rang. It was Wayne. He was pleasant, almost cheerful, having solved the riddle of his wife's location simply by calling the nearest hospital. Her hands shook as she gripped the telephone.

"How're you feeling? I'm sorry about the little argument earlier, but things were just a little out of control. You know how I get when I'm under too much pressure," he said.

"Your bosses called. They said they hope you're doing better. I guess they can't wait for you to get back so you can finish working on the books, and I think that would be for the best, don't you?" Her husband was so cool, her teeth chattered from the memory. He sounded calm and natural, teasing her with thinly veiled threats. All of it under a smarmy veneer of pleasant chatter.

Resolving then to get away from him, the next evening, she left the hospital with the clothes on her back, pain pills from a sympathetic nurse, and the money in her purse.

She'd run to the nearest bus station. The next bus out was destined for Atlanta, Georgia. Noelle rapidly counted her money. She had enough—barely. She boarded that bus, and rode into a new life. A life lacking the fine china, heavy silver, and other amenities she'd known in Shaker Heights, Ohio. A life offering her freedom from the pain she had lived with for so long.

Shame quivered a cold line of goose bumps across her skin. Strange, how even with the passage of so many years, she still felt dirty from her time with Wayne. She almost felt like it was sticking to her skin, like anyone who looked at her could see it. The indignities, she thought, and bit her lip to keep from speaking aloud. It was hard, even now, to believe they were behind her.

"Miss? Are you okay? You looked a little . . ." The man was tall and slim, wearing a blue polyester FoodMart jacket, and a name tag identifying him as Ralph. Noelle jumped away from the hand Ralph extended.

"I'm fine. Thanks."

He squinted through wire-framed glasses. His furrowed brow pushed his already receding hairline higher.

"I just got a little turned around." Her vision cleared and the past faded wispily. "I see what I need right over there." She could feel the man watching her back as she turned the corner into the next aisle.

In Atlanta, Noelle shielded herself from all sorts of potential pain. She learned who she was with the support of a good friend, but there were things that she'd never fully told anyone. Even Pat. Things she probably would never have the words or the courage to tell.

She secured her divorce in nearby Florida but the aura of Wayne's filth still touched her. Her only remaining connection to her family was the occasional letter she mailed to them several times a year from different locations around the country— she'd gotten good at having coworkers and acquaintances mail them for her when they traveled.

She wondered again why she bothered with the letters. Even if she included a return address, she wondered if she really wanted to hear from Mattie or Louis Perry. She wondered what her mother was like now. If she had gray hair pulled back in a bun, and spending her spare time busily baking cookies for the neighborhood kids. "No," she shook her head denying the fantasy. "My mother is as chic and trendy as ever, probably out playing tennis and chairing some committee."

Noelle looked over her shoulder. Ralph was pushing a cart past her aisle, still looking like he thought she might be dangerous.

Even now, in her heart, Noelle knew she hadn't forgiven her mother for her casual abandonment. She could overlook her stepfather's betrayal because he had always treated her as an accessory. Never really like a daughter. But, her own mother. That was different. Noelle wanted to believe that a stronger bond should have existed between a mother and daughter. It still hurt her to know that no silken emotional code ever linked her to her mother.

She couldn't continue this private life forever. Eventually, she knew she would have to let someone in.

She thought briefly of the warm little girl waiting for her at

Pat's house. Admittedly, she was lonely. At some point, she knew she was going to have to learn to trust someone. It would be so wonderful to find someone to love. Pat warned her . . . Noelle let the thought hang. She pushed a cart over to a display of soft drinks and loaded it. Adding chips and ice cream, she headed for the checkout.

"If I continue to hide out like this, Wayne and his meanness will win. He gets to hold me prisoner," she muttered to herself, smiling back when the elderly lady in front of her looked around with a suspicious smile.

"It's not fair and I'm not going to live like this anymore," Noelle hissed to herself. "And besides, I'm not just alone anymore, I'm lonely. I feel like I'm still paying for a crime I didn't commit. I feel broken, damaged. I want the 'happily ever after' part of my life. I'm ready for a man, a companion, in my life. I'm ready to be happy, and to share that happiness. I'm ready to repair this part of my life and that's what I'm going to do."

The elderly woman eyed Noelle, and moved two steps farther away, her smile wavering slightly.

Jamal Harris was an ideal choice. He was attractive, sensitive, bright, single, and—if yesterday was any indication—he loved children. If she could stop building walls and closing him out, maybe he was as interested in her as she was in him.

Could it be that all he needed was a chance? Maybe, if she could just keep her foot out of her own mouth long enough to give him a chance . . . Maybe, she sighed, he's deserving of that chance. Every man in the world wasn't like Wayne. Some were better. Noelle was betting that Jamal Harris was better. It was a bet she wanted to win.

"Okay," she told herself sternly, "nothing beats a failure but a try. So, I'll try." Grabbing her bags, and stepping around the cautious elderly woman, she headed back to Pat's with conviction in her heart.

# Eight

"Sounds like a car."

"Wonder who it could be? Jamal, can you see who it is?" Pat shifted in her lawn chair to reach her glass of lemonade. She twisted further to her left, straining to see the new arrival.

"She's baaack . . . ," Jamal whispered as Noelle rounded the corner of the house, bags in hand.

Weaving her way through the dancing, eating, chattering crowd, Noelle made her way over to Pat and Jamal. Angel paused—still clutching Kermit—to wave happily.

"With this crowd, I figured you could use more munchies." Noelle hoped she sounded calmer than she felt, and she turned quickly away.

Pat's strong fingers snaked across the short distance between her chair and Jamal's to quickly pinch his arm. Her head jerked in Noelle's direction. Twice. He caught on and followed her quickly.

"Let me help." From behind, he grabbed two of the bags.

Here he was again, helping her. Conviction wavered for just a moment. How hard, she worried, was she going to have to work to find out what he wanted from her?

Raw panic crept through Noelle's already trembling bones. Oh God, she prayed, what if I misread him? What if all he really wants is to be a good Samaritan? She stepped ahead of Jamal, crossing the bright kitchen, feeling heated blood warm her face and neck.

"Noelle?"

She paused, balancing ice cream against one hip, to look at him over her shoulder.

"Have I done something to offend you?"

His slow, careful, southern drawl seemed to wrap itself securely about her. No. Jamal Allen Harris was anything but offensive to her. "Why would you think that?"

"I think you're a pretty nice lady. I'd like to know you better, but I get the feeling I make you uneasy. Do I?"

"Oh, no!" She said it too quickly. Turning her back to him, she pushed the ice cream farther into the freezer. "I'm just getting to know you, and there are a lot of other things going on in my life right now."

"But, I would like to know you better," she said into the freezer.

Hot damn! He had her now. At least she was standing still and talking to him—even if her head was in the freezer. She had even said that she was willing to know him better. The attorney in him surged forward, pressing a known advantage.

"One way to learn more about a person is to spend some time together," he said gently. She was still facing the freezer. "I eat pretty regularly. How about you?"

She giggled into the freezer as she nodded her head. *Good,* Jamal thought, *a sense of humor helps.*

"Do you think we might manage to eat at the same time? Like maybe in the same restaurant? I'd even be willing to spring for a sitter. . . ."

Noelle turned from the freezer, slowly closing the door. "It's just that I don't date much."

"It hasn't changed recently. I trust your basic social skills will suffice, and anyway," he warmed her again with his stunning smile, "I'd enjoy the company."

"Really, it's nice of you to offer, but . . ."

"James! Pick it up!" Pat yelled as she burst through the back door. "I'm not going to tell you again!" Her eyes continued to follow her son even as she reached behind her.

"I need that big platter, with the potato salad on it." Wiggling fingers prompted Noelle. "And the bread." Noelle found them. Pat passed the large basket of bread out the door to the plump lady standing on her porch.

"James! You boys stop scaring the girls." The boys had found a small snake and were terrifying a delighted group of little girls. "And get it out of here—I don't like it either!" She passed the platter through the door.

Pat's entrance gave Jamal an idea. A double date. That ought to work with Noelle. No way could she reasonably refuse, besides Pat's personality and temperament were ideal for Morgan. *He'll do it. He's a pal, a buddy, a friend. Besides if he doesn't, I'll cripple him,* Jamal thought.

"Pat," he reached out to catch her arm, "we're going out to dinner tomorrow evening." Jamal was talking fast, trying to out-talk Noelle's objections. "I thought, maybe you'd like to join us." He was nodding, willing her to take the hint. Pat was nodding, caught in the rhythm of his words and his bobbing head.

"A date?" Pat looked horrified.

"Yeah Pat, date." The teasing voice grated on her nerves. "Like the man who'll pick you up, and spend the evening in your charming company. Date."

"Noelle," Pat said dryly, "I used to consider you a friend." One eyebrow inched upward. "A blind date? With a strange man?" She shook her head. "I don't know."

"He's not that strange, and you'd be doing me a real favor. Morgan's a good man, he's got no plans, and needs a good excuse to get out in public."

"What is he? Some kind of hermit?" Pat's face twisted. "You make him sound very attractive. I think I'll pass, besides the kids . . ."

"Will be fine with a sitter," Noelle crossed her arms firmly across her chest.

Pat watched Jamal's encouraging nod. *What a good-looking*

*man,* she thought. His voice was so convincing and earnest. Pat bet he worked the hell out of a jury. "Well . . ."

It was Jamal's turn to pinch. "Sure. It'll be fun. A chance for you ladies to dress up and spend an evening on the town. Say yes." He looked meaningfully at Pat. "You'll have a good time."

"Well," she drawled.

"Oh, come on Pat. It could be fun. I'll go if you will."

Pat had to look twice. Could this really be the reclusive, re-tiring, monastic Noelle she'd known for so long? She almost sounded excited. This man was even more persuasive than he seemed before. He must really be one heck of a lawyer!

"Okay," Pat agreed uncertainly. She'd always hated double dates, but this one was for a good cause.

Satisfied, Jamal finally released her arm, and she sank into a nearby chair. Pat rubbed her pinched arm and looked suspi-ciously up at Jamal.

"Great!" he clapped his hands together—like it sealed their deal. "Your date, Morgan, will pick you up at eight. How's Dailey's? Down on International? Maybe the City Grille if you'd rather? Or somewhere else? You choose."

Pat looked dazed, "Dailey's is fine." Noelle nodded.

James erupted into the kitchen. "Horseshoes Jamal," he screamed. "We're ready to play! You promised."

"I really did." He looked apologetically to Noelle and Pat and silently blessed James.

They both waved him out the door.

He wanted to cheer. Jamal couldn't remember a courtroom victory that had been more significant than his effort to get some time with Ms. Noelle Parker. Perseverance paid off.

"I got a date." He said it to no one in particular.

"Who with," asked James.

"Oh, with your friend Noelle."

"Aw-right!" crowed James. "She's nice and she's fun. You'll have a good time. You gonna take my mom too? She could use some fun. You know, grown-up fun."

The little guy was wise beyond his years. Jamal grinned and

looked around the large crowded yard. "Where're those horse-shoes, anyway?"

Noelle poured herself a glass of lemonade. Sitting across from Pat, she looked at her friend.

"Dinner. Do you believe he just conned us into dinner?" Noelle grimaced distastefully. "Why'd it have to be dinner?"

" 'Cause you would've found another excuse if he had sug-gested lunch, drinks, or a movie. Besides, what's wrong with dinner?"

"Well excuse me for thinking, but most people are not at their most attractive choking down food and chewing like cows."

"I see. So, now you want to be attractive?"

"Pat! You know what I mean."

Eyebrows rose. "Do I?"

Noelle slumped back in her chair and gave up. Pat was like water, given enough time, she could wear out a rock.

"So, what are you going to wear tomorrow?" Pat giggled.

Noelle huffed in mock indignation. "I have no idea," she said.

Angel trudged across the kitchen, face and hands sticky from ice cream, still hauling Kermit. She paused beside Noelle's chair and looked from Noelle to Pat and back again. She closed her eyes and smiled as Noelle's hand gently traced the soft line of her warm forehead. She reached for a damp towel to clean the little face and hands.

"Girl, you know you do that almost too naturally."

"Maybe, but it's fun, and it needs to be done," Noelle replied.

"Yeah," Pat agreed.

"The blue dress is pretty," Angel said.

"What!" both women exclaimed, jaws dropping in unison. Noelle never felt the towel drop from her stunned fingers.

The child tipped her head and blinked quietly. Unimpressed by the effect of her now-broken silence, she sighed.

Pat leaned forward. "Baby, what did you say? Tell Aunt Pat what you said."

"I said to my mommy, the blue dress is pretty."

Noelle found the dropped towel and folded it neatly. "Did you call me your mommy?"

Angel smiled and nodded. "You want to look pretty like the ladies on TV? Wear a pretty dress. Blue dresses are pretty," the child repeated patiently.

Still blinking in disbelief, Noelle faced Pat. "I guess I'll wear the blue dress."

Angel threw both arms across Noelle's lap, then followed with one short leg. Noelle helped her into her lap.

"You're talking?"

"Yes."

"You didn't talk to me before."

Angel calmly arranged Kermit in her own lap, then looked up. Her brown eyes were huge. "I didn't have nothing to talk about. But, now I do." She smiled and rearranged Kermit.

"Well, I'm glad you decided to talk to me. Did you talk to James and Kelly?"

"Yes, when we played the game. I talk to you because I love you." She looked up and blinked again. "It's good to love your mommy."

Pat's lips parted in surprise, but she said nothing.

"Where is your mommy?" When the child smiled brightly, Noelle immediately corrected her. "Not me. Your mommy."

"Other mommy? I don't know, maybe in Heaven." The women exchanged startled looks.

"Sweetie," Noelle waited for the child to look up. "Where do you live?"

"Dunno." She paused to think, then looked clever. "I live with you."

"Do you go to school."

"Uh-uh." Further questions only seemed to confuse the little girl. She seemed to have accepted her change in circumstances, and liked the idea of having Noelle as her mother.

"Angel, I just can't believe you saved all this up," Pat told her. "Is there anything else you need to say?"

The little girl nodded and looked up at Noelle. "I like J'mal," she announced. "Do you like J'mal?"

Noelle looked to Pat for help, but her friend was studying the child. "Yes," she finally answered, "I do."

Pursing her lips, Angel looked up again, this time including Pat in her solemn gaze. "That's very, very good. He likes you too. And you know what?" She leaned close to Noelle, her small finger beckoning to Pat, "J'mal would make a good daddy for us."

" 'Out of the mouths of babes,' " Pat whispered.

# Nine

"Okay. Fine. I've made this about as difficult as I can." Noelle had thrown every excuse she could think of from her formidable arsenal at Jamal, and the indomitable Mr. Harris had risen to each occasion. They still had a date.

"It's too late to leave town. I wanted a man, and now I guess I'm committed." She caught sight of herself in the mirror above the old yard-sale dresser she'd refinished last summer. Her face was flushed and excited. "Girlfriend, you've got a date. Get a move on."

Noelle's fingers pulled and smoothed the lacy strapless bra over the smoothly blushing, cocoa-colored skin of her breasts. Her blue silk dress fit too closely to tolerate wrinkles or bumps underneath. Stepping into the wispy matching slip, she allowed it to settle over her taut hips and flat stomach. Her fingers dipped low to straighten the long, beribboned garter holding her hose in place.

"Maybe he's seen me in too much blue already," she whispered to herself. Raising her eyes to the mirror, catching sight of the teal-blue silk against her skin, she changed her mind. Rich color enhanced the subtle tones of her skin. Angel was right. The blue dress was pretty and it would look great tonight.

She could hear Angel giggling with the baby-sitter in the living room as she slipped the blue dress from the hanger. Angel. . . . Now, there was a puzzle. The previously silent child was now a regular chatterbox. She couldn't seem to keep quiet for more than a few seconds at a time.

Noelle still wondered why the child had chosen to break her silence at Pat's. Willing to speak to other children about other things, she still hadn't told anyone her real name. Apparently she liked Angel just fine. She didn't seem to know her correct age, but she was good at alternating between one, three, four, and five fingers.

Noelle and Pat had questioned Angel for more than an hour, trying to determine whose baby she really was. When asked about parents, Angel smiled an adorably sweet smile and replied with certain finality supplemented with child-logic, "My mommy went to sleep. She's gone now."

Gone where? If she knew, Angel certainly wasn't telling.

When asked where she lived, the child smiled inscrutably, snuggled deeper into Noelle's lap, and continued to reply, "with you." That settled all questions as far as she was concerned.

So, where did she come from? "Home," Angel stated simply as though it was perfectly obvious.

Noelle stood turning the dress in her hands debating what she knew of Angel. Her mind drifted across the few facts she knew until she caught sight of the clock. Running late, she dropped the dress on her bed, and began a flurry of activity.

Her robe, shoes, jewelry, and perfume flew like things in a Disney movie. The doorbell rang as she grabbed for her dress, silk whispering along the floor as she stepped into its full skirt, pulling the strapless bodice higher.

"Miz Noelle, your date is here," the baby-sitter sang around the door. Sticking her head and an arm into the room, Pam winked and signed, 'ok'. Giggling at Noelle's self-conscious grin, the girl ducked back around the corner.

Zipping as she moved, Noelle seized her handbag and matching jacket. Stepping into the living room, she wasn't fully prepared for the sight of the penultimate *GQ* male. To say that he was handsome and neatly attired was almost like calling Niagara Falls "a little dripping water."

Jamal looked like a model for one of those liquor ads she'd grown up seeing in magazines. An ad for the genteel and elegantly luxurious "good life." Her breath caught in her throat as she tried to speak.

The dark Armani suit was tailored carefully, with beautifully detailed stitching. It fit his tall, athletic frame with delicious intent accenting all the positives of his athletic physique. The pale pink of his shirt played up the tan he'd earned at yesterday's cookout, while the bold pattern of his tie drew her willing glance to his broad chest.

He was so comfortable with looking good, Noelle admired. He looked like dressing this way was second nature to him. She'd seen him in several other outfits, but happily admitted she liked this one best. He was a vision of sartorial splendor, and she liked it. A lot.

Pam, was obviously captivated by Jamal's abundant gorgeousness. From the moment he entered the room, he was the sole focus of her attention. Her already large eyes had widened then narrowed, lashes fluttering all the while. Now she was circling him as though he was something good to eat, and she couldn't figure out where to start.

Not even Angel was immune to his obvious charms. She was doing her bit to draw his attention, as well. Generously, the little girl even offered to let him hold Kermit again. Noelle figured his best defense was an introduction to Pam.

"Y'all sure do look nice tonight," the teenager was obviously directing her comment to Jamal. Noelle watched the girl flirt and preen under his attention. When it was time for them to leave, she looked like she took it a little personally. Pam actually pouted a bit as she closed the door behind them.

"You do look lovely," Jamal agreed warmly as they left the apartment.

Escorting Noelle to his silver Lexus, Jamal appreciated the subtle shift of her hips beneath the iridescent silk. He tried not to be obvious as he casually noted her way of moving. She walked beside him with a lithe, long-legged grace. Her movement was smooth and flowing, lending a pleasant swing to their combined steps.

A woman used to going places, he thought, not necessarily in a hurry, but with efficiency and dignity; she didn't bother with the erection of coy, mincing facades. She obviously didn't need to. Jamal enjoyed her unpretentious nearness.

He'd always considered himself immune to the sting and burn of obvious feminine beauty, but this subtle woman had a way of getting to him. She touched him in ways that he thought he'd long since forgotten and now remembering, found altogether too hauntingly pleasurable. Opening the door, his hand slipped to her slender waist, and he withdrew it reluctantly as she settled into her seat.

When he'd touched her, he'd been struck by a heated psychic image of what might be contained by the delicate silk. Intuitively, his fingers knew that her skin would be warm and pliant, smoother even than the material beneath his hand. He also knew that her flesh would be firm and tenderly yielding.

His hand had tried to stall its departure, wanting to stray further, knowing a mannerly need to move away and a human need to indulge. His sense of touch made him long to trace the slight shiver he felt when he'd touched her arm as she folded her body into his car.

Jamal felt a romantic rush of envy for the hair sweeping the gentle bend of her shoulder, and the sheen of light brushing her cheek. His hand ached to follow the light along the sweet curve of her breast.

Her perfume seemed to fill the air around her, and he wanted to discover all the private places she'd applied it. He wanted to caress the soft curves of her body and tell her exactly what was on his mind, but he knew better.

He knew, too well, the effects of her approach-avoidance conflict where he was concerned. He didn't want to frighten her away again. The car seemed unbearably warm and oppressive. He hadn't felt like this since his teenaged years. Sitting so near her, air conditioning was a major necessity. He started to drive.

"I'm glad we settled on Dailey's. Before we go though, I want to make a quick stop. I need to check with a client," he looked over, happy to meet her provocative eyes. *I'm acting like she's the prom queen,* he scolded himself.

"Sure, that's fine." Her voice was level as she averted her eyes. She wondered if her heart had lurched visibly beneath her silken bodice. "Where are we going?"

He drove skillfully, talking along the way.

"We're going to Grady Hospital. I've got a young client there. A lot of things have happened around her over the past two days, and I'm guessing she's a little scared right about now. Probably wondering what's going to happen, and I just want to fill her in a little."

Turning onto Butler Street, he pulled into the parking lot using a coded card to activate the gate. The lot was abandoned, and sheathed in shadows. He peered through the windshield— no guard in sight. There seemed to be a lot of cars, but no people.

"Do you think," Noelle asked, "that your client would mind if I came in too? I mean, I wouldn't want to violate her confidentiality or anything, but . . ." she looked around warily.

He looked at Noelle. He looked at Noelle in that dress. No way he was leaving her behind.

They found Andrea Pierce playing a card game with the evening duty nurse. She eyed Noelle suspiciously, taking careful note of every detail.

"Guess I'll just collect these," the nurse folded the cards easily into her hands. "You talk to your lawyer honey," her dark hand patted the girl's leg as she smiled at Noelle, and excused herself.

Andrea continued to check Noelle out.

"Well Andy," the girl's eyes shifted hungrily to Jamal's when he spoke, "how're you doing?"

"Pretty good, 'cept it was kinda lonely. I haven't had much company, just you an' Mr. Dennison," the girl said slowly. "Who's she?"

"A friend," he grinned and the girl shrugged her shoulders. Noelle took a breath and stepped into the curve of his arm. Though she'd never imagined herself taking such a bold step, she couldn't imagine being anywhere else, right then. "She's a good friend," he assured Andrea.

Obviously liking his tone, Andrea brightened. "Oh! I got it," she announced. Finality and triumph mixed dreamily on her thirteen-year-old face. "She's your lady. Your girlfriend!"

Mortified, Noelle began to count the tiles on the hospital room floor.

*Don't I wish,* Jamal thought, and changed the subject.

"Andy, they're releasing you on Monday."

"Yeah," her little face lost its brightness, and her voice dropped, almost as though someone had flicked some internal switch.

"I gotta go home. Sure was nice here though," she looked wistfully around the room, pleating and smoothing the sheet as she spoke. "Quiet, and it's pretty clean too. Food wasn't that great . . . but no bugs. The nurses were real nice," she sighed, ". . . just nice. You know?"

She looked from Jamal to Noelle and back again, willing them to understand.

"I know," Noelle said almost to herself, understanding the kind of home that could make a hospital stay seem pleasant.

"I know," Jamal said, remembering the loud, dirty, over-crowded Pierce home with the abusive mother and the revolving door policy on boyfriends.

"Andy, the reason we came by tonight . . . the reason I came by tonight is to try to explain some things to you."

Noelle drifted over to the orange vinyl-covered chair next to the window. Andrea looked closely at Jamal's face—silently questioning. He seemed to be organizing and filing thoughts as he spoke.

"So," Andrea looked at Noelle again, "you a lawyer too?" Her voice was strained as she tried to ignore the subject. It was evident she didn't want to hear Jamal's explanation.

"No," Noelle almost whispered.

"She's a caseworker. She works for the Department of Family and Children Services," Jamal detailed. "Maybe," he looked into Noelle's watchful eyes, "she can explain some of the things I'm not making clear."

"Oh. You mean you're like the lady who does the food stamps and Medicaid and stuff? My mother gets a check for us." Her eyes brightened with understanding as Noelle nodded. "We get all that stuff at home . . ."

"You're not going home. Yet."

The girl's eyes squinted, distrust slid easily onto her narrow face. "Where am I going Mr. Harris?"

"We went ahead and got a warrant for your mother and Larry's arrest. Do you understand what that means?"

"Who's we?" she asked cautiously.

"We is Mr. Dennison and me. You met him this morning, remember?" The girl nodded. "We are your lawyers. Under state law, we represent your rights, and one of those rights is not to be beaten like you were."

"Okay. So, like, why'd you get my mother 'rested?"

Both the adults flinched at the girl's question, but she deserved an answer. Professionally, logically, they understood the psychology of the abused child. Typically, the children always loved their abusers. Andrea was no exception, even with the beatings and neglect that were a regular part of her home life, she was still concerned about her mother.

"Andy, the biggest reason is because you're important. Your mother, any parent, has an obligation to protect and take care of their child. Your mother didn't do that."

Noelle found his fervor very sexy. For just a moment, she wondered if Jamal did everything with this same level of intensity. Her eyes traveled the length of his body. She just wondered, . . . *Get your mind out of the gutter,* she scolded herself, and turned her attention back to what he was saying.

"Another of those rights," he was forcefully warming to his

topic, "is that you don't have to have sex with anyone you don't want to. Besides, you're a minor. That means . . ."

This was bad. He hadn't told her about the depth of Andrea's problems. Noelle rose quietly from her chair, and tugged gently at his sleeve. He had been so caught up in making sure that Andrea understood, he hadn't noticed how uncomfortable he was making her.

"You get the idea . . ." Andrea nodded at him and he tried to make the rest of his explanation simpler, a little easier. Andrea waited silently.

"The sheriff's office is going to use that warrant I told you about to pick up your mom and Larry tonight. We've got a foster home ready for Pietta, Michael, and you."

"Together?" Her voice trembled, and a tear shimmied its way down one brown cheek. The girl suddenly looked very young and defenseless. Noelle patted the tear away.

"Yes. Your brother and sister will be with you." Jamal's voice was husky and infinitely kind. "Yes, we want you safe and together."

"What are they? I mean, are the foster people like us?" Her voice was sharp. "Mixed up? 'Cause they might not understand about us if they're like just plain black or white or brown."

"How about if they're just good, honest people who like kids?"

Her lips parted in a relieved grin. "That'd be cool," she agreed settling back on her stacked pillows. This kid recovered quickly.

"Last time we checked, that's exactly what they were." Jamal laughed. Noelle smiled, watching the exchange. He was good at his job.

"You know," Andrea tilted her head judgmentally, "you two look good together." Her head tilted again, straight black hair swept her shoulder. "Real good."

"Did y'all hear that little bell? Well," the nurse propped the door open with her foot as she entered with night medication, "visitin' hours are over, and Miss Andrea needs her rest."

Fifteen minutes later, Noelle watched Piedmont Road flash by in an urban blur from the front seat of Jamal's car.

"Andrea's a nice girl," she shook her head. "Too bad she's in such an awful situation. Did I hear you say that her mother and a boyfriend had abused her?"

Jamal nodded.

"There's so many good kids in bad situations. I know you can't help them all, but here, in Andrea's case I can't help but wonder, how will you prosecute?"

Jamal handled the car expertly, and continued driving as he spoke. "We have the mother on abandonment, assault, negligence, child endangerment, and sexual battery of all three children now. Before, it was only one child and there was no prosecution. The next time, she plea-bargained her way out of it. Got parole.

"This time Larry, the boyfriend, is an ex-offender with a history of physical battery and this is a violation for both of them. Besides that, we've got this one documented up the . . ." he stopped, aware of the very ungentlemanly phrase he'd been about to use.

Anger crossed his face as he thought about the Pierce children and the two dozen or so others like them he'd seen during his ten years with the state agency. It had never made sense to Jamal—this abuse and manipulation of innocent, dependent children. He took his cases personally. Often, he was all that stood between the children and brutality of their broken families.

"At least with this case, we can make a difference for those kids," he said almost to himself.

Noelle was moved again by his intensity.

She'd seen her share of abandoned and abused children at DFACS. The children always suffered. Noelle was glad Jamal was one of the good guys. He could help the Pierce children, and he was going to. She could see it on his face as he talked.

Noelle was seeing him in a whole new light. He was more than just a good-looking man with an excellent body. She could see where the authority and arrogantly forceful attitude she had resented earlier were needed in his job. He was an intelligent and goal-oriented man. He was dedicated to his job and his child-clients.

She liked hearing the conviction in his voice, the assurance of his expression. She liked it a lot. She found herself drawn as much to this as to his obvious masculinity. For a hot minute, she thought about reaching across the seat and drawing him into her arms to deliver the kiss she felt etched upon her lips. *Down girl,* she silently warned herself. *You've got an entire evening to get through.*

Jamal parked carefully, and swung out of the car to open Noelle's door. Proceeded by those long, elegant legs, she rose easily to stand near him. Her perfume drew him again. *Chill homeboy,* he warned himself, *you've been lucky so far but don't rush it.*

"Noelle!"

She'd never know if it was just one of those fortunate accidents or just spectacularly good timing. Noelle's head jerked in response to her name, and Jamal bent forward to catch the jacket she almost dropped. Their coincidence was too right to have been planned.

At his slight movement, Noelle turned her head. When their lips met with sweetly shocking brevity, they both tried to think of an immediate way to prolong the contact, but couldn't. Jamal moved away first, surprised by her gentle response, and aware that someone had called her name. His lips burned desperately, branded by the accident.

Noelle stepped back, her eyes following Jamal. Her tongue lightly traced the track of his kiss. Her upper lip still tingled from the brush of his mustache. She felt like a fairy-tale princess waking to the new possibilities of reciprocated love. Stepping gracefully away from the car, Noelle turned to look in the direction of the caller.

"Noelle!"

Tipping her head, Noelle could see Pat coming toward them

dressed in cool, sleeveless peach. She was accompanied by a tall, bearded man who had to be Morgan. Noelle and Jamal waved as their friends drew near.

Noelle remembered her jacket and turned to take it from Jamal. Her fingers met his with an electrical jolt that rocked them both. She folded the jacket over her arm, and carefully put her hand in his. A bold move for her, but he liked it. He stood waiting with her as Morgan and Pat joined them. The evening was looking more promising by the minute.

# Ten

". . . so, anyway, there we were standing with this big group trying to look like we belonged." Morgan laughed aloud at the punch line to his own story. Noelle and Pat were nearly in tears as he finished. Other diners turned to smile and stare at their group hilarity. That just made the whole thing funnier.

"No. No. That's really not the way it was," Jamal protested, trying to fit a serious look around his own laughter. He failed miserably and broke into further laughter.

"Oh, really," Noelle teased, "now you wanna tell it like it really was, huh?"

"No, he already told the big lie. You'll never buy the real story." Jamal had tears running down his face.

Noelle reached across the table to dab at the rolling tears, and the laughter broke out anew.

"Lord," Pat was shaking her head and calming herself. "Noelle, I need to make a quick visit. Come with me?"

She stood and Noelle, still giggling, followed her to the ladies' room. Once through the door, she whirled on Pat.

"Well?"

"Well, what?" Pat serenely moved to select a stall.

Noelle followed her. Pat quickly shut the door in her face.

"Tell me what you think of him."

"I think Morgan is tall and totally incredible. I think he's funny and . . ."

Noelle's kick at the stall door silenced her for a second or two. Over flushing water, Noelle heard Pat laughing to herself.

"You didn't say which 'him' you meant," Pat sassed. She took her time selecting a sink. "For a man you kept running from, he certainly seems to have your full and complete attention now."

"Tell me what you think of him," Noelle repeated.

"What does it matter, what I think? Okay, what I think is he's tall and drop-dead gorgeous," she grinned at Noelle's threatening look. "Seriously, I think Jamal Harris is one of the most charming and handsome, articulate and intelligent men I've ever met. I think he's so bright he could light up a room with a spare thought."

"I think that if you've decided to end your celibacy, he's the one you should do it with. I think that if you're planning a long-term relationship that includes him, you should give him every opportunity to prove he *is* Mr. Right."

"He's very convincing when he speaks and I'll bet he could talk you into almost anything, but he won't. He's got ethics and integrity and morals and standards. You fit them. I think he's also as taken with you as you are with him. He's a good, kind man. That's what I think!" Her pouting lips showed that she'd finished her statement.

"So, how much did he pay you for that endorsement?"

"I was paid quite well and totally in full, thank you very much." Pat feigned indignity. "I got Morgan."

"You like him?" Noelle giggled.

"Are collards green? Is a pig pork? Honey *please!* I could love that man . . ." She turned to her reflection in the vanity mirror before adding, "with a passion!"

"This is an interesting development. . . ." Noelle raised her eyebrows.

"He *is* an interesting development . . . for me. . . ." Pat let the words trail off suggestively.

Noelle sat on the small wine colored velvet stool and watched Pat try to arrange her unruly curls. She waited as Pat dug out blush and lipstick to repair her makeup. Pat even took the time to adjust her slip and her hose.

"How interesting a development?"

Pat smiled coyly. "Very interesting. I plan on seeing a lot of that man. If you know what I mean," she leered.

"Oooh, girl!" Noelle laughed, clapping her hands.

"Get your mind out of the gutter. . . ." Pat smiled primly. "What does that dirty little mind of yours suggest to you about Mr. Harris?"

"You know me too well for that. I haven't thought that far ahead."

"But you *are* going to see him again?" Pat insisted. She just wanted a little reassurance.

"I guess," Noelle's tone became wistful. "I could speculate, but I'm afraid to jinx something that could become good. Really good." Her tone brightened. "Let's get back to those two hunks before a couple of stray women come along and scoop them up."

"You mean like we did?"

"Exactly!"


"What're you grinning at?" Jamal asked before the women returned.

Morgan's grin widened above the small coffee cup. "My brother, you are a fine man. You not only find an earthly angel for yourself, but you bring along a friend for lonely little old me. Yes indeed, a fine man." He set the cup down, folded his hands across his well-muscled stomach, and leaned back in his chair with a satisfied sigh. "Yes, indeed. *Mon frere!*"

"That means you like Noelle, and Pat's alright too."

"That means I like Noelle, and I'll be seeing a lot more of Ms. Patricia Stevens and company."

"You met her kids?"

"Right. If I ever get tired of Pat, I'll consider falling in love with that cute little Kelly. And by the way, someday when we go into our own practice, do you think we could set aside an office for James? That little guy's as sharp as a tack. He's gonna make a terrific lawyer someday—when he's a little taller." He sipped more coffee, still beaming around the cup.

Jamal sat back in his chair and eyed his old buddy. "Man, I am not going to beg you for your opinion. You see, I have made up my own mind on this one. The more I see of her, the better I like her."

"I can understand that. I like what I've seen of her too." He grinned salaciously.

"Man," Jamal shook his head. "Once a dog, always a dog."

"Arf! Arf!"

"Fool! What do you think of her?"

"Jamal, my brother, you have done worse. Much worse. I've seen it. This lady's different, though. She's smart, and pretty, a little on the shy side, or maybe she's just slow to warm up? I gotta give you credit though, she's a fine lady. A definite keeper."

"I think she just might be that complement we talked about."

"You're still stuck on that, huh?" He looked up as the ladies approached the table, "I always did say you were too good at math to be an attorney. Ladies!" He stood to pull out Pat's chair, winking at Jamal over her shoulder.

Once Noelle was seated, Jamal turned to her. "How about a little dancing after dessert? Maybe at Caribbean Sunset?"

"Oh, I'm a lousy dancer." *Damn,* thought Noelle, *old habits are sure hard to break.* "It's just that I don't want to publicly embarrass you. People will think bad things if you dance with me," she warned playfully.

"I'll take my chances," he smiled back.

"Dancing sound good to you?" Morgan asked Pat.

"Is Caribbean Sunset the club in Underground?" Pat asked the question like it would help to determine the fate of the free world. When Morgan smiled into her eyes to say yes, Pat's smile showed that his answer determined a lot of things as far as she was concerned. Noelle shared a knowing smile with Jamal.

"Why else would I have worn these shoes?" Pat stuck her silver-shod feet into the aisle, tapping her toes rhythmically.

"Then dancing it is!"

*Now what?* After the time they'd spent together, Noelle couldn't fake a headache, slip through the door, and hope Jamal would call again soon. On the other hand, should she take a chance on sounding like an old movie cliche and invite him to, "come up and see her etchings"?

Stepping from the Lexus, Noelle wasn't surprised to find her palms moist as she gripped her keys and purse.

*I knew dating was a bad idea.*

Noelle found she had a little trouble breathing as she inserted the key into her door. *Now I'm going to be alone with this stunning man. I don't want to blow it.* "Sometimes it sticks a little," she said aloud. "The key, I mean."

*Why aren't there how-to manuals on what comes next in a date?*

What was next, she wondered. *A kiss.* Oh, that earlier impromptu kiss had been sweet, but all too brief. And now? An accidental repeat was too much to hope for.

"Let me help." His hand slipped over hers, guiding and warming it as he pressed the key home, then turned it. Noelle felt her knees turn to jelly.

She pushed the door open.

The sleepy baby-sitter was nodding over a bowl of chips, wedged into an armchair with Angel and Kermit sort of in her lap. The sleeping child was snoring like a trucker. Noelle managed to get her arms under the little body.

"I'll be right back. I want to get her into bed," she whispered.

Jamal roused the sitter. Pam looked disoriented as she blinked stupidly into the handsome face before her. Suddenly she remembered that she was almost sixteen—almost a full-grown woman. When she finally recovered, Jamal paid her for her services and watched from the door as she walked home. It amused him that she seemed to make most of the walk back-ward.

Turning from the door as Noelle returned to the room, Jamal marveled again at the way she looked and moved. Even if she told him to go away, never call her again, he knew that he wanted to carry the memory of the way she looked right then with him, forever.

"Why are you smiling like that?" she asked from across the room.

"I was thinking about my father," he replied softly. No lie. He really was. His dad had once told him and his brother about meeting their mother. He'd also told them about their first date and how she'd looked and acted.

Noelle seemed a lot like the graceful young woman his mother might have been. His dad had finished his story by saying that if the boys ever met a woman like that, they should marry her as soon as possible because she was too rare a jewel to be lost. His dad had always made a lot of good sense.

"Can I get you something?" she offered.

"No, thanks." It wouldn't be polite to ask for what crossed his mind.

"What were you thinking about your father?" She drifted closer.

He looked around the room before answering. "Just that he would have liked you. He would have liked this room too. He enjoyed indoor gardening and reading," he gestured to the plants and stacks of books.

Noelle felt herself blush. The lusty, Gothic, bodice-ripper romance lay on top of the stack nearest him. Her hand found the book and fumbled to put it behind the stack.

"Jamal, I had a really good time. Thank you for asking me out."

"I'm glad. It's late though." He stepped toward her, then backward to the door. "I'm sure you need to get an early start with Angel in the morning. You will be in the office Tuesday, right?"

"Absolutely," she assured him, coming closer.

"How about lunch? I'll be in the building around one."

"Sounds really fine. That's my usual time."

Pulling open the door, he smelled her maddening perfume again. What in the world was that stuff? The scent was softer now. Warmed by her body heat, it was muskier, more heady than before.

Suddenly Tuesday seemed an eternity away. "How about tomorrow," he blurted.

"Okay."

"We could . . ." *Could what?* He only knew he wanted to see her again as soon as possible. It didn't matter what they did, as long as they did it together.

"What time?"

It was time to go. He wanted to pull her close and trace the scent's path along every curve of her body. Almost wickedly compelling, his senses screaming, Jamal fought its call. It was really time to go.

Without thinking, Noelle reached for his hand. It rested in his for just a second longer than either of them would have thought necessary under other circumstances. Her eyes caught and tangled with his for just that second, and she thought the fleeting summer breeze might have been his hand at her cheek.

Maybe Pat was right. In that second, Noelle knew that she would only survive Jamal if she trusted her emotions. The lessons of her past simply would not apply to a man of this caliber. He was beyond those lessons, and in the sultry heat of the Georgia night, so was she.

Noelle took her first step of faith with her lips. Soft, slightly parted lips led her to the breathless discovery and exploration of his. Her hands moved along the line of his arms to his shoulders, lingering at his collar where her fingers teased his skin. His sigh cued her fingers and they joined, closing at his neck, drawing him closer.

Jamal thrilled at the touch of her fingers and her nearness. He fought the urge to clutch the desirable scented softness and heat that were Noelle. *Pull back,* his mind warned. *Better move slower,* he thought. The last thing he wanted to do right now was to scare her off. Right then, he wanted only to hold Noelle forever.

His hands moved to her body, as though they'd always known the way. He held her as though she might escape or somehow fade from his grasp. Echoes of an earlier dance seemed to presage her nearness, in fact, to make it inevitable. The narrow tightness of her waist and the curving softness of her breast called him with an answer to a hunger he'd felt all his life.

The soft silk of her dress echoed the blood-rush roaring in his ears. He wanted more of her. Like a man dying of thirst, he wanted to go deeper, to drink her in fully, and to remain there forever. In Noelle, he knew he'd found a home.

Her knees felt weak, almost nonexistent, and she swayed gently against him, letting him take her weight and her caution. Oh God, she nearly gasped aloud, what was she doing?

The silk of her dress rustled, whispering of the passion it hid. The long search of his burning kiss touched her tongue and her teeth. *How did he do that?*

The deliberate probe of his tongue against her willing lips demanded surrender of all those inhibitions Noelle had spent the past five years hiding behind. She felt walls of fear crashing with soundless abandon. She willingly let them tumble, break, and blow away on the summer breeze.

Noelle offered no protest as the kiss built and redoubled itself. The warmth and firmness of Jamal's lips silenced everything except her pounding heart. The trace of his tongue, teasing and tormenting her tender lips drew her deeper along a path of swirling heat—and she let it. How long had it been? Had she ever been kissed like this? Had any woman ever endured such sweet torture?

Trembling, elegant hands traced his jawline, then cradled his face, so close to her own. His heated lips seemed to kindle a consuming fire inside her. How could she send this man away, tell him he had no place in her life. How could she be sure he would not suddenly turn into Wayne?

It was a wonderful, swooping, triumph of a first kiss; a genuine shared man-woman experience. The kiss finally wound its way down to a series of small, tender, intimate little pressings and suckings. Noelle's arms were wound tightly about Jamal's neck, her head resting against his shoulder, and he found he liked that too.

"That was nice." Her voice seemed to stroke his ear with a feathery grace. Her eyes closed slowly, and her body relaxed gracefully against his, emotionally spent.

He found himself nodding. It was very nice, indeed.

When they finally parted, he was touched and pleased by her breathless, shy smile. Closing his eyes, he knew that he wanted more, much more from her. That kiss was only the beginning. It was definitely time to go. He could ask for no more. Not now. To do so would be to lose her, to chase her away—and he would not do that.

Her hand touched his chest then rested there, her smile grew a little broader. Placing his hand over hers, he asked, "Lunch?"

She nodded, as he stepped through the door. "Call me in the morning. We can plan something for later in the day." Her tender fingers traced electric lines across his cheek. It was Jamal's turn to smile and nod as Noelle disappeared behind the closed door.

# Eleven

"Thinking of teaching that technique to the Braves? They might never have traded Gant or Wiggins if they could do that. You fell into that chair like a runner rounding third for home."

"I'm ignoring you, Pat. Can you tell?" Noelle tossed her purse into the drawer at the side of her desk, and wheeled her chair around to grab the telephone on the second ring. Pat paused at the corner of Noelle's desk.

"You're late." She tapped her watch meaningfully. "What's up? Things okay with Angel?"

Noelle drew a finger across her lips in a silencing motion. "Good morning, Fulton County DFACS. How may I help you?" She got it all out without gasping for air.

"No, I'm sorry," she told the caller, "Alice Morton is on vacation this week. Is there anything I can help you with?" She grabbed for scratch paper and a pen. Pat continued to stand at the corner of Noelle's desk.

"Okay. Yes, Ms. Dalton. Would you give me your case number? Uh-huh, uh-huh, was that four-four-three-two-seven-one?" Noelle waited and listened to the extended complaint. Ms. Dalton's food-stamp voucher had been delayed by the holiday, and of course she was concerned. Money was tight and food was low.

Noelle turned her back on the distracting Pat as the client repeated her case number.

"I'll check the case for you. Can you hold on for just a moment?" She depressed the hold button and moved to the computer.

An unexpected whisper made her jump. "What happened after we left you?" Pat, eager as ever for all the news, had followed her. Her round face glowed with suppressed excitement. "I'll tell you what we did, if you tell me what you did," she teased in a singsong stage whisper.

"Things went very well. Thank you very much." Noelle returned to the client on the phone. "Ms. Dalton, I just checked and the benefits were issued last Thursday. Has your mail run yet?" She waited while Ms. Dalton explained the rigors of mail service in the inner city. "Okay. Well, check your mail today."

Pat made exaggerated faces and pantomimed a hurry up sign. When that didn't work, she stood drumming the edge of Noelle's desk impatiently. Her head twisted annoyingly back and forth to the tempo of Noelle's voice, and she was mouthing words almost under her breath.

"The voucher should come today." Noelle fanned her hand at Pat to shoo her away. Of course, Pat twisted her mouth to the side and stayed.

"I'm sorry, what did you say? Oh, well thank you," she laughed quietly, "but no ma'am, I can't move you to my caseload. No ma'am, I don't think they'll give me a raise for helping you, though it would be nice. Okay, call me back if you have any other problems with this. I'm Ms. Parker." She listened a moment longer while Pat continued to puff and blow from the corner of her desk, "Okay Ms. Dalton, you too. 'Bye."

"Okay, now for you." Noelle plunked the phone into its cradle and swiveled her chair toward Pat. "You really ought to see a doctor about that nose problem of yours."

"I called you yesterday. You were out."

"Jamal, Angel, and I had a picnic. There's not much more to tell." She averted her eyes and Pat knew that contrary to what Noelle was saying, there was indeed a lot to tell.

"Oh, well that's just fine. A picnic. Don't bother to fill me in. Keep it to yourself, why don't you?" Pat was intent on getting a satisfactory answer.

"We're going to have lunch today."

"Well, that accounts for the glow on your face," Pat commented tartly. "You've seen him every day since you met him, haven't you? Really, you look happy and you ought to be excited. Nothing perks a woman up like a new love."

"Who's in love? Who said I was in love? You ain't heard no such talk coming from me, girlfriend."

"Noelle, I can't remember the last time you had a date, and now you're going out with this adorable, intelligent, sexy man who obviously adores you. That man's got a voice that could tell me anything I wanted to hear. He's attentive, sensitive, and all the good things you could ask for. He wants the things you want, he likes the things you like, you have a lot of the same kinds of goals. He's perfect. What's not to love?"

"Pat, I wish you'd get that word out of your mouth, Noelle warned. "I don't know him well enough to commit to that kind of ongoing relationship. He was great with the kids. He's fine for a night out. Lunch will be enjoyable, but you know the last time I fell in love, it was with a man who talked a good game. I don't want to do that again. I'll be in love when I find a man I can trust and depend on. I'll let you know when I find him."

"Say what you will. This may just be the beginning, but it looks like love to me. All I know is all I know, and I know it looks like love from over here." Pat began pulling records from the file cabinet. "You have many cases to see today?" Pat kept referring to the list in her hand.

"Yes. Twelve this morning. Just trying to get a jump on next month." Noelle consulted her own list.

"How was Angel this morning? Was she okay when you dropped her off?"

"She didn't say much at first. She just looked kind of sad. I think she thought I was giving her away. Then she discovered James and Kelly. Those three renegades at once, I don't know how anyone can take it." Noelle shook her head in mock amazement. "It was good of your sitter to take her on such short notice."

Pat nodded. "She's pretty flexible if she knows you, and as long as the child is healthy. That's one of the good things about home-based childcare. What did Caren say when you talked with her?"

Noelle looked away, suddenly busy with the files in her hands.

"Noelle?"

"I never reached her," she said quietly.

"I should have known."

"I called like I said I would—three or four times, but she never got back to me."

"You're stalling. You don't want to deal with this, but you know you have to. Legally, you know you're on thin ice. What are you going to do about her today?"

"I'm not sure." Noelle bit at her bottom lip. "I guess I've waited too long as it is. But, I don't want Angel in anybody's care but my own."

"Yeah, she's a doll all right."

"She is. Pat, I don't want them to take her away. Angel's more than just good company. I'd miss her so much. And, if she's really been abandoned, I'm more than willing to keep her."

"Noelle," Pat shook her head from side to side. "This is very shaky. Tell me what I need to do to help."

"Let me think a minute, organize my thoughts, then I'll call Child Protective Services." Noelle looked like she'd rather eat glass.

"Be sure to talk to Caren Whittaker when you call. She's good at what she does, and she's understanding. Not like some of those other Harpies. Caren will be sympathetic to the situation. I'm going to the breakroom to match these up." Pat lifted the stack of case records and computer sheets and she was gone.

Noelle pulled a stack of food-stamp applications from her file cabinet. Locating a stack of verification request forms, she checked her appointment book. Twenty minutes before her first

client was due. Ample time to make a quick call to CPS. Dialing
with her right hand, she dug out a pen with her left.

"Child Protective Services." The voice was flat and officious.
*Go right ahead,* thought Noelle, *just make me feel welcome.*

"Hi, this is Noelle Parker. I'm downstairs in Eligibility." No
answer. "I've got some questions I need to ask. Is Caren Whittaker there?"

"Yeah."

"Do you think I could speak to her?"

The phone clattered to the desk as whoever answered went
to find Caren. Noelle waited, idly drawing mindless patterns on
scratch paper. Five minutes later, the paper was filled with doo-
dles and she was ready to hang up. A woman's voice came on
the line.

"Hello? Can I help you?" The voice was cool and professional with an edge of intolerance. It was a feminine, but somehow androgynous voice. Not a friendly voice, but Pat said this
woman could be trusted.

"Yes Caren, my name is Noelle Parker. Pat Stevens suggested
I give you a call." Pausing, she moistened her lips. "Last week,
after the office closed, a little girl was brought into my office.
She was alone and I was unable to find an adult caretaker."

"No adult? Is that why you're calling us? Where is the child
now?"

*Why is she jumping on me?* The woman's intimidating tone
made Noelle feel she had to hurry. "Give me a moment to tell
you the whole story. I was about to leave, when the janitor came
in."

"I thought you said there were no adults around?"

This interrogation was ridiculous! "What I said was there
was no caretaker. I checked, the janitor checked—no mommy,
no daddy. To make a long story short, there was no one available
in your office . . ."

"We're on call twenty-four hours a day."

"I know, but Caren, if you'd seen this child. She's special,
and she's very young. When I got upstairs to your office, I saw

the people there, and—and the child wasn't responding to any questions."

Almost out of breath, Noelle finished her story. "So, I still have the child. I don't know if there are any other people out there looking for her. I mean, it hasn't been in the papers or on the news or anything. I watched and listened all weekend, but I have yet to hear anything. Do you get any reports like that? I mean, if there's no family, I'd like to become at least her foster mother. I want to keep her. She's a sweet baby and I love her already. You know how it is, bonding just happens. I really do want to keep her Caren . . ."

"You still have the child?"

"Well, yes." *Didn't these people listen to anything?* "I already told you . . ."

"Hold on," and before she could say anything else, Noelle found herself back on hold.

The phone was picked up again, three minutes later. "Where are you? You said downstairs? Eligibility." Noelle had no chance to answer. "Hold on." Noelle was listening to dead air again.

More time passed, and this time a man picked up the line. Noelle felt her stomach try to shrink and double over onto itself. Something was wrong. This was not the way things were supposed to go.

"You said you're in Eligibility?" Noelle was tempted to hang up the phone, but she needed to know what to do. "How long have you been with the agency?"

"For. . . . wait a minute." Slow to anger, Noelle suddenly realized she didn't even know who this demanding stranger was. Beyond that, she'd been on the phone for more than fifteen minutes and still had no more information than she started out with. This didn't feel right at all.

"Who are *you* anyway? And why do you need all this information all of a sudden?"

"Hold on." Dead air again.

Noelle sucked at the inside of her cheek for the next two minutes. Two minutes after that, she was still on hold. That was more than enough—this being on hold was getting abusive. She hung up the phone.

Knowing she still needed to resolve the situation didn't help. CPS was obviously too busy to help her out, and staring at the phone wasn't making it any better. Maybe walking up on her break was the way to go. *And waste my time because they can't see me?* She shook her head. Wasted time was not an option, and Noelle folded her elbows on her desk, everything else she thought of had a drawback.

Better not to think about it, at all.

"Did you call?" Eager for resolution, Pat planted herself in the chair next to Noelle's desk.

"Yeah, I did," Noelle shrugged impatiently, "for all the good it did."

"What does that mean?"

"Well, I called and got shuffled from one person to another, and when I finally got Caren," Noelle shrugged again, "she was awful. I mean it was like going through a meat grinder—accusing, and brusque—ugh!"

"That doesn't sound like Caren. She's very professional. She's compassionate and sincere. I've never known her to be rude, but that's beside the point. What about Angel?"

"I don't know. This is giving me an awful headache."

"Well how about this, put it off until tomorrow. I've got a heavy day today, but I'm free tomorrow. I'll go up to the CPS office with you, and we'll get this all settled. In the meantime, you and Angel come home with me for dinner. We'll get a video, the kids can enjoy each other, and you can relax."

"I can't do dinner, but thanks for asking."

Pat's hands settled indignantly on rounded hips. "No?"

"Angel and I have a date."

Pat sucked air in through smiling lips. "A date? Jamal! Lunch and dinner? Where are you going? Call me later!"

Hopeless. A good and reliable friend, but hopelessly and undeniably romantic.

"No way!" Noelle had to smile back.

The telephone rang again, and she reached for it. "Yes Ms. Dalton, this is Ms. Parker . . ."

"Honey, I am a made woman," Minnie Raymond chortled gleefully. "A made woman," she repeated reaching for the telephone directory.

"What do you mean?" Her coworker peered at her over the rims of his Ben Franklin glasses. Minnie was happy. It always scared him when she was like this.

"That call was from a caseworker holding a child, not her own, in her home. No parents, no permission, no nothing—illegal custody. You know what that means."

"Uh-uh. What?"

Minnie looked up from her paging. Her full lips with their unnaturally pink coating of lipstick pushed their way to the side and held. "Rob Blackwood, you're stupid, you know that?"

"Well Min, just cause I didn't know . . ." Rob tugged nervously at his vest.

"Here it is, *Journal-Constitution*." Minnie copied the number, then leaned back in her chair. Her good humor was restored. Rob shivered.

"You know," she said, "I came here as a secretary—a typist, not even a real secretary. I had to work my way up from there. I didn't just walk in. Not like you with your degree, that your mommy and daddy paid for. I just had to turn over every stone and do what I could for myself. Not like you at all."

Rob had the grace to blush bright red. He knew what the office gossips said about his rapid rise to supervisor. He'd only been with DFACS for two years compared to Minnie's twenty, and they held the same position.

"But this is my ticket," she grinned. "It's my time to rise."

"I don't get it Min. What are you talking about?"

*Of course you don't get it,* Minnie thought meanly. *If I'd slept my way into a job, I might not get it either.* She blew a hotly exasperated blast of air at nothing in particular. Just blowing off steam. When she finally spoke, her voice was softer as she clearly enunciated each word as though speaking to a slow child.

"I'm talking about exposing the worker, saving the child, in other words doing my job—and taking full credit for it. That ought to get me the promotion I've been waiting for."

Blackwood peered at her again, his mouth sagging open. "Who is the caseworker, do you know her? What did she ever do to you Min?"

"Nothing. I've never met her—wouldn't know her from Adam's house cat."

"Min, that worker will lose her job—maybe never get another one in this field. That would destroy everything she's ever worked for—just toss it all away. This could ruin her life."

"Personal problem. She should've thought of that before," Minnie replied, dialing.


Noelle thanked goodness Pat was tied up on an interview when she made her way to her desk after a morning of visiting clients' homes. Peeling paper from her plastic straw, she pulled her cup of iced tea closer. She shook her head, she couldn't stand the grilling she knew Pat would give her about last night.

Last night. Noelle tried to keep the smile private. She pressed her knees tightly together, and tried not to dance in her chair. Last night had been more fun than she could have imagined. Her smile burst forth. Jamal and Angel clearly adored each other. Even better, she thought happily, they both seem to care for her. It felt good to be included in family type love.

Now that she was thinking about him, it was hard to believe she had known Jamal Harris for such a short period of time. It had taken him less than a week to breach her defenses, and she had no regrets.

But, she did have a telephone number. *I can call him if I want to.* She couldn't remember when she had dropped his card into her bag, but there it was. He was as close as a telephone call.

Propping the card against her calendar, Noelle closed her eyes. Seeing him in her mind's eye was easy—almost too easy.

They had exchanged no more than kisses, but each time his hand touched hers or his lips came close, Noelle thrilled to the rush of emotion his nearness evoked. She refused to give voice to or even frame the hazy thoughts of anything beyond the sweetness of his kisses.

Sweet kisses and more. It was how those kisses were delivered that mesmerized her, the graphic promise that lay so tenderly behind them. The intoxicating thought of his skin against hers made her dizzy. Yet, she dared go farther, to almost imagine how the hands that closed so naturally on her waist might feel closing on places she concealed, even from herself.

The heat of her thoughts rose in her body. Flushed, Noelle gulped thirstily at her tea.

And if Pat asked, as Noelle knew she eventually would, Noelle would immediately deny she was hoping for more.

Another deep sip of tea proved it would take more than a cold drink to help her recover from a morning under a hot Georgia sun in July. A major headache in full bloom, Noelle dug through her desk drawer for aspirin.

"Noelle, I need to talk to you."

"Oh, hey Dennis. What did you need?" The aspirin packet looked like it had been in the drawer for a very long time, but it would at least take the sharp edges off her headache.

"I need for you to step into my office." He held the door open for her to enter.

"I see you've got your supervisor face on. Did I screw something up?"

"Noelle, I just got a very disturbing telephone call."

"Disturbing? About me?" She watched him curiously.

"I understand," he walked around his desk to his chair, "you found a young child here in the office?"

"Yes." It was that simple.

"You found a little girl, in this office, took her home, kept her all weekend, failed to report her appearance . . . where is she now?" He looked at her as though she'd just announced her arrival from Mars.

"She's with a sitter. What did you think, I'd leave her alone? That's why I took her home with me."

"What were you thinking of? You're good at your job. You know better than this. I know you know the consequences of your actions. Not to mention the legal implications . . . where in the world was your mind?"

Dennis's forehead was almost painfully worried, heavy wrinkles were crowding one another for space. His eyes pleaded with her to tell him he'd misunderstood. Noelle wished she could do exactly that—but as luck would have it, she couldn't.

"What were you thinking about?" He was almost pleading with her.

"Dennis, you're right. I do know the consequences of my actions. I know that what I did was wrong. I can only tell you I did it for the right reasons. I know the problems I've caused."

"No. I really don't think you do."

She shrugged then smiled bitterly. "Aw, Dennis. She's such a little girl. She needed someone, and I was the only one here."

"Noelle, I'm afraid that's not good enough."

"Dennis, I waited around, but no one came for her and there just didn't seem to be any other better choices to make. I even got as far as the CPS office, but the environment was all wrong for a child—especially one as young as this one.

"Look, I made a professional judgment, it wasn't the right place for her. Not over a holiday weekend. Then there was that whole thing of her not being able to, or not wanting to talk. The idea seemed too traumatic to subject her to. I tried to do this as right as I could, but . . ."

Her mind was just coming up to speed when the thought hit her like a runaway train. "How did you find out?"

"I got a call from Minnie Raymond up in CPS. Of all the people in the world, why would you call her? Why would you tell her instead of me? At least *I* like you!"

"What?"

"You couldn't have picked a worse person to talk to if your life depended on it. It took her twenty years to become a supervisor, and now she's so defensive of her position she'd tattle on dust behind the refrigerator if she thought it would gain her someone's favor or influence."

He blew out heavily, shaking his head. "What a mess. For the life of me, if you couldn't talk to me I don't understand why you didn't talk to one of the other workers up there. You could have talked to Caren . . ."

"Whittaker? But I did!" Noelle almost screamed. "I specifically asked to speak to her, and I had to wait a long time for them to go and find her. When she finally came to the phone, I called her by name. She answered and . . ."

"And you talked to Minnie, who immediately smelled a chance to promote her own agenda. Baby," Dennis shook his head sorrowfully, "you've stretched your neck out way too far this time. Minnie's got a sharp knife out for you."

Sitting, thinking of what her next words should be, Noelle let her eyes take in Dennis's office. He'd been with the agency for twenty-two years, and this little office with its patched and crack-veined pale green walls, limited privacy, and ancient splintered chairs was what his tenure merited.

Book-filled shelves climbed the walls on three sides of the room, and his paper covered gray metal desk was angled into a corner. A green and white philodendron sat daringly on a stack of books, making a valiant display of stunted leaves. Dusty windows all but strained sunlight into the narrow room, and Noelle wondered if this was worth fighting for. Maybe not, her heart told her, but Angel certainly was.

Noelle began quietly. "Why would she have done this to me? Minnie doesn't know me. We've never met. And, I didn't steal or molest this child. One of the reasons I called was to try to find out if there was a way I could become her foster parent, for now. And if she was really abandoned, I wanted to ask how to go about adoption. I told her about that when I called. Dennis, I've only had Angel a few days, but . . ."

The ringing phone stopped her.

"Dennis Avery." He waited, glancing tersely at Noelle. "I've discussed it with her . . . yes . . . that doesn't fully cover the situation. It would seem that there are extenuating circumstances. Perhaps this would be better handled if . . ." He sat listening, shaking his head slowly from side to side. Moving his right hand in the air, he tried to make his point. "Don't you think you're blowing this out of proportion? The child's interests are not necessarily best served in that case. As I've said, there are extenuating circum . . . I see. I'll tell her."

He hung up the phone with obvious distress. "Noelle, I have to tell you that call was from the attorney general's office. They're demanding you be released from your job immediately. Of course an investigation will follow. That includes possible civil charges."

"But Dennis, why? It's not as though I'm a career criminal or anything. I don't steal children as a hobby. I would never molest or hurt a child, you know that. I really don't understand how my helping . . ."

"In spite of what I know about you, Minnie apparently got real busy, real quick." Regret ran deeply through his voice as he continued. "That's not the worst of it. The state will be recommending charges at a later point. Where is the child now?"

"Now? I told you, she's with a sitter. Dennis?" Noelle felt her throat close. She didn't have the words to finish her question.

He sighed and shook his head again. "You need to get your things. That was my order to escort you from the building. Of course, they'll want to pick up the child sometime this afternoon or early tomorrow, I imagine. This is a damned shame."

Stunned, Noelle simply nodded, stood, and walked from the office to her desk. Vaguely, as though in a dream, she gathered her things, obviously her good intentions hadn't mattered at all.

Dennis stood silently framed by his office door. "Pat," he finally said, "can I see you for a minute?"

"Sure, Dennis. What's up?" Confused, Pat paused in mid-stride, dropping the files she carried. Casting a cautious glance at Noelle told her nothing. She placed the recovered files on her desk.

"Just come in here." Dennis motioned urgently, then closed the door silently as she entered.

Several caseworkers had their heads together when Pat emerged from Dennis's office. They separated quickly. Nobody wanted to be caught actively gossiping. They didn't mind doing it, they just didn't want to be caught.

"Noelle? Girl, are you alright? Dennis just told me." Pat walked reluctantly forward, her arms open for a consoling hug. Noelle angled her body away, avoiding contact. Comfort seemed wrong now, too. She was too numb to appreciate it.

Noelle felt as though she was moving in slow motion, through thick, viscous air. Her feet seemed to weigh a thousand pounds each. Her chest felt small and tight like it wasn't really hers. It was hard for her to breathe, and her mind was locked on denial. None of this was real—this simply couldn't be happening, she thought.

Noelle opened her mouth, and wasn't surprised when no words came out. She cleared her throat and tried again. "I'm leaving now, Dennis. I'm really sorry for the problems I've caused." She walked past him and through the door like a woman in a trance.

Pat watched her friend's back. For the first time in her life, she didn't know what to say or how to comfort Noelle. Her escaping sigh caught the interest of the office gossips. They knew Pat was feeling sorry for her dear friend. They knew she was crying tears of blood for Noelle.

Here Noelle was, just finally opening up to the world, and this had to happen. There were three or four quickly surmised stories of where the child had some from, but it was plain to see that the possibility of losing her had distressed Noelle.

The whispers were spreading wildly, and sometimes loudly, now. She'd never work in social service again, at least not on the state level—and the shame was that she was one of the few caseworkers who liked her job and was damned good at it. Probably would be prosecuted for kidnapping. Wasn't it just too bad her call had been directed to Minnie by mistake? Everybody knew Minnie was a glory-seeking busybody. It was just a pity, they all agreed, but Minnie was just doing her job.

Noelle was gulping air, trying to steel herself to cross the office lobby. She knew that by now, all the secretaries had heard the story of her folly. They all knew she'd thrown away her job, and probably figured she'd wind up being arrested and maybe even doing a little jail time. Oh, boy, fresh gossip for lunch!

"There she is! There's Parker!"

She was prepared for whispers and stares, but not for the bright, hot spotlight that struck her as she rounded the corner into the lobby. The numbness that carried her from her desk was no longer sufficient to sustain her dignity. Startled, Noelle reflexively batted at the microphone that was jammed into her face, and quickened her steps toward the door. Who in the world would have called reporters?

A woman tottered along behind the migrating reporters, trying desperately to gain their attention. "Ladies and gentleman," her voice was loud and commanding. "May I have your attention, please." A few heads turned in her direction.

Electing to make the best of the limited attention she'd attracted, the woman stood taller. Her severely cut gray suit was hiked high on her wide behind and dipped low in front to accommodate her abdominal girth. Thin legs posed unsteadily atop once fashionable stiletto pumps, and one plump arm was waving for attention while the other clutched a large, black binder to her ample, heaving bosom.

"My name is Minnie Raymond, and I am a supervisor for this agency, charged with guarding and implementing the law. This is the personnel manual of the State of Georgia. It explains in detail all of the regulations that apply to this case. Every employee of the State of Georgia receives a copy when he's hired and it's their duty to be governed accordingly. Ms. Parker has clearly disregarded these regulations."

*So,* thought Noelle, *this is Minnie Raymond.* The reporters shuffled anxiously, and looked back to Noelle. When she moved, so did they.

"May I have your attention . . . please!" Minnie followed the reporters begging for a little more consideration. She was totally ignored.

The reporters were seasoned and swift, they knew a hot story when they saw one, and they were unwilling to let it get away. Noelle was soon surrounded. Trapped in the hallway between the elevator and the stairwell, Noelle cringed at the loudness and the bluntness of shouted questions.

"Ms. Parker! Over here! Did you kidnap the little girl, like you're accused?"

"Ms. Parker, are you aware of the regulations you violated by keeping the child?"

"Where is the child now? Where have you hidden the child!"

"Ms. Parker, you have no children of your own, do you? Is that why you stole the little girl?"

"Smile Noelle! You're gonna be on TV!"

"Whose baby is it!"

"Have you ever done anything like this before? Stolen a child, I mean . . ."

One of the reporters, a pretty, very familiar looking auburn-haired woman matched Noelle's pace, then took a calculated step in front of her to block her. She wore a microphone clipped to the front of her stylish crepe jacket.

"Lark Allister, Peyton Communications," the woman said brusquely. "How did you come into contact with the child?" Noelle looked blank but managed to step around the reporter.

Four quick steps and Lark again blocked her quarry. "What did you plan to do with her? If you planned to steal her, how did you hope to succeed in documenting things like her birth?"

"I didn't!" Noelle stopped walking. The shouted questions and accusations were sensationally ridiculous. Angered, she wanted to turn on her pursuers and tell them to get away from her, to go find some real news to chase. She wanted to plow over Lark Allister like an Army tank. She wanted to cry.

"Of course I've never done anything like this before," Noelle snapped. "Can't you see the child just needed someone who cared? Wasn't it obvious that I had only had Angel's best interests in mind when I took her home with me?"

A slim, oily faced man placed a tight hand on her wrist. "Mack Carpenter, *Constitution.* Tell me how you attempted to use the resources of this agency to . . ."

"I've never misused my position." Noelle pulled her wrist away from his grasp. She could see the reporters were determined to physically detain her, if necessary. They obviously didn't want to hear a rational, calm explanation. Hysterics was more like it. They wanted to film her screaming and crying, repenting a crime she had not committed.

Their accusing numbers seemed to be growing by the minute—the TV people were joined by radio and print reporters. What could she tell them that would make them go away and leave her alone?

"Noelle, how did you get custody of the child . . . it's a girl, right?"

"Where did she come from?"

"How do you feel about losing your job?" The Allister woman was so close now that Noelle could almost count the fine, silver-tinged hairs resting against salon-perfect red-blond waves.

Confused and disconcerted, she wanted to say the right thing, and escape. She took a deep breath and opened her mouth to speak. A supportive, steadying hand gripped her arm. Noelle looked up into Jamal Harris's gravely handsome face.

His authoritative voice cut through the noise and pressure of the scene in the hallway. "Ms. Parker has no statement at this time."

"Who are you?"

"Where do I know you from? Aren't you an attorney? With DFACS, right? What's your involvement in this case?"

"Are you her lawyer? Did you help her steal the kid?"

Jamal's grip, tight at her elbow, propelled her through the

door and down the stairs. Noelle stumbled, then started toward her car, but Jamal towed her to the silver Lexus.

"They've probably already checked your tags and can recognize your car. Let's take mine."

Traveling west on MLK, Jr., Drive, Noelle felt calm for the first time since making her phone call.

"Where did you come from?"

He smiled. "We had a lunch date, remember?"

"Right—I forgot. Thank you for the rescue."

"No problem. What did I rescue you from?"

"I don't know if I should tell you. You may have to prosecute me. This may wind up being a conflict of interest. Besides, it's embarrassing too." She looked wary. "You're an officer of the court, aren't you? Maybe 'anything I say can and will be used against me'."

"Nah, the Miranda only works for cops. You sound as if you think you need a lawyer."

"I think I do."

"Have you got a dollar?"

"Yes, why?"

"Just give it to me."

She sniffed deeply and blinked impending tears. Pulling the crinkled bill from her jacket pocket, she handed it to him.

Deft fingers captured and folded the crisp bill. He tucked it into an inner pocket, and glanced at her from the corner of his eye. She studied her hands, and didn't meet his eyes. Jamal continued to drive.

"What was the dollar for," she finally asked.

"Let's call it a retainer." His voice was quiet and capable. "You just hired legal counsel. Tell me what happened. If I can't handle it or if it is a conflict, I'll simply tell you to stop."

She sighed deeply, and knotted her hands in her lap.

"I promise you'll get your money's worth."

Noelle turned her face away from Jamal. It seemed to her that it would be easier to tell her story if she didn't have to look at him. She didn't know how to start her story without making herself sound stupid.

"It's about Angel. You see, she's not exactly mine."

# Twelve

"When I left the office, the place was a complete madhouse. Phones were ringing off the hook." Pat's voice was as frazzled as her rumpled curly hair. "Speaking of phones," she reached for the one on the kitchen wall. "I need to call my neighbor to check on my kids." She dialed quickly, pinning the receiver against her shoulder with her chin.

"Reporters everywhere. They were asking everybody about this mystery kid." Her raised hand interrupted the flow of conversation. "Louise? Yeah, this is Pat, and I just wanted to . . . oh, really?"

Her eyebrows lifted as she turned to face Noelle and Jamal. "The police were at my house, you say? Uh-huh and they asked you about my friend Ms. Parker? Uh-huh. Oh! Lark Allister? Isn't she the reporter from WCRD? Yes. . . . She said what?"

Pat's brows worked furiously as she rolled her eyes. "Well, this is still America, girl, and everybody is entitled to an opinion, no matter how stupid or biased it is. You know what they say, 'opinions are like . . .' " she laughed, letting the unsaid line dangle. "Oh, you heard that one, too. Well, I'll be there by six or a little after. Thanks, Louise!"

Pat turned, planting her hands firmly on her hips. "Well, everybody's talking about you, girl! Reporters and the police were at my house looking for you and Angel. Child, they were at the office askin' everybody, even the clients about you. Have you heard from the CPS unit yet? Are they coming to pick

Angel up? Where do you think they'll put her? What did Dennis have to say?"

"Slow down Pat."

"I'm just asking."

"Just don't say 'I told you so'." Noelle looked tired and worried. The corners of her mouth turned down in a determined pout as she recrossed her legs for the fifth time.

"Never," Pat swore.

"We haven't heard anything from CPS. At least, they didn't call before we stopped answering the phone. Jamal wants me to surrender Angel on my own instead of upon demand."

"I think it'll look better, more cooperative in the long run," he said.

"And I'm sick over it," Noelle finished miserably. "I need time to prepare her, to let her know that she's not being given away."

Pat thought they looked comfortably like a couple sitting on the couch. "Speaking of prepared . . ."

"Noelle's been explaining how all of this happened," Jamal's voice was low, protective.

*And you're still here,* Pat thought.

"I've already called Morgan. He's going to call us at three this afternoon," Jamal checked his watch. "He's filing a hearing request for us. We're trying to locate the janitor . . . Mr. Jackson?" Noelle nodded.

"So, how does it happen you can do this for her?" Pat eyed him suspiciously. She wanted him to do right by her friend.

*Because I think I'm falling in love with her—okay?* Jamal only thought it, he'd never say it out loud. Not to Pat. Not today.

"As it happens, this case might eventually come into our office, but my particular area is concerned with physical and sexual abuse of children. Judging from what I've seen of Angel and Noelle, that's not a factor here. This case is potentially criminal. Kidnapping. No conflict there, because we don't handle those cases. No overlap.

"The other thing is that Morgan and I have been planning

on opening a private practice. This is just our first case." His arm lifted, and traveled across the back of the couch, settling around Noelle's shoulder. It was a claiming gesture for him, a calming one for her. Pat watched as Noelle settled peacefully into his embrace.

"I guess you're going to have a pretty rough time with this, though. Minnie Raymond went crazy on her phone. She's so desperate for attention, I do believe she's called every television and radio station in town. Do you know, I even saw Lark Allister at the office this morning? And Louise said she'd been at my house this afternoon."

"Lark Allister! Did you get a look at that hair?"

Pat shook her head slowly from side to side, and stuck her tongue in her cheek. "We all know the type, girl. Body by Fisher, mind by Mattel."

Jamal tried not to smile. So, anyway, what about Lark Allister?"

"She's got a reputation for doing her job well. You know she only handles heavy stuff—national stuff. Minnie called all the local newspapers too. She's giving interviews left and right. I don't know for sure, but I think she's even called the mayor's office and the governor's office, as well."

Noelle moaned and closed her eyes before answering. "Pat, this is madness. You're trying to tell me that these people I don't even know are working overtime to convict me of a crime I didn't commit. People I don't know are following me and accusing me of being a kidnapper." She shivered and pressed closer to Jamal's side.

"Hey," Pat shrugged, "go figure."

"The most I'm guilty of is bending the law in support of a child in distress. Jamal believes I'll probably never be able to work for DFACS or the Department of Human Resources again, but I won't have to go to jail. What I want though, is to find out if there is any way I can gain legal custody of Angel."

"Custody?"

Noelle sat forward eagerly. "Pat, you've seen her. You know

what a sweet baby she is. She's just started talking to us. I can't imagine being without her now."

"Do you really think a judge would give you custody—now?" Pat shook her head, and looked to Jamal for an answer. "How likely is that to happen?"

"There's always a chance." Jamal looked into Noelle's trusting eyes. He wanted to put her case in the best possible light. It was important that she trust him, but he wasn't going to lie to win that trust. "We need to round up a few witnesses, including you and the sitter."

"Is Angel still with the sitter?"

Noelle nodded. "We thought it might be better to leave her there for now—until some of this excitement dies down."

"I still don't feel comfortable with this. You're willing to go to the mat to get custody of this child, but no parents or other caretakers have been heard from yet? It just doesn't feel right."

"Until they contact us, I'm more than willing to continue taking care of her. You've seen her Pat. She's at ease with me and I can meet all her needs, at least until her mother shows up."

Conversation stopped at the rushed sound of several vehicles stopping, their doors slamming, in front of Noelle's building. Heavy feet ran up the stairs to her second-floor dwelling. The doorbell sounded, then pounding on her door.

Noelle stood and tiptoed to her front window. Her heart sank as she peeked through the blinds.

"Reporters?" She nodded.

Jamal moved to stand quietly behind her. Her breath hissed between clenched teeth.

"The vultures have landed." He pulled her gently away from the window, noting the tears rolling freely down her cheeks. "Do you want to stay here?"

"No," she didn't give herself a chance to think it over.

"I'll help you pack bags for yourself and Angel, and you can come home with me," Pat offered, walking into the bedroom. "If they can't find you, they can't serve you, and that should give you a little more time with Angel. Besides, this is too nerve-racking for any sane individual."

"No Pat, she can't go to your house. Yours is the next place they'll look for her." Jamal held his breath. What he was about to say almost scared him. He hadn't known he was going to make this instinctive offer but, it was the right thing to do. He knew he wanted to help Noelle, and besides, she needed to lean on someone now, whether she knew it or not. *And if she's going to lean on anybody,* he promised himself, *it's going to be me.*

"You and Angel are coming home with me."

"With you?"

"Yes, Pat is right. It will give you a little more time with Angel. It's a temporary solution, but only Pat will know where you are until the dust settles and you can make a formal answer to any charges."

"Great," Noelle swiped at her cheek with the back of her hand. "What about my reputation?"

"I can't speak to that, but it'll certainly enhance mine." The brightness of his teasing smile almost made Noelle feel better.

Pat peeked through the bedroom blinds. "Well, both your reputations are going to be flashed over the airwaves with film at eleven if you don't get out of here."

"So, what do you say? My house?"

"Jamal, I can't ask you to put yourself out like this for me and Angel. You've already jumped into a breach the size of the Grand Canyon for me. Thank you. I'm grateful, but I can't ask you to do anymore."

" 'Ask' me? Noelle," he pulled her into his arms, "you still don't get it do you? For a smart woman, you can be pretty slow, and you do say some dumb stuff sometimes." Offended, she pulled away from him, staring open-mouthed.

He caught her before she completely escaped. "Noelle, you're not asking me to do anything. Baby, this is the way it is: I'm here because I care about you, not because you're a professional obligation. With you in this predicament, there's nowhere else for me to be. We haven't had a lot of time together, but I'm convinced this is right. For both of us."

Jamal hesitated before going further. Pat's dark head popped back around the corner and bobbed there listening—not quite out of his range of vision. He knew he was about to make a serious commitment and he wanted to be sure Noelle recognized it for what it really was.

Noelle's head dropped to rest against his shoulder, and she mumbled something against his chest. If it was a protest, it did no good. He hugged her close and held her there. Dropping a kiss on the crown of her head, he enjoyed her warmth a moment longer. She was no longer crying.

"I haven't known you long, but I believe I'm what you've been waiting for. . . ." He felt her inhale, as though she intended to say something, but she didn't. "I also believe you're what I've been waiting for." He paused again. "I think I'm falling in love with you, and if I'm right, there's no way you're going to get rid of me easily. You've got me for the duration."

"Duration?" Noelle smiled against his chest.

"I figure at least fifty good years."

Her eyes glistened with unshed tears, but her voice was clear and determined. "Mr. Attorney, that sounds like a plan to me."

She packed quickly, efficiently. Among the clothing she gathered for herself and Angel, she included a child's picture book and a thick paperback novel. Jamal watched, realizing how little he knew about her, how little he needed to know. He began picturing her as a far more lonely, more complicated person than he had first thought.

Chauvinist, he chided himself. Just because she's beautiful doesn't mean she didn't have a life before you, and it certainly doesn't mean she can't be lonely.


Peachtree Street, far below, had lost its daytime rush. Evening traffic, mostly expensive cars, aggressive taxis, and horse-drawn carriages, inched along July-heated asphalt. As dusk gathered, spilling sapphire across a cloudless blue sky, Lark Allister sat alone—in conference with herself.

Incredibly sheer, almost invisible hose whispered as one caramel-colored, well-toned, booth-tanned leg crossed over the other before snugly kissing at the knee. Beautifully sculpted navy Chanel pumps gleamed subtly in the waning light. Leaning possessively into the turquoise leather of her chair, Lark fingered the pink message slip. Her manicured fingers folded, creased, and refolded it as she thought.

Brushing professionally honeyed, carefully cut, tone-on-tone hair from her face, Lark looked around her, drawing strength from the decorator inspired beauty of her office. If expense had been spared in the decoration, one would never know by looking at the suite. Nobody got an office like this, or went this high, this fast in Peyton Communications unless they had a lot on the ball.

At thirty-three, Lark Allister had a lot on the ball. She was still good-looking, though the years from secretary to on-air anchor had leached the softness from her face. She'd come to WCRD, Peyton Communications's Atlanta station, right out of grad school. She'd been a good student, a good staff writer, and an award-winning reporter. Trophies and plaques testifying to her carefully honed skills lined her walls.

Ambition was the drug she thrived on. It had led her from the little one-horse, red-dirt town she'd been born in, and fueled her professional rise. Like any other addict, she sought her daily fix in ever increasing doses. When she'd begun her career, her ambition had been the sumptuous salary and designer clothes she now counted as her due. Along the way, her hungers had increased to include fast cars, high-profile men, and name recognition. Now she craved star status. The national television anchor spot.

She licked her lips hungrily. High on ambition and poised for success, Lark knew it was only a matter of time. She chose her assignments carefully, but it was still a matter of time. Time and luck. Lark believed they were both on her side. Rather,

Walters, Chung—when the time came, she'd make them memories. Faint, distant, unimportant memories.

But to make memories, you had to have important, memorable stories. Smoothing the pink note against the pale gray marble desktop, Lark decided. There was something about the Parker woman that might make her an important story, but what?

Someone from DFACS had called earlier, dangling unsubtle clues. Taking a chance, Lark decided to follow up on the tersely worded memo. The pencil eraser hit each number unerringly as Lark punched in the phone number. Let this woman be lying to me, and I'll eat her for lunch, she promised herself.

"Ms. Raymond?" Her voice was a sarcastic drawl, friendly enough, but warning too. "This is Lark Allister. I'm returning your call."

The woman on the other end of the line inhaled, sharp and quick—obviously awed. *She'd better not be playing with me,* the reporter thought as she tried to reign in her notorious lack of patience. Flexing her fingers, Lark resettled the receiver under her chin.

"This has to do with the Parker case, does it not?" The ingratiating, fluttery voice on the other end was so sweet Lark could almost feel her teeth ache.

"What's goin' on Ms. Raymond? Why is child custody in dispute? Whose child is it, and why do you think it's newsworthy?"

Minnie nervously cleared her throat. Lark grimaced in irritation as the echo grated through the phone line, rasping against her ear.

"Ms. Allister, I would like to thank you for returning my call. I would also like to state for the record that I am currently employed by the State of Georgia in the Department of Family and Children's Services as a supervisor in the . . ."

"I know what DFACS is, and I am aware of your position. You identified yourself and your credentials on your initial call."

Lark could just see the woman's posturing in her mind's eye.

She knew the type well, and despised them in any guise. *A brown-nosing, self-important, little tin god who needed to get a real life.* She didn't say it out loud. There was no payoff in antagonizing a source, however self-serving it might be.

"I was there earlier when Parker left the building."

"Then you saw the guilt written all over her face. The woman is as guilty as sin."

"That remains to be seen. Make your point, please."

"Right! Well, it seems . . . that is, it has come to my attention that as a worker in my agency . . ." Minnie seemed to think a moment, then desperately back-pedaled. "Not one of my workers! Not in my department. Absolutely no one under my supervision would ever . . ."

"Your point. Make your point." Lark's Timex, a low-tech high school graduation gift from her grandmother, read 8:42 P.M., and this Raymond woman was still babbling. Impatient, Lark's self-assured southern lady's voice wasn't lilting now.

"She took the child! Just stole her, knew it was wrong, did it anyway! We have got rules about stuff like that! It's not legal . . ."

"That's sure the impression you're giving. People like you call offices like mine every day of the week. I talked to the woman myself, and she's no Mad Ax Murderer or Kiddie Madame. I strongly suspect this is a witch-hunt . . ."

Minnie's online sputtering only added fuel to Lark's frustration. "Yes, I said witch-hunt! And I suspect it's designed to rid you of some interoffice rival. Or maybe it's a promotion you're after?"

"In a city, in a country that's had to deal with so many children's problems, and so much other violence, I should think you'd be ashamed to even try a stunt like this—and you have the nerve to do it in the name of the law?"

"I'm not making this up Ms. Allister."

"No? Then I ask you again, why bring this to me? Why not call *Hard Copy,* or *Atlanta Today,* or *Georgia Online*? Why, I b'lieve this might be more in the line of *The Tattler,* or one of those other gossip sheets."

"Because they deal with sensationalism, and this is news. It's a blatant abuse of the law. This woman, Noelle Parker, has to be stopped. This isn't the first time she's done something illegal. Personnel wouldn't tell me details. They say she's protected by the Privacy Act, but it has to be investigated. Besides, there's the child. She's still holding on to the child.

"What if the child's being molested or involved in some other pornographic abuse like those poor little babies we heard about up North last week? They were news, and so is this. If this little girl doesn't have family, she's supposed to be in state custody, and she's not. You said your feeling was that Noelle Parker wasn't a kiddie madame or anything, but what if you're wrong. Just, what if? Well, somebody's got to help me!"

"You could go to the *Journal* or *Constitution.*"

"The newspaper is too slow. This situation needs more urgent, hard-hitting attention. This needs the kind of attention and follow-up that only the electronic media can give it. It also needs the attention of a reporter who will stay with it and dig up all the facts. And because this is a child-related problem, I think the reporter should be a woman—a woman like you."

Maybe it was the shrill desperation in the woman's voice. Maybe it was just a slow news week. Maybe it was the sixteen-hour day, but Minnie Raymond started to make sense. It was scary.

Lark reached for an engraved Mont Blanc pen and began sketching her trademark, abbreviated, marginally legible notes. "Start at the beginning . . ."

# Thirteen

Angel was asleep almost before Noelle could pull the covers over her.

Noelle hoped the child would sleep through the night in the strange room with all its dark, oversized, masculine furniture. Draping the pink scarf over the lampshade for a makeshift night-light, she was struck by a strong sense of déjà vu.

Actually, she corrected herself as she walked down the hall toward the den where Jamal waited, it was more a sense of déjà-almost-vu. A couple of nights before, hadn't she done almost exactly this same thing? That had been her first night with Angel. She'd tucked the little girl in and then found herself fantasizing a warm, loving, responsible, waiting man. A man of her own.

Tonight, for a change, there really was a man. So what if he was not really her man? A woman should always be able to dream. It was nice to pretend the fantasy was real.

Cocooned by the domesticity of the early evening, Noelle couldn't help but wish she could somehow force the creation of her ideal family. As it was, she couldn't. But she did wonder what she was walking into. Her hand touched her hair just to check it. Could it be that Jamal Harris was her loving man?

*Dream on,* she thought to herself, *he's just an awfully nice man.* To be sure, he was more than just considerate of both her and Angel. All evening he'd met their every need, after first rescuing her from the madness of the office, then driving the getaway car from her apartment.

He entertained Angel. He ate her lousy cooking, burned chicken and watery mashed potatoes, without complaint. He'd insisted on doing the dishes while she got Angel ready for bed.

Time with a man like Jamal was what Noelle imagined when she'd stood next to Wayne Sterling, dressed in white, and murmuring, "I do." Being with him tonight had been so like the marriage she'd coveted. It felt better than right, it felt perfect. Like coming home at the end of a long journey. Jamal Allen Harris felt like home—warm and comfortable, forgiving of human frailty. Perfect in every way.

Then there were those eyes that quietly and assuredly followed her movements. Somehow, the touch of his glance could make her smile from across the room Were men supposed to be able to touch your heart with the flick of a brow or the merry crinkling touching the corners of his eyes when he laughed? Noelle didn't remember that happening in the novels she'd read.

The authority and resonance of his voice no longer irritated her. To tell the truth, she couldn't remember why she'd ever thought him aggressive and invasive. Now, she found his voice and his presence to be both soothing and comforting.

"This is sick. I'm fantasizing over this man as though all my dreams were going to come true," she whispered detouring into a cream-tiled bathroom.

The dark sweep of Boston ferns crossing broad, frosted glass windows filtered subdued light from the night beyond. Lacy, fresh green fronds seemed to fly in the dusky light with an effortless grace. Pressing the door softly closed, Noelle admired the neatness even darkness could not hide.

*Organized.* That was the word that came to mind as her hand brushed the light switch. Cool, ivory tiles accented with a deep-red-and-gold-veined mosaic covered the walls around her. The colors were calm but intense, like him. Crisp folds in a matching shower curtain pressed against the shower walls, so neatly Noelle could almost sense the touch of a woman's hands at work.

Yet, he lived alone. There was no other woman, not even a housekeeper. Alone with his neat, organized life. She sighed, he was a lot like her. Why didn't that make her happy? Instead, she felt nervous and unsure—like a fat woman charged with the task of walking on eggs.

Facing herself in the mirror, she quickly turned the faucet, hoping the water would give her thoughts focus. *Besides, the sound might keep him from hearing me talk to myself.*

"The last thing I need is for him to figure I've lost my mind." She let the water splash harder.

She met her own eyes in the vanity mirror. Wide and deep, they were eyes she'd known all her life, but tonight they told her nothing. Rather, those intense eyes tightened a little at their tilted corners and asked questions. Too many questions, and her heart beat fast. Questions were frightening, but it was the answers that most terrified her now.

"Girl, what *are* you walking into here?" The lurch of her heartbeat almost made her gasp. "Don't read too much into this. He's a nice man who's come to your rescue. A nice, sexy, easy-to-fall-in-love-with man. He probably rescues puppies and kittens too."

The woman in the mirror raised an eyebrow quizzically. Obviously, she was not a believer.

"I know, I thought I was over that—that I could do it alone. But I want more. I want some happily ever after, and I want it with a man like him! Scratch that. I want it with him!"

"I used to think I knew what love was, but maybe I was using some colorful mixture from my novels and television." The woman in the mirror pouted sarcastically.

"But now, I've lived a little more and taken time to think it over—shoot, I survived Wayne. I know there's light at the end of the tunnel and I just want to see a little of it. I've met Jamal, I've seen the difference in what he has to offer, and I have a new definition." The eyes in the mirror still didn't look fully convinced.

"Love is the subjective condition where the welfare and hap-

piness of another person is essential to one's own happiness."
Noelle's heart sank. The definition was so clinical she couldn't
even meet her own eyes in the mirror. "It still sounds like I'm
running away from myself."

"Shucks, I know I really do want Jamal, but what if . . ." she
looked into the mirrored depths of her own eyes, "what if I
can't give him the kind of love he deserves ?" The hot choking
feeling of her heart leapt into her throat and made her look away
from the mirror.

Flipping the lid down, she sat on the toilet, chin in hand,
balancing an elbow on her knee. Slipping off her shoes, Noelle
rested her feet on the coolness of the tiles. She studied the
contrast of her cocoa-colored skin against the reddened floor-
ing, and providing no answers, it didn't help.

"I want to try."

*Jamal, Angel, and me.* It would be nice if the three of them
were a real family. Noelle sighed into her cupped palm. No way
they were going to get the chance to be a real family now. She'd
screwed that up for good. Then of course, there was Minnie
Raymond to thank for the crowning public relations touches.

Shoulders slumped, she sighed again. "Face it Noelle, you're
in love and you don't have a clue how to proceed. On the other
hand, maybe you've been so alone for so long, maybe you're
just in lust, and don't know the difference."

Chancing a look up at her reflection, she saw the image nod
wisely. She thought about it, then agreed with herself. "Okay,
that's true too. I am in lust, but I think I love him, too. At least,
I know I could."

*Noelle, you're asking too much,* she worried. *You know you
always get in trouble when you ask for too much.*

*I don't care!* "I want to know what he feels like. I want to
feel his skin on mine. I want to know if he tastes as good as
he smells. I want him to do more than know me legally. I want
to keep him with me forever."

"But you know," she stood and looked at herself squarely,
"if he ever touched me, I don't think I'd ever want him to stop.

I can imagine being a little old lady with him, sharing Kodak moments, and loving grandkids. I'd even pick up his dirty socks—willingly."

"I am falling in love, if I haven't already fallen. What am I gonna do?" she moaned. Her reflection, shaking its head, looked as confused as Noelle felt, but offered no help.

"What good are you?" Noelle chided her reflection. Turning off the water and lights, she headed for the den.

"Yeah Mo, I heard you, I'm still listening."

Jamal heard the door to the bathroom close behind Noelle. He could hear the water running even as he tried to listen to Morgan. Having her this close was a definite, but welcome distraction.

*She's under a lot of pressure because of her legal problems,* he rationalized, *she needs time to adjust to the development of our relationship.* Now, Jamal sounded like the ultimate, sensitive, nineties kind of guy. He grimaced.

Reaching across the desk, his fingers found the five-dollar gold piece his grandfather had given him as a child.

"For luck," the old man had said. "My granddad gave it to me for luck when I was just a sprout like you, and it's been with me for all the good things in my life."

*Mine, too,* Jamal thought as he watched his fingers close over the brightness of what he'd come to think of as his good-luck charm.

He hoped there was just a little more luck left. Enough to bring Noelle into his life, and keep her there. His thumb caressed the golden eagle, then pressed tightly against the solidity of the coin. *Give a listen to me,* he almost laughed aloud, the woman barely walked through the door, and he already had her looped into a relationship.

"Jamal? You still there?"

"Yeah Mo, I hear you," he lied, and tried to wrangle his errant thoughts into line. The effort didn't work.

She's got a lot on her plate, his mind blurted. Not to mention this case. Jamal didn't want her to come to him out of gratitude. Nothing permanent could ever be built on a weak foundation. He didn't want to crowd or rush her.

"Jamal!"

"Sorry, man. I guess I wasn't listening. I'm afraid my mind was wandering. You wanna repeat that for me?"

On his end of the line, Morgan shook his head. His partner was in deep—and this was good. He couldn't help but wonder at Jamal's level of emotional involvement. Usually, when they worked on a case, it was Morgan whose mind wandered off on unrelated tangents—never Jamal.

In fact, in the whole time they'd been friends, he'd never seen him like this. What was it he'd said the other night over dinner, while they were waiting for the women to come back to the table? Something about Noelle just being right. Something about her being the complement he'd waited for—for so long.

"But, in the meantime . . ." Morgan said. "I was able to get the hearing scheduled for next Wednesday. The good news is that that's going to give us a little more than a week to pull this all together. The bad news is that it looks like the state might want to add some other nice things to the list of charges."

"Oh? Like what?"

"Like maybe molestation and child endangerment, for starters. Stuff that can carry mandatory jail sentences, we won't know 'til later."

"They're blowing smoke. I think we can answer those charges pretty effectively. After all, they've elected to wait until next week to test Angel. They must figure she's safe enough for now. And the kid's healthy, she'll test fine."

"I like your optimisim. Seems like that Raymond woman's trying to marshal the media. You know, get them on her side."

"Oh, you mean all those reporters at Noelle's?"

"No my brother, more than that. Ever hear of Lark Allister?"

"The reporter?"

"The hotshot, go-for-the-throat, determined-to-be-a-star reporter. She gave me a call earlier, and she was definitely hot for this little story. Said she's doing some digging into Noelle's background. Anything there we ought to know about?"

"I doubt it, but I'll check." Jamal remembered seeing the commercially attractive woman on television, but she hadn't made an impression. "Star, huh?"

"Yep, she's got the look and everything that goes with it."

"And you say the Raymond woman started all this uproar, huh? Why? What's in it for her? Noelle says she doesn't even know the woman—never met her."

"Why does anybody do anything? In the meantime though, we're definitely going to have to make arrangements to get the little girl into a temporary foster-care situation. It'll look better for Noelle that way."

"Yeah, but I know Noelle's going to hate that. She loves Angel like she was her very own."

"She's a cute kid. I don't see any way of getting around it though. It's gotta be foster care, and you know the state's going to demand . . ."

"I know, it's just that . . . we'll miss her."

"Yeah. I'm sure you both will. I talked to Tom." Jamal heard him flip pages in his notes. "He thinks he can arrange to get her placed with a family who lives near you. He even hinted the lady might even be amenable to letting Noelle visit . . . I know that's not a part of the rules, but I can't see totally wrenching that child away from someone who cares about her at a time like this. I mean, it's like she's already been physically abandoned. She shouldn't have to be emotionally abandoned too."

"You're right. I'll talk to Noelle and we'll plan it from there."

"Has she been served yet? Tom seemed to think a court order would go out any minute."

"Man, you know Tom. He's an alarmist."

"Jamal, how's she doing? Staying at your house and all?"

"What do you mean?"

"Well, when you bought that house, you were planning on

marrying Marie and living there with her. Didn't she pick it out?"

"Aw, man." Jamal was laughing so hard now that he was choking. "You know damn well she did, but that's ancient history. Marie may have picked this house out, but I've paid for it. Every stick of furniture in here belongs to me. It's my house, okay? And, no, I haven't told Noelle about Marie. That's what you really want to know, isn't it? It just hasn't come up yet."

"Of course, that's what I really want to know. I'm just trying to watch your back, my brother." Morgan was laughing too.

"I'll tell her. I'm not sure when or how, but I'll tell her. Let's do this, I'll check on the janitor and do the office follow-up and we'll touch base tomorrow around noon."

"S'fine," Morgan mumbled around the pencil he held in his mouth. "I'll also talk some with Pat."

"I hope it won't be a hardship," Jamal verbally leered over the phone.

" 'Bye fool!" Laughing, Morgan ended the conversation with a click.

Sitting at his desk, Jamal twisted in the chair to comfortably throw one long leg over its leather-covered arm. Idly, he flipped the gold coin again. He wondered how Noelle would feel about Marie.

Noelle probably would have simply ignored Marie. Written her off as a silly, shallow, wannabe socialite, made a charitable donation and gone on about her business.

Marie, for her part, would have hated Noelle. At least, she would hate what Jamal knew about her—too altruistic. Too mysterious and too smart. Marie believed a woman only needed to be smart enough to catch a wealthy man, and never hesitated to let people around her know it.

Jamal blew a hard breath between his teeth. *I just wish I knew more about her, period.*

He pulled a long yellow legal pad across the stained cherry-wood surface of the desk. Parking the gold coin at the top of the page, he grabbed a pen. Patiently, he listed the things he knew about Noelle.

It wasn't a long list. "I know about her problem with Angel, her friendship with Pat, and that I've fallen in love with her. I know nothing."

Doggedly, he continued writing. "She's already told me where she was raised, where she went to school, and how long she's lived in Atlanta." He was struggling to come up with something other than her obvious physical attributes.

"Nada," he said aloud, reviewing his list.

Okay he told himself, if he looked at the good, he had to look at the bad. He started a list of what he didn't know. It was considerably longer than the first list.

"There's no way this is supposed to work," he whispered to himself, fingering his talisman. "Just no way I should care this much about a woman I know nothing about. It's not as though we have a past—I've known her less than a full month."

He stood, squeezing the gold piece tightly in his palm, and walked to the window. Staring out at the peach trees he'd planted earlier in the year, he wondered about Noelle. He'd had dinner with her. A couple of afternoons, and a run from a mob. Now, he'd brought her into his house. For the first time since he bought this place, it felt like a home, like the home he grew up in. Like the home he always knew he was meant for, and he honestly felt like it was the only place in the world for her. For them.

He brought a hand to his chin, then slowly drew it across his face. Looking out into the purpling night, Jamal was haunted by the beauty of her eyes, the soft curve of her cheek, and the determined independence of her stance in keeping Angel.

He even sounded like he was falling in love with her, in fact, I guess I've sounded like that almost from the first time I saw her standing there with Angel. Love at first sight—it's crazy. That's the stuff late-night movies featuring Lena Horne and Bill Robinson were made of. They were both too practical and logical for that, too much a part of their times. And, their times were crazy.

Finally, he gave up and watched the summer night grow darker. Seated at the desk again, he grew angry with himself. "Making lists—you're taking this too far." He grabbed his Noelle lists, viciously crunching them into twisted balls. "You're going to nag this thing to death, being so analytical. Just give it up. You love her." He tossed the balls into the trash. "You love her, and the hell with the rest of it."

# Fourteen

Jamal's full lips were drawn into a tight, thin line as Noelle walked into the room.

"Something wrong?" Noelle's face creased with worry. "Is it the charges against me? Am I being arrested? Did they call about Angel?"

"Hey! No. Not at all. That was just Morgan on the phone. We were planning strategy based on what we know right now."

"What do we know right now?" She was watching his every move. "That shrug doesn't do a lot for my confidence."

He stood and moved around the corner of the desk. Noelle leaned against the sofa, trying to relax. She liked the way he looked standing there, his hip propped against the corner of his desk.

They stood there in the dusky room a heartbeat longer, before it occurred to Jamal to turn on a light. Noelle was struck by the length of his arm and the refined economy of his movement as he reached for the desk lamp. The glow of the lamp gilded their skin and found them smiling companionably. Neither wanted to be the first to speak, so they just rested there, sharing a gentle smile.

Noelle finally interrupted the silence. "Penny for your thoughts," she offered.

"How do I know you're good for it?"

Noelle slipped her hand into the pocket of her faded jeans. She had to dip along the smooth curve of her hip twice before she located the coin. Wordlessly grinning, she extended it to him. His hand closed on her fingers, the coin was still warm, but his hand was warmer.

"Well, lemme see," he drawled. "I was thinking about you."

"And it made you frown like that."

"No, that was something else. Tell me about you. What were you like as a little girl. Tomboy?"

"Tomboy? No way! I was a dainty little darling." She turned her nose up, and Jamal fought an urge to kiss its tip. "I've gotta admit though, I didn't take crap off boys." She made a muscle to prove it, then laughed. He liked the sound, soft and throaty.

"Oh, I'm sure you really kept the boys in line with that."

"Doubting Jamal," she teased. "Any other questions?"

"What did you do before you found a home in lovely Atlanta?"

Her face closed. There was no trace of the secure grin she'd worn just seconds before. She shifted her hip and walked solemnly around the sofa to sit on the cushion. Sober and thoughtful, she took a deep breath and looked at him.

"Just drifted," she said.

"Oh, that sounds like a real career move. Tell me something personal."

"Like what?"

"Pat says you were married."

"When did she tell you that?"

"Her house—at the cookout. We had a chance to sit and talk a while when you went to the store."

"Pat may have said too much."

"Come on, don't be mad. She's a good person and she only told me because I pressed her."

"Like you're pressing me?"

He grinned, took a chance and moved closer. Noelle sat very still as he drew her closer, deeper into the circle of his arms.

"I can't even imagine pressing Pat like this."

It felt better than right and more than natural to be closed in Jamal's warm embrace. His lips, ardent and firm against her own, bound them together in a fusion of emotions. Reluctantly, Noelle pulled away from the lure of his lips.

"Was it that bad?"

"No. Actually, it was kinda nice." She sat a little straighter, hoping to cover her embarrassment. "It was just more than I was ready for."

*I'm ready enough for the both of us,* Jamal thought. She still rested in the curve of his arm, a good sign. "So, are you going to tell me about you, or what?"

"I was married, now I'm not. What's to tell?"

Jamal leaned forward to watch her. It was amazing! She still wasn't sure about him. He could see her emotional balancing act. Was it all men she distrusted, or just him? What scared her so badly?

"I almost married once, but it turned out to be the wrong woman."

"That can be bad—marrying the wrong person." She was thoughtful now. "I found out the hard way." She looked up at him, believing the honesty in his face.

"Can you talk about it?"

"I guess I should. You're my attorney."

"And your friend?"

"And my friend."

She smiled and Jamal felt the rush that the soft curving of her lips automatically brought. He knew this was a turning point—she was weighing him. Maybe, she was even measuring his ability to understand what she needed to say.

*She's still trying to decide if I can be trusted. Lord please,* he found himself praying, *please don't let me come up short. Let her trust me enough to talk.* He needn't have worried. Noelle had decided days ago that she could tell him about her past, but it was difficult to get the words out.

"I told you I had been married." Her chest rose and fell sharply with deep breaths. "I told you it was bad."

Jamal nodded, and pulled the gold coin from his pocket.

"I guess, maybe there's a kind of woman who can take the

kind of man Wayne was," she stuttered and laughed nervously, "Is. He's still alive, as far as I know."

"You sound kind of distant. Did you love him?"

Her eyes flashed to meet his, then just as swiftly darted away. Brass lamps and heavily masculine dark wood seemed far less threatening than Jamal's attentive curiosity.

"Maybe I shouldn't have asked. There are some things too personal to be told."

"You asked, and you deserve an answer." He felt her sigh deep in his own chest. "Did I love Wayne?" She looked at him for a long time, working at phrasing her reply. "I wanted to. More than anything else in the world, I wanted to love him, and I tried."

"Even when he got started with the other women, I wanted to love him, and I tried to stick by him. I suppose I was really naive, but I tried to talk him into counseling and I kept making deals," she shrugged, "but it never seemed to work the way I thought it would."

Sitting quietly by her side, Jamal continued to toy with the gold coin. Maybe its luck would hold, and she'd continue to talk. His thumb pressed hard against the eagle's likeness as he willed her to keep talking.

"How much more of this do you want to hear?"

"How much more do you want to tell?" His thumb passed across the face of the coin again. His voice was encouraging, his smile tender, and Noelle began to speak slowly.

"I went to work for Hawkins, Crockett, and Gray. They were a pretty good size accounting firm, and they needed a secretary." Her sidelong glance was only a little coy.

"Don't you think that's funny? With a degree in psychology, I wound up as a secretary—and not a very good one at that. Anyway, I was good with numbers. Better with numbers than with a typewriter, and I was hopeless with a word processor, so they made me a junior accountant.

"Meanwhile, Wayne was spending every penny he could find, usually on his girlfriends. It didn't matter if I borrowed extra from my folks or earned it working overtime. We just never had enough money. Whenever I complained, he ignored me, and I think that hurt most of all.

"I married him because I thought I could love him, that we'd be together forever. I thought we'd grow into that kind of comfortable togetherness you see old people with. I don't know, I guess I thought we'd love each other, our kids and grandkids, till death did we part—but, it didn't work out that way. Jamal, do you have any idea what it's like to be truly alone?" Chewing her bottom lip, the expression in her dark eyes was smoky, like the depths of troubled water—totally unreadable. "That's what my marriage was like."

Her eyes and voice shifted subtly. Years of practice spent wading in denial and pain shaded them. "The first time it happened . . ."

"First time?"

"Yes. It happened two or three times before I figured out what I had to do to save myself."

Jamal listened. His face carried no traces of the revulsion or pity she feared.

"It was scary the first time a strange woman called our home. Married six weeks, and you'd better believe nobody prepared me for that." Her eyes dropped. "I guess I was about as innocent as a new bride could be. I promised myself that I would try to be better—you know, sexier, sweeter, more responsive, whatever it took to keep my husband at home."

"The next time, a strange woman came to our door while Wayne was out of town. She wanted to know why I wouldn't free him from our 'loveless marriage'." Noelle paused with a deep sigh. " 'Loveless marriage'. That was news to me."

Jamal's thumb turned the gold piece over and over against the taut skin of his palm. Oiled by the friction of handling, the warm coin turned easily as he willed her to keep talking.

"We had been married for two years, and everything I had hoped for was falling down around me. Meanwhile, I kept working. I kept ignoring the women, and then I made a discovery."

"I'm not sure how he cooked up his scheme. Wayne got a group of the Hawkins, Crockett, and Gray clients to put up money for a block of foreclosed properties down on the river-front, and I found the records."

Jamal's brow furrowed, and Noelle paused in the telling of her story. She sucked lightly at her front teeth and continued softly.

"I know. In and of itself, there's nothing wrong with buying foreclosed properties. It's only when they don't exist, in a po-tentially lucrative part of town like The Flats, that you have problems. And you can bet the amount Wayne got was a good bit more than my next paycheck.

"I started to get weird headaches. Something a little worse than migranes. Blurred vision, excruciating pain, and confu-sion, that sort of thing. Nothing the doctors gave me worked, and all the tests came back negative. They said it was all stress-related." She made a bitter sound that may have been a laugh. "What stress did I have?

"To make a long story short, I got a promotion that put me right in line to see exactly what Wayne was doing. I confronted Wayne with what I'd found. He wasn't very happy with my discovery. Foolishly, I believed I could save him—save us—from his folly. I thought if I just did the right thing, I could make it all better."

Her chest seemed to freeze as she held her breath. Suddenly cold, Noelle wrapped her arms tightly around herself. She guessed this was the point where Jamal either eased out of her life because of her stupidity and abundance of problems, or started to feel sorry for poor little Noelle.

"We fought like cats and dogs for a week, but Wayne refused to give the money back. He'd already spent most of it, and we had nothing to spare. The only thing left was to rework the books to cover Wayne's tracks."

Now, she was a thief, albeit a stupid one. An admitted thief. *Oh, please, please don't let him treat me like a specimen—*

*something to observe.* She squeezed her eyes shut, willing him to speak, and praying he wouldn't.

She didn't want to hear accusation and judgment in his voice. She didn't want him to send her away or tell her he couldn't handle her case. She didn't think she could stand it if he did. She couldn't stand to see pathos In his eyes. She sat silently, waiting for a reaction.

He let her sit until she could continue.

"The hard part," she finally said, "was trying to explain to my parents. They resented my suspicions, defended Wayne, and didn't want the news to get out. But, the worst thing was their disappointment in me. They knew I knew better, and so did I. My boss was an old golfing buddy of my stepdad's, so of course it was socially embarrassing too." She shrugged and fell silent.

He didn't interrupt or try to offer advice when she finished. He had never been the kind of man Wayne Sterling was and they both knew it. Jamal just let her talk until she finished. And, because he let her talk, she told it all. She even told him about her late-night exodus.

"That's pretty rough," he finished for her.

Noelle exhaled visibly. "Yes, you could call it that. Pretty rough."

Trying to ease the mood, Jamal stood and stretched. "How about a Coke," he offered.

"A Coke? After what I just shared with you?"

"I didn't think you were the bourbon type, and besides it always seems to work in the commercials."

"Commercials? Just for that, yeah. I want a Coke, In a glass. With ice." Noelle's eyes belied the demanding tone of her voice.

"Anything for you, dear. I think I can even arrange a straw, if you like."

"I like," Noelle giggled.

When he brought the drinks back, Jamal's lanky body folded itself on the sofa near her. "I saved the best for last." He sipped the Coke, and Noelle was entranced by the tip of his tongue as it traced his lip catching random drops of cola just below his mustache.

"What's the best?" She smiled around the glass.

"Tell me what you like."

"Like?" He nodded.

"This is silly, being interviewed like this. Frankly, I would have to think about it. Nobody's ever asked me that before."

She looked blank, then made up her mind. At first she talked because she felt that she owed it to him to at least be a little entertaining. After all, he'd been so understanding and supportive.

"I like reading."

"Me, too. Favorite book?"

"That's easy," she grinned. *"A Tale of Two Cities."*

"My favorite too."

"You're kidding? Isn't it more trendy to say you love something by Achebe or Alice Walker or E. Lynn Harris or even Tom Clancy?"

"Not if what you really love is Dickens. 'It was the best of times . . .' "

" ' . . . it was the worst of times.' " She finished the quote with a disbelieving smile.

"That's great! What else do you like?"

"Movies, swimming, especially snorkling."

"Really? Me too. Ever snorkeled in Aruba?"

"No, my stepdad preferred Florida."

"Guess that's what comes from living in the cold northern lands. You take whatever warm water you can get." Jamal shook his head in mock pity.

"Well there are other places I'm sure, southern boy. I said it was my stepdad's choice, not mine. But, what do you know about making snow angels?"

He laughed, "Never heard of 'em. Besides, I'd swear you're making that up. What's a snow angel?"

"Am not! It's the imprint when you lie on your back in the deep snow and move your arms and legs, like this." She stood and demonstrated. "Actually," she dropped onto the sofa, "it's only one of the reasons I moved to Atlanta. Much warmer climate."

"Is that the only reason?"

"No. The economy, the housing," she shrugged, "The schools, and . . . other things."

"Like?"

Coy shyness caught her off guard. The look in his eyes was making her warm in unexpected ways and places. "Like, what do you mean?"

"Like, I was hoping you might consider the people in Atlanta a reason for being here."

"People? Like you, for instance?"

"For instance." He grinned and shrugged, trying to look innocent.

"The people are an especially wonderful part of living here." She leaned closer to place a brief press of warm lips against his cheek. "People like you."

She smelled of springtime and other earthy things, and Jamal felt his body react with a lurch. He cleared his throat, and hated his body for betraying him. "You want another Coke?"

"No. I'm fine," she sighed. "In fact, I'm better than I've been since this whole crazy mess started."

Relaxing, Noelle slid across the sofa. Laughing, her hand found his thigh, patted it, then rested warmly there. Jamal wondered what further temptations he'd be challenged with this night.

# Fifteen

"What's so funny?"

"Coke."

"Coke?"

"Uh-huh. When I first moved here, I knew Atlanta was where Coke originated. I kind of thought it was like the official city drink or something." She giggled at the memory.

"That is silly." He pulled her into his arms and she snuggled against his warm, solid chest. Their shared laughter felt good. The laughter grew softer, quieter and his arms seemed even more secure than before.

Noelle felt a moment of panic when she realized how completely satisfied she was. This home, the sleeping child in another room, and the comfort of the man beside her all felt natural. What must she have done right to deserve this natural, peaceful interlude, and what would it cost her in the not-too-distant future?

"Jamal, I think I need to say something. Wait." She used both hands to push away from his chest, hoping that distancing temptation would make this easier to say.

"We need some ground rules, just for my peace of mind if not for the sake of anything we're about to start. I need to tell you that I'm not used to one-night stands. I've never done anything like that before, and that's not what I want with you. Is that where we're heading? Because, if it is . . ."

He shook his head, denying her words, and his smile, touched with sadness, grew tender. She was afraid of being hurt or damaged again, and she had a right to be. He folded her into his arms. His fingers traced the curve of her cheek as he held her close.

"Noelle, I've told you that you mean a lot to me. I know that it takes time to learn to trust fully, and I accept that, but I'm going to do everything in my power to help you learn I mean every word I've said.

"I am not Wayne, and I am not about to abandon you—not physically or emotionally. I'm not claiming to be perfect, but if you trust me, you won't be sorry. One night stands? That's not my style either. I told you before, I'm in this for the long run."

"This," he called it. What is "this"? An affair? A flirtation? Love? Noelle sat quietly. She wasn't sure what, if anything, she should say to him, and less sure of what she wanted him to say to her. She settled for lifting her face to receive his kisses, and returning them in kind. Tightening her arms about his broad shoulders, he sure felt like the right man.

"Okay, you say you're serious, and I'm feeling . . . but what if we find out we're not right for each other?"

"Honey, that's down the road." He dropped a kiss on her forehead, "and it's a chance I'm willing to take."

"Jamal, I have to confess, I haven't been with a man for more than five years." Embarrassed, she focused on a point somewhere above his left eye. Willing her voice not to tremble, she was pleased when it didn't—much. "What if, well . . . what if I've forgotten how?"

Her confession made her all the more special to him. Most women would have died before making such an intimate confession. He held her closer, his grin so big she could hear it in his voice. "It's like riding a bike," he assured her through a light rain of dizzying kisses. "You never forget."

His face was closer, his kisses consuming, and for a dizzy moment she felt like he was going to kiss the gloss right off her lips.

"You're that sure?" At his nod, she returned soft kisses.

Folding her hand into Jamal's, she followed as he led her along the shadowed hall. Her steps slowed as she accepted the idea of the room spread before her. They stopped when she saw his enormous bed. The custom-built, double king-sized bed, with its carved mahogany head and footboards dominated the room. Noelle was awed by its magnificence.

She thought of her own small, pink-sheeted, virginal, single bed, and her eyes questioned his. The bed was such an obvious symbol of commitment to a man she'd so recently come to know, that it gave rise to second thoughts, in spite of her desire.

"If I touch it, there's no turning back, is there?" Her voice was small in the dim light.

"Noelle, do you want to turn back? Do you think you need to turn back? If you're not sure, I don't want you to do anything you're not ready for. I can wait as long as I have to for you to make up your mind about us, and to fully and freely accept me."

*No pressure.* The lack of it made her feel light-headed and almost weightless. Vivid images of Wayne sneered at her, daring her to go on without him. He defied her to lay her hands on the vital loving life being offered her. His challenge was dry and pithy, sour to the taste.

With Jamal's hand still warm on her arm, and the remembrance of his kisses sweet upon her lips, Noelle made her choice easily. Wayne disappeared with an almost audible pop.

"My mind is already made up. I am exactly where I want to be" she said.

At the press of a switch, bedside lamps glowed gently. Softly inviting amber light bathed the room, and bronzed Jamal's handsome features. Hands on her shoulders, he drew her closer. Her eyes still questioned him.

He bent forward, kissing her neck, shoulders, and the tender lines leading lower. Pressing her closer, he felt her hands against the back of his neck. She radiated heat, he could feel through her clothes. Her breath thundered into his ear.

"Jamal . . ." she whispered, "I'm so scared . . ."

He drew her down onto the edge of the quilt, easily unbuttoning her blouse. His finger traced the sweetly inviting curves of her breasts.

"It's been so long." Her fingers trembled against his skin.

Kissing her lips, he watched the gentle flutter of her lashes, and the lazy drift of her closing eyes. Slowly, he bent low and kissed her throat where the pulse beat hard and fast.

"Noelle," he whispered, loving the feel and sound of her name crossing his lips. Her name was a hymn, a song, an incantation—a promise of anticipated fulfillment.

His hands were deft as he undressed her. Exquisite breasts with darkly saluting, insolent nipples molded themselves firmly against her chest, rising and falling with the flow of her breath. She was so achingly beautiful, his heart almost stopped.

"I love you," he heard himself say.

He felt no fear—none at all—of saying the words to her. He had never trusted a woman like this. Not since Marie, but he felt himself falling freely, slipping willingly into the familiar dark mystery of woman, where no man has a guiding light. But he was not afraid. Her fingers pressed tightly, possessively against the small tightly bunched muscles of his back.

"Oh, please," she breathed, infusing the words with more passion than she had imagined possible.

He pulled at the quilt, and magically, they slipped beneath cool, tangling sheets. Arms and legs fell naturally into the patterns of the eternal weave of human sexuality. He was all molten heat and massive sensation crowding need and hunger from beneath her skin and out of her life.

Noelle lost all sense of herself as he breached the walls she had built. Things were melting, slipping away, and changing proportion forever. All the problems, the loneliness, and confusion became ashes in the burning rush of his assault on her senses.

Her voice, murmuring words of urgent thanks and christening new emotions, came as softly to has ear as a newborn kitten's first cry. Jamal heard himself answer with the words he'd never spoken to another. Infinite tenderness might have been the ultimate goal as his fingers, lips, and hands traveled the course of her body, unraveling the tired threads of ancient inhibitions as he went.

A small moan burst unchecked from her lips, another, then a gasp. She felt herself meeting and dissolving within him, sailing endlessly down a broad midnight river, riding wave upon wave toward a great unknown ocean.

"Noelle . . ."

Time unfurled itself like an unending bolt of cloth, its folds assuring unhurried exploration and surrender. Now, it was his breath and his urgency thundering, roaring in her ears, and pressing to conclusion. He called her name again, convulsing within the darkly intoxicating confines of her offering. Then like her, he was silent. He lay against her and did not move.

Finally closing his eyes, Jamal knew he had arrived, at long last, at the place where he had always wanted to be, with the woman he'd always known was right for him. They slept through the darkness turned like matching spoons, body to body, holding safe their intimate discoveries.

# *Sixteen*

The old saying was true. Time really did fly when you were having fun.

Noelle smiled, rising on her elbow to check the bedside clock. Luminous numbers told her that miracles could indeed last longer than mere minutes. Time flew when you were falling in love. Snuggling low beneath the covers to fit her body closer to Jamal's, she rested her head against his chest.

Tempted to make a telephone call, to broadcast what she felt, she stopped herself. Who, besides Pat, would she call? Beyond that, she couldn't imagine the words she might use to explain the magic of what had happened here tonight.

Nothing beyond this huge bed seemed important, nothing meant anything anymore. It was as if she had no past, and her future was inexplicably and inexorably tied to the man beside her.

Holding the memory of their shared intimacy, Noelle found herself comparing Jamal to Wayne. Every way she looked at it, Wayne was a poor second. She'd never been able to talk to Wayne and God knew, he'd only condescended to talk *at* her.

She'd never been able to convince him that she also had emotional, physical, or sexual needs. Mostly because she'd been too embarrassed to say the words. Even if she had been able to get him to talk, there was no way he would have believed he'd not satisfied her every conceivable need beyond doubt. His ego wouldn't let him believe anything else. Closing her eyes, allowing herself the luxury of a body quaking stretch, Noelle again coiled herself against the now familiar, relaxed length of Jamal.

There was a quote, she remembered, that described Wayne perfectly. *He's a legend in his own mind.* That said it all, and seemed to render memories of her now ex-husband impotent and unimportant. She pressed moist lips to Jamal's warm chest. He stirred lightly in his sleep, a slight smile forming on his lips. She wondered if he was dreaming. She hoped he was—about her. His slight movement seemed to be all around her, and she recalled how much she had initially resented his closeness. That felt like a long time ago.

Watching him was easy. He was beautiful in repose, sleek golden skin, tightened over relaxed muscles. Sculpted features etched and echoed in shadow, engraved themselves indelibly in her heart. Her finger lightly traced the boldly squared planes of his cheek and chin. He was a gentle man.

"I love your gentleness," she whispered, molding herself more firmly to his warm form. "I am so grateful to finally have you in my life." And what would I have done, who would I have become, if not touched by you, she wondered. "I adore your touch," she celebrated, sliding her fingers delicately beneath his, and wanting to scream with delight when his hand tensed, then closed over hers. "You are so good for me."

Jamal Allen Harris was good for her, she'd known that last night. Last night. The thought made her giddy. All she had room for in her memory was last night. The grace and sensitivity Jamal demonstrated had been long awaited and almost desperately needed in her life.

Pat was right, she thought. Noelle never dreamed she would someday just run into a man like this. A man who was even better than the heroes in those paperback books so faithfully collected over the years. If only she'd known about men like Jamal before Wayne, the evil twin with his dark magic entered her life. But, she had Jamal now.

Her fingers moved lightly, with a proprietary touch, sweeping his skin again to be sure he was real and as good as she remembered. "I have him now," she whispered to herself.

Such a special man. He'd been more than a gentleman. Generous and encouraging, he was all the things she had never known before. Impatient, she wriggled closer. Admiring the strength of his face, her wanton fingers traced his lips. Drowsily, he licked at her intruding fingers, and continued sleeping.

From start to finish, she thought lazily, he'd been responsible. Even down to condoms. Wayne always refused to use them, claiming they diminished his pleasure. *Mine never mattered,* Noelle pouted, then corrected herself. What he'd really said was, 'I can't feel anything.' He always managed to imply she had done something wrong, and left her feeling guilty and hurt, and assuming she was somehow inadequate.

Jamal moved slightly at her touch.

*It's okay Wayne, I understand now. All you were is all you are.* Her lips curved with satisfaction. *I'm better now, and it's okay. I can let you go, and never feel the space you left behind.* Jamal Harris erased that tiny space forever. She felt ready to explode with remembered joy spilling from her soul.

"Wake up."

He stirred slowly, stretching his long body beside her. Heavy lidded eyes opened slowly. Prayer truly worked. Delighted by his deliberate movements, Noelle lowered her face to receive the gentle caress of his lashes against her cheek. Eyes still closed, slow smile dawning, he shifted subtly to enfold her.

Easing closer, holding the moment and knowing the security of his love, she tensed eagerly, ready to receive all that he offered. His arms tightened around her shoulders and she felt reverberations of the strength that earlier had inscribed her body with undeniable evidence of his passion.

"Did you want my attention?" His voice was husky and suggestive, utterly provocative. Delighted, Noelle only nodded. Being here with him, like this, she reclaimed and rejuvenated herself. Lord, she celebrated, this was a healing man! She was with him because she wanted to be, not because anyone had manipulated or shamed her, and whatever happened after this, she knew she was able to love him fully.

She felt free for the first time in years.

Jamal's hands traveled slowly over her shoulders. He seemed encouraged by soft moans escaping her parted lips. Sensing rising passion, his fingers found their own path, touching her face and teasing the hardening peaks of firm breasts. His hands felt huge as they moved gently, deliberately to her legs. Her body twisted and virtually shimmered with delight at his touch.

"Noelle," he whispered, softly calling her name. His body seemed to vibrate in perfect tune with hers. As her long leg traveled the course of his hip, they both knew the path their yearnings would take.

The feel of her satiny skin was everything he remembered, and nearly more than he could bear. He fought hard for control, wanting to move slowly, to savor her look and feel. It was a battle he was destined to lose. But his loss was their triumph, its ungentle conclusion rocking them beyond their combined essence.

An urgent blue-white flash of lightning glazed the lines of their joined bodies, leaving subtly negative afterimages printed against closed eyes. They lay quietly listening to the quickening sounds of rushing wind tinkling through chimes outside his windows. Noelle loved where she was.

"I do love you," she whispered.

"I love you, too, Noelle. God help me, I think I always have." And that was enough.


He woke slowly, letting his soul fit itself gradually back into his body. He kept his eyes closed while he gently touched and turned his memory, replaying who he was and where he was and all that had happened. Stirring slightly, his fingers met firm flesh, and he grinned. Satisfied that she was more than a dream, he opened his eyes.

Jamal looked around the bedroom, studying it for change.

The lightning and thunder had ended. It was too dark to see clearly, but he recognized the four familiar enclosing walls and the furniture he had selected on his own, though the room was forever changed for him. Pushing the sheet aside, he swung his feet to the floor.

Through curtained windows, he noticed the moon was down. Straining to see far to the southwest the sky was starless, but brightening. Maybe, there'd be some light from the cloud-shrouded moon before too long.

Yawning, and stretching, Jamal was tempted to scratch himself, when he remembered Noelle's presence. No need to gross her out, he decided as he headed to the bathroom sink.

Drinking a handful of water, warm from the tap, he noted the air even smelled different with her in the house—not perfumed—but better. Sniffing, he separated her scent from the gently moist smell of summer rain and damp soil. Yeah, the air smelled of rain, as it had for weeks. But, there was also the clean, healthy smell of her hair and skin.

He ran a little more water, splashed his face, then found his old green terry robe on the back of the door. *Maybe I should check on Angel.*

The thought came unbidden, and he tried to defend it. A little kid in a strange house, the thunder and lightning, the early morning hour—couldn't hurt to check. The defense of the notion, he decided, was unnecessary. Nothing wrong with liking kids. He'd always liked kids, and this one happened to be special. The little girl was so quiet sometimes, he worried, though he loved her laughter and sweetly chiming voice.

He yawned again, then shambled down the hall to the room where Angel still slept peacefully. She looked tiny, lying with Kermit in the full-size bed. One fist clutched the sheet tightly under her chin, while the other arm was blithely flung above her head on the pillow. Her breathing was softly moist and marked by childish, intermittent sucking sounds. It was clever of Noelle to have improvised the scarf shielded night-light. It made the room more homey.

"G'night baby," he whispered from the door. Dreaming deeply, she smiled and tucked her thumb into her mouth with a sigh. Jamal almost imagined she'd heard him.

Without thinking, Jamal returned to his bed on tiptoe. Kneeling, he watched the spill of dark hair curling across Noelle's cheek, and remembered how he'd envied that very curl its caressing proximity only—was it weeks ago, or merely days? His finger discreetly traced the curl to its delicious destination. The luscious pout of her lips pressed his finger for the barest part of a second before he withdrew it.

Exquisite, he thought. Sliding into his still-warm spot beneath the sheets, he wondered how some people turned their back on family. He looked at Noelle's still sleeping form, thought of Angel, and smiled to himself. They were so like a family, the three of them in this house together.

*My family?*

The sweet ease of the claim made his heart swell in that familiar way that makes some men question their manhood. Jamal never wavered. The love he was feeling, he knew, was a big part of what made him a man.

"I guess this is why those people in musicals just suddenly hear music and start singing and dancing. Sudden, stupifying happiness." He had to admit he did feel a little foolish confessing to a sleeping woman.

He was still smiling as his arms arranged themselves around Noelle and she snuggled close against his chest.

What fool would throw away such miracles?

# Seventeen

It was beyond understanding. How did one average woman inspire such unbending loyalty in people who hardly knew her? The crime Minnie Raymond had alluded to may or may not have really existed, though if these people had their way, Lark would never know. Minnie was by all accounts, a thrill seeking glory-hound.

But, Lark could feel it, as subtle as a sheer silk slip beneath lace. Something hidden below Noelle Parker's glassily perfect surface. What it was and where the proof lay hidden, well that was something else again.

It was almost as though Noelle Parker had a fan club, and it had banded together to protect their star and her cool reserve with a code of silence. Kind of like the "Omerta".

Lark's beautifully manicured fingers played across the computer keyboard. Moving the mouse easily, she accessed first her own, then the investigative team's notes. The research was professionally thorough, and page after page flashed in golden letters across her terminal. Every lead they'd tried hit the same dead ends. Nothing, or at least nothing usable. Frustrated, she slipped her foot free of the soul-soothing Valentino pump, and moved the mouse again. Reading, rereading, then re-rereading, she still found nothing.

Leaning back into the womblike comfort of her chair, Lark freed her mind to work on its own. Some people called this brainstorming, but it felt brain-calming as she let her mind impose order on the randomly disconnected information she'd gotten from her computer.

"Talked to the mother, no comment." Actually, the mother had quite a few comments for the reporter she'd talked to, Lark remembered, and none of them were politely quotable. The nicest thing she'd said was good-bye.

"Moving right along," Lark fingered the mouse's controls again. "Talked to the mother's current neighbors, don't know the daughter. Old address, new neighbors. They don't know her either." Lark leaned forward to check a note on her screen.

"Lived in an eastside condo with husband from . . ." Lark's smile tightened her lips into a straight line, pulling only at the corners. It was the only indicator of the idea she was hatching.

Without looking, her hand hit the intercom.

"Jane, get me the management for Ville du Lac in Cleveland, Ohio." Eyes barely moving, Lark continued to scan the line that had caught her attention.

"Can you check on evictions too? I think we may have one here. Either in the name of Noelle Parker, or her ex, or . . ." Lark's eyes narrowed in direct proportion to the broadening of her smile, "Perry. Try Louis or Mattie Perry, and it would be, oh I don't know, five, six years ago."

Jane murmured something, then disconnected.

Lark sat back to wait. Nothing satisfied her more than a good day's work. Absolutely nothing.


"Everybody else pays," he whined. "I happen to know that some of the tabloids would pay serious money for my story. I don't see why I can't get a little cash advance. Your company can surely afford it. Besides, I've seen your national reports, don't you need me to tie up a few loose ends for you about my ex-wife's past?"

Flipping the library copy of Wayne Sterling's photo over like a playing card, it was easy to see why any woman, including Noelle Parker, would have been attracted to this man. At first glance, the chiseled features and cinnamon colored skin, blinding smile, and dimpled chin would have sent most women rushing for sheer lingerie. Lark's respect for Noelle Parker grew again.

Good-looking though he was, and young and inexperienced as Noelle had been back then, she still had seen through his pretty facade. She may have married him, but at least she'd had the strength and intelligence to survive him, and to get on without him.

*Same as I would've done,* Lark told herself. *Besides, Sterling, I've seen your replacement and it's no contest.* From all she could see, Jamal Harris was a special man. Noelle Parker was no dummy.

Lark tucked a leg beneath her, admiring her Enzo sandal, and swung her chair away from the door of her empty office. She let Wayne Sterling talk himself out, knowing it would net more information.

It hadn't been hard to find him after Jane dug up the eviction, and accessed the *Plain Dealer* files for the time in question. In fact, the story began to piece itself together nicely, bit by interesting bit once Lark turned the key. She silently blessed the information superhighway again.

The condo had been listed in Noelle's stepfather's name. Louis Perry had given them the condo as a wedding gift, and Sterling would probably be living there today, if not for his conniving little money games. Everything else was a matter of public record. Even the fiasco with Hawkins, Crockett, and Gray, the company Noelle had been employed by.

Lark was glad she'd thought to record the conversation, though Sterling didn't seem to care one way or the other.

"I probably should save it for my book," he said.

"You're writing a book?" Lark let her voice drip magnolias and honey.

"I'm writing my life story. After being in here, I realize I've got a lot to say."

"Oh." Lark let the word flutter over the telephone lines,

knowing it would have the same effect on a man in the Ohio State Penitentiary that it had over drinks at the Three Dollar Cafe or Pano and Paul's up in Buckhead. She fought down a ridiculous urge to suggest titles for Wayne Sterling's upcoming literary tome.

"That's right. Does your company have ties to publishing? I mean, that's usually a part of these communications empires these days, isn't it? Maybe you could recommend me to an agent."

"Hmm," Lark made commiserating sounds in the back of her throat, and Sterling continued to talk. It was easy to understand why Parker had gone back to her maiden name after leaving Wayne Sterling.

"I saw in the papers where she turned up in Atlanta. With someone's stray child. If I'd gone looking for her, I never would have thought to look there. Atlanta." He snorted, then spoke to someone in the background.

"Hey, I've got to go. They only give you so long to talk, you know. Anyway, you get back to me. Okay?"

The call disconnected.

"In your dreams, buddy." Sitting silently, Lark stared at her hand resting on the still-warm receiver.

The slim bangle at her wrist reflected golden sparks in the afternoon light. Her Timex read 2:26. Sterling was no prize. Nobody could blame Parker for getting out of her toxic marriage; away from her husband and his delusions of grandeur.

Pulling the yellow legal pad closer, Lark started sketching notes, moving bits and pieces of information into line with her pencil point. She always thought better when she recorded information the old-fashioned way. Much as she hated to admit it, she still didn't fully trust computers. Trying hard to fill in the blanks, she numbered the items. It didn't help. Sterling had shed very little light on what she already knew about Parker.

He confirmed the parental estrangement, and seemed genuinely relieved to hear that Louis Perry was deceased. He had tried to control the conversation, steering it into areas of creative darkness. He was a talented manipulator, with a tendency toward self-service, and Lark was always careful of that in interviews.

Sterling said Noelle Parker was a quiet woman, and he painted her moody. He said family and roots were important to his ex-wife, but he couldn't supply the names of her friends from so long ago. She wanted children, he didn't. Sterling hinted there was nothing Parker wouldn't do to get what she wanted—even if she had to steal. In fact, he said that was one of the reasons they were no longer together. Lark could think of others.

Sterling, like most convicts, also said he was innocent.

Lark drew a line under the last words of her notes, then casually thickened it with broad strokes of her pencil. WHAT NEXT? She wrote the words in large block style letters.

Minnie Raymond said Parker committed a crime, but she didn't know what it was. Staying with Wayne Sterling would have been a crime, because he was certainly no prize. Lark shook her head at her notes—no need to editorialize. The information she'd gotten could point to spousal abuse, but did that lead to kidnapping?

"A better question is, does that lead to tonight's story?"

Brainstorming is tremendously underrated. Minnie Raymond's name was her first thought, it had to be the right one. Reaching for the telephone, she pressed the buttons and waited out the ringing.

"Ms. Raymond? This is Lark Allister."

"Ms. Allister! How nice of you to call, I was just thinking about you. I was wondering where we stand on the Noelle Parker investigation."

*We?* "That's actually why I was calling. I've hit a bit of a dead end."

"A dead end? Dear me. Umm . . ."

"Yes?"

"I'm just wondering if perhaps that lawyer . . . That Mr. Harris might be involved somehow."

Instinctively, Lark went with her gut on that one, knowing it missed the mark. "I doubt it. Harris is a new factor in this story. Didn't he only recently meet Parker?"

"Maybe so, but he's constantly involved with children's cases. Usually little girls, and right around puberty. More importantly, he spends a lot of time alone with the children in his caseload."

"No. I think you're reaching for signs of impropriety there."

"He was recently part of a case where the girl was hospitalized at Grady . . ." Minnie let the words hang, suspended by threads of innuendo.

"What was the girl's name?"

Minnie nearly clapped her hands as the reporter rose to the bait. "I really can't remember offhand, but it was right around the fourth of July. Wasn't that about the same time this little Angel was taken by Ms Parker?"

"Actually, it was. But, I don't know. Can you think of anyone else who might be involved with these children?"

"Of course I can," Minnie said. "I've heard Pat Stevens has children of her own, but she and Noelle are very close, so you can bet she's a part of any plan or plot. Pat would know for sure."

"On the other hand," Minnie continued slowly, "there was a woman in Jamal's life sometime back, I heard. Flighty little flirtatious thing, I heard. They were engaged, looking at houses and furniture, that sort of thing, then nothing. She left suddenly. There was some talk about her taking a high-profile job overseas. Maybe there was a child . . . ? Out-of-wedlock, naturally."

"Really?" The alarm on the reporter's instincts went off with a flip of her stomach. She reached for her pen. "What was her name? What else do you know about her?"

On cue, Minnie began to rattle off her arsenal of facts. "I believe her name is Marie, with an e on the end. If it's not Marie, then it's Mary with a cute spelling, but her last name is Campbell. I think her family's originally from Cedartown. Anyway, she went to work for the World Health Organization about five . . . yes it was five years ago when she finished her internship with the DFACS Home Health Unit."

"I don't suppose you know where she was posted?"

"Oh, yes. She made a big deal out of it, told everybody she was off to bigger and better things. She left Atlanta for New York City. I heard she made some mistakes though."

"Mistakes? What kind of mistakes?"

"You know the kind her sort always makes. In the wrong place, at the wrong time, with the wrong somebody's husband. You know. And from there, she wound up in North Africa."

"North Africa?" Lark scribbled furiously.

"Malawi."

"Is she still with the WHO?"

"Sorry, I don't know." The woman's voice held genuine regret.

"I see. Well, you've been very helpful," Lark said graciously. Hanging up the phone, she decided to pull the new thread Minnie Raymond dangled before her.

"Jane," she pressed the intercom button. "Tonight we're going with the people around Noelle Parker. Heading the list is Jamal Harris. Let's look at Pat Stevens too. Keep all the kids out of it—for now."

She checked the Timex—3:44. If she worked fast, she could just make it before DFACS closed for the day.

"One other thing Jane, what's the telephone country code for the African nation of Malawi?"

# Eighteen

"I don't really think I can help you Ms. Allister." The cultured voice had a texture like buttermilk—thick and creamy, with small golden nuggets of her southern past occasionally visible.

"That may be Mrs. Doshon, but we won't know until we talk, will we?" Lark matched her with carefully rounded, velvety tones of her own. Peyton Communications did not pay her to be shy or coy.

"Jamal Harris was a very long time ago for me. He was my past."

"That may also be true, but the past has a way of impinging on the present and shading the future."

"True. And now, you want to rummage in my past. How do you suppose that will affect the future?" The woman smiled, adjusted her large green-tinted shades, and tilted her head to follow the movements of the small golden skinned boy playing on the broad expanse of manicured lawn before them.

"If we don't talk, we may never know." Lark smiled pleasantly.

Shifting her slender body, the former Marie Campbell of Atlanta, Georgia, conceded. "Alright, you have thirty minutes. I hope they're worth the airfare."

Lark hoped so too. It had taken five days of telephonic confusion across three continents, and then a rushed flight to Virginia when the woman refused to talk on the telephone, but here she was. A small, powerful recorder sat on the table between them, and Lark pressed the play button.

Marie Campbell Nyong Otrou Doshon had not been easy to track down. She had moved through several African and European countries to finally land in this great old white-columned mansion in Arlington, Virginia.

Thrice married, with a small child, Marie Doshon was a beautiful, gracefully feline, elitist social climber who claimed wealth and position via matrimony. Her latest spouse was a genteel, landed ambassador whose old money and exotic family background gave her the local cachet of royalty, something she obviously cherished.

Deep at heart, Marie was just an old-fashioned kind of girl who shed her last name as easily as a snake sheds its skin, and left it up to her man to take care of her. Timeless beauty was the insurance policy. The flawless blue-white Van Cleef & Arpels diamonds at her fingers and the man who provided them were the only allegiances she would ever hold.

"Mrs. Doshon, you were once involved with Jamal Harris?"

"Involved? That is such a nebulous term, don't you agree?" Marie shook her head with an amused smile. "Already you are wasting your time. Asking the obvious." Her chuckle was mocking and made Lark wonder how she'd snagged those husbands whose last names she strung onto her own with the ease of an add-a-bead necklace.

"Alright. Perhaps relationship is a more precise term. What can you tell me about your relationship with Jamal Harris?"

Marie shifted her glasses against the glare of the afternoon sun. Lark was rewarded by a glimpse of large, heavily mascaraed, startlingly emerald eyes of the sort that are always considered astounding in people of color. They glittered like flawlessly cut jewels against her dark skin.

"I was engaged to Jamal Harris some years ago when we both worked for the Department of Family and Children Services in Atlanta. But, you already know that. That is why you came looking for me, is it not?"

"If you want me to say that he is a horrible degenerate who drank excessively, beat me, spent his spare time carousing with wild women, and misspending my money—then I repeat, you are wasting your time. He is a very special man, a gentleman in every sense of the word. I have never known a kinder man, or a gentler, more understanding and skillful lover."

Chuckling softly at Lark's widening eyes, Marie shook her hair back from her face. "Does my candor shock you in some way Ms. Allister? I thought in these MTV-Generation-X days, I could be frank with a member of the press."

She leaned forward in a soft hiss of taupe and ivy-colored linen to fuss over the silver tea service. "May I offer you tea? It is a wonderful Darjeeleng-based blend. One of my personal favorites." She poured exquisitely at Lark's assent.

"Jamal Harris is genetically coded to be decent, upstanding, and forthright—in short, a Boy Scout." Lark couldn't tell if the other woman's expression was wistful or desirous, though it changed fleetingly beneath the dark glasses. "He would have made a wonderful husband, and an even better father. Is he still handsome, charming, and tied by honor to the department?"

"I'm afraid he is," Lark replied.

"That is exactly what I would have expected." Marie lowered the Beleek china cup and saucer just in time to catch the laughing, tousle-haired child who ran screaming to her lap. Lark was reminded of another child. A little girl, who turned to another woman with exactly the same openness and enthusiasm the little boy demonstrated.

Hugging the child to her breast, Marie Doshon selected two small cookies from the silver tray nearest her. Offering them to the child, she fixed him with an adoring and indulgent mama-face. "What do you say, darling?"

"Merci, Maman." The cookies disappeared efficiently. The child slipped from her lap as a small, heavy-set woman approached. He ran shouting into the open arms of his caregiver.

Marie watched as the pair crossed the portico to reenter the house.

"That is my son, Ethan. We are working on manners."

"And how old is Ethan?"

An eyebrow lifted gracefully. "Ms. Allister, you could use some work on manners, as well. Again, you are wasting time, and you are out of line. Jamal Harris is not my son's father, no matter what any wicked gossip might have inferred. Jamal is far too honorable to father a child out of wedlock. I would have had to marry him in self-defense, if only to ameliorate his guilt. And never, would he fail to acknowledge his child—if Ethan were his."

Lark weighed the words, wondering what emotions lay beneath them. "What caused the rift in your relationship?"

"One might say it was Mr. Nyong, Mr. Otrou, or Monsieur Doshon. It doesn't matter which, you see. Our 'rift' was a matter of conflicting life philosophies. Jamal wanted to be all things to all people thereby making all things equal. I wanted to be all things to one man who would adore me, making me more than equal. It would seem we've both gotten what we wanted."

She removed the dark glasses and regarded Lark with ice in her green eyes. "To be sure you understand, I repeat, Jamal Harris is not my son's father—neither legally nor naturally. There are no questions of legitimacy where my child is concerned. Paul Marc Doshon, my husband, is in fact Ethan's father."

"You defend Mr. Harris like a woman in love." A flash of pain rushed behind Marie's lovely features before she regained composure, and Lark was sure she'd guessed right.

"I think your time is up."

Lark's teeth played against her lip as she reached for the recorder. "There is one last thing I need to ask before we conclude."

She hated having to ask for permission, but if it got her question answered, it was worth it. "You've already said that you believe Mr. Harris to be above impropriety." Lark's breath caught in her throat. "What about collusion?"

"What?"

"Could he aid someone in the commission of a crime?"

"You're very insistent. I suppose he could, he is loyal enough, and he certainly knows the law well enough to avoid pitfalls. But he would not. His moral sense is too strongly developed. Who do you suggest he might help?'1 She slipped the green glasses on again.

"There's a case in Atlanta, involving a woman. A case worker accused of taking a child, and . . ."

"Taking a child?" Wonder infused Marie Doshon's cool voice. "We have heard about that in the news. Paul and I discussed the case just this morning. I had no idea . . ." Her mouth closed slowly, as she shook her head in astonished denial. "Somehow, you think Jamal Harris is involved?"

It was exactly the answer Lark had anticipated. Astonished confusion. She'd reached another dead end. Tucking the recorder into her bag, she glanced at her Timex. She could still make an early afternoon flight back to Atlanta. She stood and reached to shake Marie's hand.

Marie ignored the hand, slipped the glasses from her face, and fixed Lark with those piercing emerald eyes. "What is she like? The woman you think he's helping?"

"She's, umm . . . Noelle Parker is a caseworker. Tall and slender, willowy like you. Rather cocoa-colored skin, dark eyes and hair. Pretty."

"That is not what I am asking. I mean what sort of person is she?"

Lark shrugged. "I don't know quite what you want me to say. Not physically? Let me think—she's a survivor who has come through some tough personal times. She's bright, diligent, and apparently enjoyed working with DFACS. She says she took the child because she had no alternative."

Marie nodded. "And she would kill for that child. She does not hesitate to go the extra distance, because she cares. She genuinely cares. Don't you see?" The green eyes bore into Lark's, daring her not to understand. "She's the kind of devoted, selfless, giving person Jamal has always needed. He is the Yin to her Yang—the perfection of her soul."

"I see," said Lark.

"No. No, you don't."

*Stupid.* Lark almost heard the unspoken word.

"You cannot possibly understand. Jamal is the kind of man who truly believes in happily ever after, and that God made someone special for everyone. He's a hero, and he will always be there to slay the dragons for his Lady Fair. I used to tease him about that, but he truly believed."

Marie Campbell Nyong Otrou Doshon bit at the fisted hand she brought to her lips, her body poised for flight.

"If he is standing beside her in this fight, know that he loves this woman just as surely as Romeo loved Juliet. He loves her because she gives him a completeness no other woman ever has—rather like a mathmatical component. I think it's called an absolute." Marie stood silently looking into the distance before she continued.

"To answer your question, though, his heart is there—where she is. And he would do the right thing, almost anything, for the woman who holds his heart."

"So, you do think he could, would, help her?" Lark fumbled for her recorder. "You think he's as guilty as she is?"

The green eyes glittered with the bright sheen of sudden tears. In an abrupt swirl of linen, Marie Campbell Nyong Otrou Doshon walked swiftly toward her massive, white columned, antebellum mansion. Lark strained to catch the words she left behind.

"No. I think she's a very lucky woman."

# Nineteen

Noelle twisted the papers in her hand again. The opposite way this time.

No way was she ready for this, she told herself. How did anyone get ready for something like this? Not to mention Angel. There was no time to prepare her for a separation. Every time she'd tried to bring it up, the child had deftly changed the subject or shifted her attention—as though she knew trouble was coming. They weren't ready. At all.

Slowly untwisting the mangled papers, Noelle read them silently again. "For the safety and stability of the minor child . . ." She didn't need to read the rest, she already knew the words by heart. It was a court order. Noelle was being ordered to turn Angel over to a designated officer of Fulton County. A court order delivered to Jamal's house, because he was the attorney of record.

The dull ache presented itself first behind her eyes, and her massaging hand brought no relief. She'd asked herself and Jamal all the insane questions last night. How could any child be more loved than Angel? And where would she be safer? Surely, nobody would believe that she'd done anything to harm or endanger the little girl?

*I'm just being selfish,* she scolded herself, *there are laws.* Even though Noelle didn't like Minnie Raymond, she was right and Noelle had let her heart lead her the wrong way. There were appropriate ways to handle situations like this, and falling in love with a child, planning the life she'd always wanted with an incredible man who felt like destiny, weren't a part of it. Tears stung under Noelle's lashes, the papers were crushed and twisted again in her hands.

Jamal's shout of surprise and the pattering sound of Angel's racing feet startled her. Noelle managed to brush her tears away just as Angel skidded around the corner and into the den. Jamal was hot on her heels.

"Save me Mommy!"

"No saving for you, you little devil!"

"Save me!" The front of Angel's blue-and-white gingham dress slapped wetly as an arm snaked around Noelle's long leg.

"You're all wet. . . ."

"You'd better believe she is," Jamal growled.

"What happened?"

"I helped!"

"Yeah. She helped alright. I was trying to clear up the lunch dishes. I sat her on the counter, where she could see what I was doing I thought she'd like it."

"I did like it!"

"Well, to make a long story short," he lifted his soggy denim shirt away from his muscular chest, "she helped herself right into the sink!" Angel giggled and dodged his reach for her.

The door chimed. "I'll be back for you," he promised as Angel laughingly hid her face against Noelle's leg.

Noelle lifted the child, swinging her casually onto one hip. "Funny girl," she smiled. "What you did wasn't very . . ." She stopped as a somber faced Jamal entered the room followed by Minnie Raymond, and a brown uniformed Fulton County Sheriff's deputy.

"You Miz Noelle Parker?"

"Y-yes." How were these things usually handled? Her mind scrambled to find an anchoring memory. It couldn't be this abrupt—and if it could, it shouldn't be. Noelle had heard stories, but never actually been present when a child was taken into state custody. Angel's head lay softly against her shoulder, her breath stroking the tiny hairs by Noelle's ear.

The deputy, a red-faced, raw-boned, sharp-voiced man, named Freeman, clearly wanted to be anywhere except here. He didn't mind backing up DFACS when the kids had to be picked up hurt or scared from the projects or alone and homeless on the streets, but this was different.

This was a nice home, in a nice neighborhood, and the man and woman looked like good folks. Then, too, there was the way the little girl, in her wet dress, was hanging on to her mama.

Freeman nudged himself mentally. It wasn't her real mama. The tall pretty woman sure didn't look like a kidnapper though, and the kid didn't look like a victim. But, according to the caseworker standing next to him, and the warrant in his hand, that's what they were.

"Ma'am," the deputy tried not to look away from the woman's hurt, accusing eyes. "I got a order here to remove the little girl from your custody."

Jamal knew they were in trouble. He felt it in the pit of his stomach. Then he heard Noelle.

"No." Her voice was soft and calm. She might have been telling them she was just going to get a sweater for Angel. Only, that wasn't what she said.

"No. I can't—I won't give her to you."

Why is it, he wondered, facing the resolution in her dark eyes, that some people can make the most extraordinary statements so easily? She had to know what she was doing . . . what she was setting herself up for legally. Didn't she? When he looked back on it, Jamal would forever have to admit to himself, things might have still gone better if Minnie Raymond had not become assertive.

"Listen," Minnie muttered, tripping on her trademark ever-high heels. Righting herself with a hand on the sofa back, she started toward Noelle and Angel again. "Listen, I have an order. That's all I need. Did you pack her things?"

"No." Noelle held her ground, not moving, still holding the

clinging child. Angel, feeling the tension, began to whimper softly, hiding her face against Noelle's body.

"Here are her things." Jamal stood in the doorway holding a small brown canvas tote bag, and an incongruously smiling green-faced Kermit the Frog.

"No!" Angrily, Noelle tore the bag and Kermit away from Jamal. Angel slid agilely down her hip to the floor. "You're not taking her things away either."

Deputy Freeman placed a thin shaking hand on the butt of his gun. Facing hysterical women was not one of the highlights of his day. Add a screaming child, and frankly, he'd rather be at Disney World.

"No, don't take me! I'll be good!" The thin, wheedling child's voice was almost unheard against Minnie's grunt, as she strained to lift the frightened child.

"I've got you," she congratulated herself. "You're going with me."

"Let me go!"

Panic quickened the child's movements as she scrambled uselessly in the large woman's arms. Minnie tried to see through the drapes while continuing her struggle to contain the child.

"I called the newspeople before I left the office—as witnesses. They should be here by now."

"Opportunistic bitch!" Noelle was still roaring as she dropped Angel's things and launched herself at Minnie. Fending clawed fingers, and flailing arms, while controlling a squirming child, from atop four-inch heels was no easy task. As the two men pulled Noelle off, Minnie ran for the door.

"Mommy, please! Help me!"

Angel's screams tore at Noelle's core. She felt the sound ripping and surging along the lines of her bones. Neighbors were peeking through screen doors and around carefully trimmed shrubs. What, they were all watching to see, could cause a child such anguish? Who, they all craned to see, was hurting that child?

"Mommy!"

The child's tiny hands were pressing against Minnie's arms and slapping at her face. Every muscle in the small body strained against confining arms. Small fingers hooked and clawed at Minnie's face again.

"I don't want to go away!"

Noelle's heart twisted as the child flung herself backward in Minnie's grasp, vainly reaching with outstretched hands. Jamal restrained her as she started forward, arms reaching for the frantic child.

"Mommy, Mommy!"

"How perverse can you be? Take the child out, now." He pulled Noelle closer. The heavy thing falling into his stomach must have been his heart.

The struggle went out of her as quickly as it had arisen. Her broken spirit seemed to leach the energy from her bones, and she stood motionless in his arms. "You've got what you came for," Noelle said over his shoulder. "What are you waiting for?"

Cold eyes calculated the scene before her. Minnie tried to shift the child to a more comfortable position, but Angel wasn't having it. Minnie continued to wrestle with her.

"No!" Angel's voice rose in an anguished howl.

The lanky, red-faced deputy looked miserably down at his scuffed shoes, then up at the still-screaming child. He knew he would hear echoes of her voice in those of his grandchildren for a long time to come, and suddenly his job gave him stomach cramps and a god-awful headache. "We gotta go." He tried to keep his tone official.

Minnie followed him, righteous indignation powering her heavy steps. She folded herself and the squirming, stretching child into the backseat of the official vehicle. Even as the car backed down the curving driveway, Angel's screams rebounded on hot summer air.

Unbelieving, Noelle watched the brown car turn the corner, carrying her baby away.

"She's gone."

Jamal reached to capture the slender hand that reached out to empty air.

Turning on him, indignant fury reborn in her face, Noelle opened her mouth, then snapped it shut. The flash of her fist was exactly that—a flashing rush of color, flesh, and forcefully projected bone neither of them anticipated. It carried all the pain and anger she felt. Jamal never saw the cocoa-colored blur until the pain exploded against his lip.

Stunned by the shock and pain in her hand, Noelle angrily cradled her fist under her left arm. Breathing heavily, she looked ready to follow up with more of the same.

Surprise and caution made Jamal fall back a step to give her space, his fingers locating the source of immediate pain. When his eyes moved to follow the sound of a car crunching gravel at the end of the long, shrub-lined drive, she turned to follow them. She heard Jamal's groan, a low snarling at the back of his throat, as she faced the approaching van.

"Now what?" she wondered aloud.

The side door of the van popped open and a black outfitted cameraman stepped onto the driveway. The auburn-haired passenger in the front seat craned forward.

"Where's the kid?" Lark hated to yell. It broke her image, but sometimes like now, it got the job done. "We need an interview!" *After Arlington, what I really need is an angle on this story.* She tried to make her walk from the van look dignified.

The cameraman raised an eyebrow. Noelle's fisted right hand was in evidence again.

"Just missed them," Jamal inclined his head to the street. "No story here."

"Maybe. By the way, I was up in Virginia—Arlington, Virginia. I had a chance to speak with an old friend of yours—Marie Doshon."

"Who?"

"Oh, I'm sorry," Lark pointedly faced Jamal. "You knew her as Marie Campbell. She's married now. She and her husband live in one of those fantasy mansions—all white columns and rolling lawns. They have a beautiful young son." She waited, watching for a reaction and could have spit when none was forthcoming.

"Who?" Noelle repeated the question.

"She was an old friend of mine. Actually, I nearly married her about five years ago." He looked disinterestedly at the reporter. "Does that answer your questions?"

"I only have one more, if you don't mind my asking." Lark fished a tissue from her tote bag and offered it. "What happened to your lip?"

"I mind your asking," Jamal drawled as he ignored the tissue. With Noelle at his side, he walked into the house firmly closing the door behind them.

"Damn!"

The cameraman turned to Lark, and shrugging, spread his hands.


"I can't believe you gave her away like that. You just gave her away."

"Noelle," Jamal started, but what was there to say?

"No. There's nothing else for you to say. You gave her away. You just gave my baby away—just like . . ." She stood stammering, choking on anger, and seeking to vent it in words that were inadequate to the chore.

"Noelle," he began again. The almond-shaped eyes he was learning to love so much he even saw them in his sleep had turned hard. Her curving lips were pressed tightly into a narrow, unforgiving line. Her tense body telegraphed only one outraged message—betrayal.

"I don't want to talk about it!"

"Wait a minute." Jamal's long legs overtook her easily as she walked away from him. "Noelle, you know what the situation is. For God's sake, you're a caseworker. You know this stuff as well as—better—than I do."

"I know that maybe I need another lawyer. One who believes in me. One who's not going to sell me out like you just did!"

"You don't believe that."

"Oh really? Why wouldn't I? What are you going to do next, Mr. Officer of the Court? Arrest me?" She thrust her wrists at him in disgust, as though anticipating the grip of handcuffs.

"No. Of course not."

"You know Angel is better off with me than being shoved into some little foster home somewhere. You know it! And you still let them take her! Why?"

Her lower lip trembled, and her lashes swept her cheek as she refused to look up at him. Placing his hands on her shoulders, he felt the tremors shaking her body. She shook herself free.

"Noelle, I'm on your side. I want what's best for you and Angel."

"Nice words. It took you long enough to say them. Maybe I should move my things to Pat's, so I don't compromise you any further. And I'll just find another . . . somebody else to represent me."

"Look Noelle, that's enough. I give my best to all my clients, and frankly I love you, so I'm going to give you about two-hundred-fifty percent effort. Now, if you can find somebody willing to give you more than that, then go with them, because I want you to have the best. You and Angel both deserve the best representation you can get."

"You know I was also ordered to surrender myself."

"Yes."

"You would have let them take me, too." The air escaped her in one great puff, and deflated, she dropped her hands, then seemed to collapse against his shoulder.

"I just didn't want her to go away, especially like that."

"I know," he said. Jamal's hands found the narrow span of her waist, and pressed her gently to the broadness of his chest, the lengthy sweep of her leg tracing his. His pressure was comforting, restoring her faith, and calming her thoughts.

"I'll turn myself in. Will you go with me?"

"Where else would I be?" The puffy lip framing his otherwise perfect smile almost made Noelle regret punching him.

The little pink sweater with its neatly cuffed sleeves lay on the floor, almost hidden by the sofa, and she bent to retrieve it. The bittersweet shadow of a smile crossed her lips as she folded the tiny garment. It was the forgotten reminder of last night's happy trip to the Dairy Queen for ice cream. Lifting it to her face, the soft scent reminded Noelle of the child so recently ripped from her arms.

"I want her back, Jamal."

"I know," he said.

"Can you get her for me?"

His lips brushed her forehead as she held the sweater to her breast, matching the tenderness of his hand closing over hers, his lips touched her again. "I'm going to give it one hell of a try," he promised.

# Twenty

"I know I said I would, but do we really have to do this?"

"You're under court order, remember?"

"I remember." Noelle shivered in spite of the weight of her silk suit as they made the walk through the heavy glass doors of the Third Precinct. She looked around suspiciously, noting the passing officers and the equipment they wore casually slung about their strolling hips. "Why isn't there a sign somewhere that says, 'Abandon Hope All Ye Who Enter Here'?"

Jamal shook his head. "It's not allowed. American jails aren't allowed to scare you to death by innuendo."

"Really. I still don't like it here."

He touched her shoulder. "I know. I may be a lawyer, but I hate jails too. They make me feel like a trapped animal." He spoke quietly.

"Most animals are free unless trapped by humans." Noelle looked at him directly. "They don't usually do it to one another, you know. And no matter what anyone else thinks, the police are humans." Jamal flinched under her stare.

Reluctantly, she followed Jamal to the counter at the front of the room. They waited patiently while the officer talked on the phone.

"Yes ma'am," the cop drawled politely. His broad gestures suggested several points to the person on the other end of the line.

"Yes ma'am," the officer repeated dutifully. Nodding while

he listened, he held up a finger, indicating that he'd be right with them. Turning his attention back to the phone, he nodded in rhythm to the speaker's words.

"Old folks," he said. Still shaking his head, he hung up the phone. "Don't never ask 'em how they doin'. God knows, they'll try to tell you." The desk sergeant finally approached them. The nameplate above his badge identified him as O. Creighton. The stripes at his shoulder identified him as a sergeant.

"How kin I he'p you?

"My name is Noelle Parker, and I've been ordered to surrender myself to you."

"I'd like to take you up on that," Sergeant Creighton grinned at her, "but my wife'd kill me." His grin broadened as two passing male officers loudly appreciated his wit. "You say you got a order, huh?"

Jamal stepped forward. "Here's a copy of the court order, Sergeant. As Ms. Parker's attorney, I represent her in the matter of compliance with this order. Can you check your records?"

"Sure. No problem." O. Creighton noisily clacked keys as he made his computer search. Seven minutes later, he returned to the counter. "We got nothin'."

Noelle turned to Jamal. "Good. Can we go now?"

"Can you search the county records as well?"

"Sure." The sergeant hitched up his pants and returned to the computer. Minutes later, he blew out a long low whistle, and pressed a button under the desk. A female officer materialized at Noelle's elbow.

"Noelle Parker? I'm Officer Jefferson. Leave your purse here, and we'll get your attorney to catalog your belongings. I'll read you your rights and process you in. You'll need to come with me."

"Process me—I'm really being arrested?" Noelle's voice was shrill with alarm. She remembered Angel's tears and panic, and steeled herself against a similar reaction.

Jamal reached for her arm and held her in place. He waited for her breathing to slow. "Noelle, we already talked about this.

Remember, walking in together was the only way to get you in here without a huge media following. This is only a formality. We'll get you out in a couple of hours."

"Could I just have a moment here?" Noelle's quiet voice was edged with a broken fringe of barely suppressed hysteria. The tall, dark-skinned, heavy hipped officer looked to her sergeant before nodding. Noelle gripped Jamal's arm and pulled him a few steps away from the desk. Officer Jefferson and Sergeant Creighton watched from the corners of their eyes.

Demurely tucking her chin, Noelle allowed her eyes to rise to meet Jamal's. Her close scrutiny seemed to penetrate the depths of his soul, and he wished she could go deeper still. The effect of her gaze was riveting, beating as it was at his professional objectivity. He led her to a recessed corner of the room.

Her hand flashed forward in a sudden grip, grasping the lapel of his jacket. "Before I go in there I need to be sure. Very sure," Noelle said.

"Of course."

"Jamal, please. Don't do that. Don't talk to me like a lawyer. Don't placate me. Don't say what you think I want to hear. Don't be professionally objective. Don't . . ." Words failed her, and she knew she was on the verge of begging. She didn't want to beg, and never intended to utter her next words.

"You're the only thing I have left to hold on to. I love you and I . . ." Looking away seemed the only way to face her feelings. When her eyes met his again, they were steady and searching.

"This loving fully thing is still new to me. I never thought I would want to even try to trust a man the way I trust you. Give me something of value in return for the trust I've given you. Talk to me like a man, a man who needs for me to walk back through those doors and into his life. Give me—dammit, make me know that you need me as much as I need you."

There was a moment, one of those little time-locked oddities that people cherish forever. A weird, shared little amorous thrill, some vagrant inspiration sparked between them, giving off an idling recall of what happened when men and women were alone. His hand found hers and closed securely.

Her heart beat visibly beneath the fragile shell-toned, vest-cut blouse she wore. He watched the dainty heart-shaped locket at her throat glint and pulse in response to her rapid heartbeats. The deliberate lift and surge of the soft flesh at her breast might have made him promise her anything.

"There's no other way for me to talk to you Noelle. If I wasn't sure you would be back before dark, we wouldn't be here now."

"That's not what I need to hear." Her smoldering whisper held him more firmly than the hands she lifted to cradle his face. Entranced, he watched her lips move. "There has to be something more. I want to hear you say it," she said.

"We're not talking about sex here, are we?" He studied her expression, and it stabbed him with a parched arrow of sensation. "No? Good, because this is deeper than that." A quick glance at the desk showed that the officers were making an effort not to obviously eavesdrop.

"Do you need to hear that I love you, because I do. Do you need to hear that my life hasn't been the same from the first time we met, because it hasn't. Do you need to hear that I've waited all my life for you, because I have." He stopped, searching her eyes for clues to explain his feelings.

"Noelle," his hands moved warmly along her arms, stamping their memory on her flesh. "Whatever you need to hear, consider it said. The law was always my passion—my only driving passion—until I met you. There is nothing, no reason I wouldn't stand by you. If I thought there was a chance you might not come back to me, that I might lose you . . ." Lost in his own words, their depth of meaning, he waited.

Again, he felt the probe of her eyes, and the fear she left unspoken. Her shift of faith was palpable as her breathing slowed, becoming less panicky.

"A couple of hours—right?"

"No more," he answered.

"And you'll be here when I come back?"

"Where else would I be?" Jamal asked.

Facing him, Noelle tried to bridge the space between them with her faith in his commitment. She concentrated on his face—the eyes and lips—willing him to mean the words he said. Her hand lingered in his, drawing slowly away until only their fingers touched. A final twining of the fingers and a squeeze of their hands, and Noelle knew she could prolong the moment no longer.

Her breathing was still faster than it should be, but she nodded and turned back to the desk. Placing her purse on the counter, Noelle allowed her feet to follow Officer Jefferson.

Jamal's fingers crawled hastily through his pockets, first the jacket then the pants. He watched Noelle through the door, then felt again, relaxing only when the gold eagle coin rested heavily in his hand. He hoped the luck was contagious.

Knowing the procedure didn't make it any easier. Jamal told her what to expect, and she knew her stay would be brief. The only difference was that now, she was *in* jail without him, and knowledge alone didn't seem to help. An icy finger of doubt traced the column of her spine, and she wondered if she would have to wear officially issued jail clothes.

Officer Jefferson ushered Noelle down a heavily finger-printed, dark green on light green, Formica-walled corridor. "I'm taking you down to a holding cell," she said.

The officer's hand guided her toward an enclosed staircase. At the bottom, they turned left and Officer Jefferson began to speak freely.

"So, you're the caseworker who took the kid, huh? Gotta tell you, I like kids myself. I have two girls, four and six. I wouldn't have no life without 'em. You did the right thing. Showed more courage than I got, and the law don't ask my opinion, but I think you did right. Nothing in the order says you can't get bail, is there?"

"God," Noelle stuttered, "I don't know. I don't think so. He said a couple of hours."

"Let's see what that nice man you came in with can do before we go any further." She offered a broad, white-toothed smile and stopped walking. "Here we are, this is it."

Embarrassed, Noelle stood outside an area that looked, to her, exactly like a holding pen for animals. Bars that ran floor to ceiling, were buried in the slick-looking gray cement floor. Wooden benches ran around three sides of the cell. Two very painted, very silent women stared boldly out at Noelle.

After a cursory search, Officer Jefferson swung open the cell door. "In there."

Noelle hesitated.

"Come on in, Princess. We don't bite nobody but the payin' customers, and then only if they ask nice and pay extra." The woman in bright red spandex propped her shoeless feet on the bench and laughed hoarsely.

"Necie, quit. Don't mind her, she so silly." The woman in turquoise spandex and sequins laughed. "I'm Joy and that's Necie. Who're you?"

"Noelle. Parker." She folded her jacket and sat on it to wait.

"What'd they pick you up for? You don't look like a working girl."

"Tsk! Necie, quit. Can't you see she's more the white-collar crime type?" Joy dropped onto the bench. "Why *are* you here Noelle Parker?"

Noelle bit her lips and looked at the floor. Nowhere in her vocabulary were words that seemed right to tell her story. "I'm here because I—I'm a caseworker and a little girl came into my office and—I kept a child."

"You kept her—what?"

"Necie, quit. She means . . ." Joy paused to look at Noelle. "What do you mean?"

Inhaling deeply, Noelle tried again. "I mean the little girl didn't have anybody. She was all alone and just wandered into the office where I worked, and I took her home with me. I'm not a kidnapper, although everybody seems to think I am." She told the story, and waited for the inevitable judgment.

"You saved that child's life, girl. They ought to be treatin' you like a hero, thankin' you an' stuff, not lockin' you up. Tha's what I'm talkin' about." Joy adjusted the flowing curly locks of her red-haired wig and sat a little straighter.

"Maybe I'm slow. I guess I need to ask again, 'cause I don't get it. What did they pick you up for? Don't seem to me like you did nothin' all that wrong. It would have been worse to leave that little kid roamin' around by herself or tossin' her in a place where she don't know nobody or nothin'.'"

"Yeah girl, you know, it's perverts out there—an' you know we know. They be pickin' up on little kids an' stuff."

"Tha's right. Hey, what you did," Necie let her hands and expression fill in the missing words. "Hey, it's all good," she finished.

"Necie, quit. You makin' the girl nervous." Joy stood and began to pace.

Noelle bit her lip again, determined not to tell Joy *she* was the one making her nervous.

"I guess you got a lawyer?"

"Yes. He's upstairs now."

"Is he any good? At law, I mean."

"Yes, I believe he is."

"Long as you believe it." Necie moved across the bench to sit closer. The red spandex inched higher on her rounded thighs, and she tugged it down. "They're not going to keep you in here long, girl. Me an' Joy, we'll just keep you company 'til they come get you, 'cause you ain't got no business up in here. Not none at all, Miss Thang."


"Okay, Miss Parker. You're out on your own." Officer Jefferson gave Noelle a quick pat on the back as she passed. "Your lawyer got you bail."

"I knew he would," Necie said.

"Keep hope alive, girl," Joy called as Noelle followed Officer Jefferson from the cell.

The policewoman led the way back up the stairs, and paused a last time before they entered the anteroom.

"Look, I know I'm not supposed to comment one way or the other, but a reporter called about you. Said she needed something about your arrest to air with tonight's news. Creighton didn't tell her anything. He said she'd have to wait 'til it was a matter of public record. He likes you, too." She dropped her eyes, then quickly swept Noelle into a consuming hug. "That child was lucky 'cause things could have been much worse. God bless and good luck. You did the right thing for the right reason."

Noelle's arms responded naturally, and she hugged the woman back. "Thank you. It means a lot just to hear that from you. Thank you." She smiled and patted the officer's shoulder, then walked ahead to meet Jamal.

# Twenty-one

He woke slowly, rising through softly veiled layers of con-
sciousness like a swimmer from the depths. He thought he'd
had a dream, but he couldn't remember it now. Stretching one
long arm across the width of the bed, he found cool emptiness
in the space he had come to think of as Noelle's.

She was gone. Gone? Jamal jerked himself to total alertness,
throwing covers from his body and rising to his feet with one
supple motion.

Beyond the bedroom door, he heard no sounds, sensing more
than seeing the mellow yellowed glow of lamplight. Rubbing
his eyes, and walking cautiously barefoot, he followed the luminous path.

The light spilled generously from the heavy brass lamp atop
the desk in his study. Noelle sat in its circle at the oversize desk,
writing. Deep in concentration, with her bare legs twined about
the chair, she was oblivious to his presence.

Barefoot, she wore only the red-and-white striped top to his
pajamas. Jamal wore the bottoms as he stood watching her. The
light of the lamp sharply defined the curves of her body against
the soft cloth of the pajama shirt.

Hers was a sincere posture drawn in intensity and tension.
The soft, busy scratch of her felt-tipped pen was audible as she
wrote furiously, covering the yellow legal pad before her. She
paused only to page through the dictionary at her right elbow,

before screwing her efforts into a ball, tossing them aside, and beginning again.

In spite of her seriousness, she made a fetching picture. He admired the careless fall of the cotton shirt across her smooth thighs, and the softly curling hair at her shoulders. Intuitively she seemed to know his presence, and turned to see him watching from the door. The seductively rounded, golden flash of her full breasts and softly shadowed cleavage made him catch his breath.

"I missed you," he said simply.

"I couldn't sleep," she replied.

Walking closer, he paused with his hand at her shoulder. "What're you working on?"

She twisted in the worn leather chair, making room for him. His long leg crossed the chair, brushing her arm and hip as he lowered himself to sit behind her, his strong thighs framing and warming hers. Relaxing against the firmness of his body, Noelle debated then decided to tell him the truth.

"I was dreaming. In bed—dreaming about the same things I've dreamt of for so long." Her hand covered his, fingers twining and holding. "Angel was there, and so were you."

"That woke you?"

"No," she sighed, "it's just that it's been three weeks since they took Angel, and I miss what we were together. I guess it was the emptiness that woke me. Funny, at one time, I thought the emptiness was all that I would ever have. I thought the void inside me was all I deserved." Her head lifted, pressing her cheek to his. The contrast of her soft skin against the night scratchiness of his stirred their mutual awareness.

"That's what woke you?" His breath was like the stroke of feathers, and she moved her face gently against his, enjoying the gentle torture.

"More. Lark Allister's still trying to get Pat to talk to her. Then there's all this," she pointed to the sheets she'd been writing on. "I've had to respond in writing to more agencies and department heads than I ever even knew existed."

"Then in the middle of all that writing, I started thinking about the way things should have gone, the kind of place I could have taken Angel in good conscience—and there were none. As a matter of fact," Noelle paged through several sheets, "listen to this. I've outlined things, the way I think they should be. Tell me how it sounds." Her reading voice was husky, but Jamal still heard nervous, quivering undertones.

She was right he thought, struggling to listen and follow her outline. The only good thing about all the official writing she had done was that it was keeping her occupied and out of jail.

He remembered the horror they'd endured when, two weeks after they took Angel, Jamal had received a phone call from Evan Roberts, the state's attorney. The department, he said, was considering prosecuting Noelle for both kidnapping and child endangerment.

She had stood by wordlessly incredulous, listening.

"I told him those charges were patently ridiculous, and he claimed there was a pattern in your behavior. When I pressed him, Roberts actually said there were a couple of warnings in your personnel file."

"Warnings?"

Jamal's face had grown grim. "Yes. It seems you bought groceries for a couple of families when their food stamps were late, and that's against the rules. You also went out of your way, in direct opposition to agency procedures, to find donations to get a lady's rent paid last year. You have a documented history of ignoring regulations, interfering, taking matters into your own hands, that kind of thing. He says it establishes a pattern of intentional disregard for authority on your part."

She said nothing, but Jamal knew Noelle was still smarting from the two hours she'd spent in police custody the day Angel had been removed from his home.

Angel. There, at least was good news. Jamal had done some serious hinting, and persuaded Tom to do a little checking on Noelle's behalf. He'd tracked down the Dixons, Angel's temporary family.

Angel, in her new foster home, had been checked and tested. The little girl was healthy and trying to adjust to the changes around her. That at least freed Noelle from accusations of molestation or abuse. The only troubling note in Tom's report was that the child had stopped talking again.

Now, Noelle was engaged in the lengthy state-dictated appeal process. As long as she continued to cooperate with DFACS and the Department of Human Resources, there was a chance she'd come out of this with no more than a lost job and a serious reprimand. He hoped.

Jamal told her this, trying to prepare her for the hearing scheduled for next week, and she'd stared into the distance, at some spot above and beyond his left shoulder.

"Jamal, tell me the truth. Am I going to go to jail? To stay?"

He'd looked at her, his lips parting to speak, when she'd stopped him with the firm touch of her finger. "Don't tell me what you think I want to hear. Tell me the truth. Am I going to jail? To stay?"

"Noelle, I'm going to do everything in my power to keep that from happening, but we have to work within the system. Right now the system says that you've taken custody of a minor child without permission, and that's kidnapping. My job is to prove that you acted correctly within the system."

Brown eyes watched his face—testing, weighing the trust factors. "You never asked me why I kept her."

"Hey, I know you," he smiled. "I already know why. My only questions for you would come if you had not done what you did."

"The system stinks," she'd finally said.

"That may be but I'm going to do my job."

Looking up now, Noelle brushed fallen strands of hair from her eyes and bit nervously at her lip, waiting for his opinion.

Hoping he'd been following closely, he tried to give her a good one.

"Yes," he said, "it makes your intentions clear, but wouldn't it be more precise to indicate the kinds of contacts your advocates can legally make, and the types of legislation you'd plan to lobby for, here?" he pointed to the offending line.

"You're right," she agreed, rewriting the line. She shook her head slowly from side to side. "When I decided to go into social service, I honestly believed I'd make a difference," she sighed. "I believed I was going to do more than push paper."

"Yeah, I know what you mean. Morgan and I talk about that a lot. Whether what we do really makes a difference in the long run, or if we're just putting on Band-Aids."

"Sometimes Band-Aids make the difference between a minor injury and a life-threatening infection, Jamal."

"Unless you hit an artery."

"You sound bitter—don't. What you do makes a difference," she nodded. "Look at what happened with the Pierce children."

"True. They are together, and last I heard doing real well. So, you could say, we win some, lose some."

"And I guess you have to believe, in the long run, that you win the important ones," Noelle said. "You know, none of this would have been necessary if CPS had been a better alternative."

"But sweetie," Jamal nuzzled her ear, making his voice a muted rumble, "it *was* the only alternative."

"But Jamal," his lips at her ear were distracting, but welcome as she continued, "that's just it. There needs to be an alternative, another level of advocacy for children in emergency situations. If I had the money," she shrugged, "which I don't, but if I did, I'd fund a temporary shelter. One that was more like a real home. A place where young children could be safe, and maybe Pat and I could . . ."

"Take on the world," he finished for her.

Lifting her head to again press her cheek to his, Noelle felt the grin escape her. "Seriously, there's got to be a company or maybe a philanthropist who could offer some private funding to an effort like this. Just think, you and Morgan could handle the legal stuff, and Pat and I could make sure the innocent suffered a little less."

"But, not tonight." Jamal pushed the papers away, kissing the tip of her nose. "Noelle, it's late, come to bed."

*Come to bed,* he said, and made it sound like the most natural thing in the world. *With me,* he didn't add, and he didn't need to. Noelle wondered if Jamal had any idea how happy he made her. Probably not, she thought, and made a mental note to tell him—no, better still, show him one day when this was all over.

Her arms folded across her chest to reach for his, and she stroked them with her open palms, pressing him close. He felt warm and solid to her touch. Jamal Alan Harris was no dream, and from where she sat, he felt like the security she'd wanted all her life.

She reached for the lamp, clicking its switch. The dark room, lit only by vague glimmers of moody outside light, cast them both in tones of sepia and shadow.

The dusky light and silent house amplified their breathing, and Noelle was gradually aware of the subtle thump of his heartbeat and his bare skin at her back. Behind closed eyes, she wondered how she had managed to be so completely alone for so long. Her skin tensed at the feel of the thin cotton barrier between them.

Moving slowly, angling to see better in the darkness, Noelle marveled at the tangle of their bodies within the limited confines of the leather chair. Her long bare legs bent easily across Jamal's to place her neatly in his lap. His hands moved familiarly along her shoulders and arms to cradle her.

"Someday," she whispered.

"Someday, what?"

"Someday, when I'm a very old woman I'm going to remember nights together, like this, and I'm going to smile and smile."

"Then I'm glad," he whispered, "because, I'll be there to smile with you, to remind you that we shared them."

As her hand lifted to Jamal's cheek, his touch coincided with her own. Fingers brushing, then lingering the contact soothed them both. Folding fingers caught and held in testimony of support. Their connection was as soft as a blush and as intimate as a lover's kiss, and Noelle knew whatever the cost, Jamal was worth it.

# Twenty-two

The number was busy for days on end, until today—probably off the hook. The sixth attempt, this morning, finally paid off, even though Mattie was deep in denial. Lark could still hear the woman's answering voice, and it grated on her nerves. Tension and a vague, thinly disguised anger were immediately apparent when she answered the phone.

Listening, the reporter could almost imagine the emotions raging across the unseen face based on the words she'd chosen.

"Alright," she'd snapped. "I suppose you'll dog me to my grave if I don't talk to you!"

Mattie Parker Perry was going to be a tough one, Lark could already feel it.

"Mrs. Perry, I'm simply trying to gather a little background, and some clarity on your feelings about your daughter's situation."

"So I hear. You've already contacted a friend at The *Call and Post,* I also hear. They sent someone to my door, scratching for dirt, first thing this morning. Were you figuring a black paper would carry gossip about my family that a white one wouldn't bother with? Or maybe you just didn't trust your contacts at *The Plain Dealer."*

"That was never my intention, Mrs. Perry, and I do apologize for the disturbance." Better to start with the kid gloves on. A good reporter could always get tough later, and if Lark was anything, she was a good reporter.

"It's just that in all fairness to your daughter, I needed to speak with you. My aim, as a journalist, is simply to establish as clear and correct a picture of her as a person as I possibly can." Lark shifted the phone and her technique simultaneously. Her tone softened, and in her southern lady voice she urged, "tell me about her."

"Oh, you're good, when your spies don't work, you wade in yourself. I want you to know that there's just nothing to tell, so you needn't try to finesse me into some admission of family sins."

"Mrs. Perry," Lark purred, "If that were true, I wouldn't be a journalist, I'd be writing fairy tales. Now, wouldn't I?"

Mattie paused, and Lark imagined the twitch of her lips. This type of woman always had twitching lips. She heard the slight hiss of air as the other woman inhaled, finally preparing to speak.

"Noelle, that is, my daughter didn't do this thing. She wouldn't."

"Unfortunately, the evidence . . ."

". . . is wrong. As I've said, Noelle wouldn't do anything like this thing she's been accused of. My daughter was raised better than that. She's had all the advantages of education and parental support. She would never do anything like that."

"I see," Lark said. *And de-nial is a river in Egypt,* she thought. Then it was Lark's turn to wait.

"I suppose you've already spoken with that horrible Wayne Sterling? My former son-in-law? I'm sure he told you several ugly things? Well, none of them are true. In no way was my daughter ever abused or mistreated. Our family was always close. Our recent separation has only allowed my daughter time to find herself, as all children must. She's always been in contact with me."

". . . and she's denied . . ."

"I didn't say that. I said, we've been in contact. Don't try to twist my words."

"You've spoken with her?"

"No. That is, not exactly. She sent me a letter, I think it was around Independence Day."

"The Fourth of July? Did she mention the child?"

"It was a personal letter," Mattie replied cagily. "If you want to know more about it, get a court order. Until then, suffice it to say, it was personal communication."

Lark felt the chill across four hundred miles of telephone lines. Shaking off the frost, she changed tactics again. "What was she like as a child," the reporter asked.

"Beautiful," the mother replied dreamily. "Just a beautiful, polite, quiet child. I'm talking about more than just the usual child-beauty, all mothers see that. Even when I first held her in my arms, I knew she was more than soft glowing features and tiny baby parts. With her dark eyes and regular features, I always knew she'd be an asset. Then, she grew up without the arrogance and cruelty that pretty girls develop—along the way."

Lark wondered if Mattie Parker Perry had been one of the pretty girls.

"She did like the water, though. You know we sit right here on Lake Erie, the city does, I mean," Mattie continued, sounding like a tour guide. "It's one of the Great Lakes. For some reason, people think you're talking about a pond or a lagoon when you talk about it, but it's called a great lake for a reason. It's really big. It stretches all the way across to Canada, you know."

Mattie sighed, quiet for long seconds.

"That's kind of like my relationship with Noelle, I suppose. Stretching." She sighed again. "Sad, huh? I had a chance to be the biggest thing in her life, but now that's a drop in the bucket. This thing you've called about is now the biggest thing in her life. Do you have children?"

"No," Lark answered carefully.

"It's just that a mother should mean more. You know what I mean?" Mattie paused a beat, then answered her own question. "No, of course you don't. How could you?"

Immediate resentment threatened to choke Lark as she struggled to maintain her objectivity. How dare this woman who could only refer to the charges against her only child as "this thing," dare to drag her into the lake of polluted emotions she was swimming in—even if it was a great lake. Support means a lot, and it's never too late. But, Lark wasn't about to compromise her interview to tell that to Mattie Parker Perry.

"I guess," Mattie said, her voice dreamy, "there's some commodity, some human connection sort of thing that was lacking in me back then. We can only be who we are, you know, and I guess I was lost in the maze of my own self. I understand, understood, she needed me, but she needed too much of me. Parenthood, especially motherhood is not always fair. I had to keep some of me for me, and for my marriage, and my daughter had to settle for what was left."

Then Mattie was silent once more. Lark watched the creeping second hand on her Timex. A full thirty seconds later, Mattie sighed loudly, then started to speak again.

"Noelle didn't do this thing—not the way you're trying to make it sound," she said. "I've already told you that, for what it's worth."

"Yes, you have," Lark agreed, sensing the solidity of the stone wall Mattie had erected, separating herself from the reporter and the truth as the rest of the world saw it.

"Well," Mattie's tone became crisply businesslike. "That's all I have to say. Except, my attorney's name is Alan Donalson, and he's very good at his job. I've already spoken to him about you reporters, and harassment charges. He's downtown in the Terminal Tower, and if you ever call this number again, I'll have him hang your ass out to dry. Believe it."

The line went dead.

Releasing the phone into its cradle, Lark became aware of how close to home this story was for her. Sitting forward, she placed her feet side by side, admiring them. It helped her think. The sleek taupe Ferragamo sandals had been a bargain at AJS— enough to calm any born shopper confronted with the puzzle of Noelle Parker.

Mattie Parker Perry sounded a lot like her own mother, if her mother had been better educated. She took pains to be totally disassociated from anything but the good in her daughter's life. At least Noelle's family had money and community standing, that gave Mattie something to stand on. Lark's family had been blessed with bills and too many mouths to feed. That meant Lark's mother had only the success of her children to live on.

In her house, Lark remembered, after her mama manipulated her like a little pet for her amusement, she'd have married to get away, too, and she'd have been stuck with her choice—however bad it was. Case-Western Reserve and any other university would have been out of the question, for her, if she hadn't made it out of there, Lark sniffed. She'd seen the old boyfriend, Bubba the last time she was at home, and he was fat and working for the chicken factory. She'd also seen his wife without her dentures.

With difficulty, Lark separated their lives. Noelle lived one, and she'd lived the other, and both were changed in many ways now. Noelle had done what was necessary to save her life—run. And that made all the sense in the world.

Needing space and movement, Lark opted for the coffee shop six floors down. She blessed the genius of the shoemaker elves at Ferragamo as she let her taupe sandals carry her to the elevator. Pressing the button, her mind rambled, searching for a new angle on her story.

"I kinda like this gal . . ." She could hear the mechanical sighing of the elevator cables and had to blink twice as her last conscious thought repeated itself in her mind.

"Nooo," she moaned aloud, realizing she had begun to identify with Noelle Parker.

"Nooo." She respected her.

"Nooo." As a matter of fact, she really was beginning to appreciate her.

"Nooo." She shook her head in vehement refusal. Understanding was one thing, empathy and developing a personal affinity was something else. Liking a subject was absolutely the wrong way to go.

"Hey! I know you!" The tall man in the dark shades had come from nowhere to stand waiting beside her. His big white-toothed grin seemed to split his face in two. Shoving his sport coat further open, he planted his hands at his waist in surprised amusement. "You're Lark Allister, I watch you all the time on the TV—I'd know you anywhere! Could I get your autograph?" He shoved a tattered bus transfer at her, and waited eagerly while she scrawled her name.

"Thanks." He tucked the transfer reverently under his jacket, into his shirt pocket. "You could say I'm a fan, a big fan. I been followin' you for years. Hope you don't mind my sayin' so, Ms. Allister, but you got real star potential, yessiree. I know it's gon' take you a long ways, long ways!"

He offered his hand, then pumped hers vigorously. "I'm Ralph Carter, and I don't see stars like you very often. It's a pleasure, a genuine pleasure. I like how your reports are always honest and you don't get bogged down in trash, like some of them others. You tell a good story, an' folks kin trust you. I like that."

The doors opened and Ralph Carter dropped her hand self-consciously. He looked to the elevator then to Lark with a gentlemanly sweep of his arm. She shook her head, and he boarded without her, but his last words echoed in her ears. "Yessir," he said with a little wave. "You got real star potential."

She watched the doors close behind him and felt powerless to move. This wasn't the O.J. case or the Jackson case or the Menendez case or the Sparling case or anything high-profile like that. Parker was simply a good person doing the best she could, and she was good for that little kid; that was all Lark would say in her report tonight. It was all she could say.

If there was more to know, if she was going to ride this horse any farther, Lark could already see she was going to have to dig deeper to find a way. If this story did in fact have star potential, it was obvious she couldn't expect any freebies. And she was going to have to distance herself from her subject.

Maybe Ralph Carter was some sort of angel doing divine

overtime, because he sure called Lark like he saw her. The man said real star potential. "Potential," Lark echoed, suddenly realizing what the word meant, and what her fan had really said. "It means bein' a star with a capital *s* is possible, but it ain't happened yet, and it won't less'n I get off my butt."

"Shoot," she said, and walked back to her office.

# Twenty-three

Pat had both hands full as she angled her full body and bulky cargo through the door.

"It didn't sound like so much when I volunteered to go get all this. Are you sure you wanted this gray suit? It's so hot out today, even for August—humidity is high, too. Must be mid-nineties at least. A dress might be better. I brought this one, just in case." She held out a militarily detailed fucshia dress.

Dumping everything else on the table, she hefted a tote bag. "Here's undies and accessories." She pulled several pairs of shoes and sandals from a small shopping bag. "I brought you a couple of purses, and this book you wanted." She dropped into a worn leather chair to catch her breath.

"It's a good thing I went to your place instead of you. Those media people are still camped out there—lurking and waiting. You'd think they'd get tired. It's been almost two whole months. Angel's in foster care, and you've been hiding out like Ma Barker or something. The excitement's over, why can't they give it a rest?"

"Aw, Pat. They've gotta earn a living, too. I guess they have a right to pursue a story whenever they can . . . even if it makes me miserable in the process."

"It's just not fair, is all I'm saying. If Minnie Raymond had done her job, instead of dipping . . . Oh! I almost forgot these . . ."

Pat pulled her large shoulder bag closer. Several business-size envelopes stuck out of the side pocket. She sorted through them quickly, returning two to the pocket, and handing the rest to Noelle.

"I figured I'd better grab your mail too. You had so much, it was poking out of the top of the box, so I grabbed what I could. I just hated to think of those enterprising reporters nosing through your stuff. Freedom of the press, and all that aside."

"Thanks. So many other things have happened, I forgot about the mail." Noelle laid the envelopes across the tote bag. "I saw Angel again this morning. Pat, she came right to me. She laid her little head on my shoulder. Said she wanted to come home with me. She didn't cry this time, though."

"I guess she's getting used to the Dixons. Mrs. Dixon said she's started talking to other people again."

"Maybe," Pat offered, "she finally has something to say again. Remember last time?"

"I remember. We couldn't have hoped for a nicer temporary family for her." Noelle tried to look composed and was almost convincing. Pat saw the rolling tear before Noelle could turn away.

"You need to get dressed, the hearing's at two." Pat checked her watch. "You've got a couple of hours. Want me to wait and drive you?"

"Nah," the voice was stronger now. "Jamal's coming home to get me."

"Home?" Pat's selective hearing honed in on that one all-important word.

"Yes. Home. He lives here, you know."

"Excuse me Ms. Thang, but is that home as in his or home as in ours?"

"Pat, you're incorrigible."

"Inquiring minds want to know," Pat chanted. Her voice deepened provocatively. "I take it things are going well. Very well?"

"Why don't you just come right out and ask?"

" 'Cause it wouldn't be ladylike. Besides, I'm not nosy, and

I respect your right to privacy," Pat oozed sanctimoniously. "I'm just a concerned friend looking out for you at a time when you're most vulnerable. So, dish the dirt, girl! Y'all doing the wild thang or not?"

Noelle squeezed her eyes shut and tried to keep the burst of laughter from her lips. It didn't work.

"You know, you have no shame! Girl, you're as nosy as the day is long."

"Annh!" Pat imitated a game-show buzzer. "Wrong. That's not an answer, and you know it." She waited and watched closely as Noelle's lips curled into a satisfied smile.

"Uh-huh, I thought so. And . . ." Pat waited again. Noelle's smile grew bigger. "And, you like it!" Pat's imagination was rapidly filling in the blanks. Noelle rolled her eyes.

"Get outta here! You love it!" Pat screamed, laughing and stamping her feet. "Does that mean this living arrangement is permanent, then?"

"Pat, you keep jumping to these wild conclusions. I haven't thought that far ahead yet. I'm trying to take everything one step at a time. We have to get through this mess first. Maybe after that, there'll be some other decisions to be made."

"So, you're the marrying kind. I thought so. Just let me know in time to get a dress and shoes. I want to be the Matron of Honor. And remember, I look good in pink. That deep shade of rose? It's perfect on me, and I wear a size twelve. A ten, if it's cut real full." Pat stood and stretched. "I'll see you downtown. Just don't forget—pink."


Noelle showered and dressed quickly. Pat was right, the dress probably would be cooler. Grabbing it from the closet door, she brushed the stack of mail to the floor. She'd forgotten Pat had brought all this junk with her.

She fought an immediate urge to step over the envelopes or just push them aside with her foot. It wasn't like it would take a long time to pick them up—she just didn't want to be bothered right now.

No time like the present, she told herself. Kneeling on the mauve carpet, Noelle casually flipped the envelopes over as she retrieved them. They were mostly bills, magazine notices, and advertisements. One letter was in a DFACS envelope.

"Now what?" Noelle felt her stomach erupt with nervous jerks. The letter was postmarked August twentieth. Three days ago.

*I don't have to open it now,* she told herself. *I can come back to it later.* But it might be important. It could be related to her case, somehow. Better to open it, deal with whatever, and be done with it. She tore the envelope open.

Inside, a hastily scribbled note from Dennis Avery, and another envelope. The enclosed letter had been mailed to her at the office, "c/o Fulton County Department of Family and Children's Services". Bless his heart, Dennis was still trying to look out for her.

What the heck was this—hate mail? She sat on the large bed she had once thought of only as Jamal's, and toyed with the envelope. The handwriting was familiar, but there was no return address. The postmark was even blurry. Her stomach quivered again with nervous anticipation.

It wasn't too late. She could still just toss it. Turning the envelope in her hands, Noelle tried to still her thoughts. She watched her finger slit the envelope. Well, it was open now. She might as well read it. The folded sheets slid easily into her hand.

Shuffling to the last page, she read the signature. *Mother.*

"Who's Mother?"

*This has to be a sick joke. It can't be my mother.* Noelle shifted back to the first page, not really wanting to read. Her stomach felt really bad now.

At first, she only stared at the pages in her badly shaking hands. It was hard to compose herself enough to read the letter. Perspiration was gathering in fat drops under her arms. Barely controlling her breathing, she followed the words on the paper.

*Dear Noelle,*

*I'm taking the chance that you'll get my letter. I'm also taking the chance that you'll take the time to read it. If you've read this far, I can hope you have forgiven me for being so short with you when what you really needed was my help and my love.*

*I have been wanting to write or talk to you for a long time now, but didn't know how to reach you. Last Friday though, the* Plain Dealer *had a story about you. I was so surprised when I saw you!*

*Noelle, you were never mean or unkind. I know you didn't steal that child, and I want you to know I believe in you. I saw your picture with the story and you looked beautiful. You looked innocent, too.*

*Do you need help with the legal fees? I didn't enclose a check, just in case you don't get this letter. Please call me if you need help. The number is still the same. Call me if you just want to talk. It may be too late for me to be a mother, but I still would like to be your friend. I would love to hear from you.*

*Louis is gone now. I'm sorry to tell you this way, but I had no way to contact you. He passed two years ago in his sleep. I just rattle around in this house like a bean. I miss him very much.*

*I miss you, too, Noelle. I deeply regret putting you aside for all those years. I always thought there would be more time. I was wrong, I admit it. If I don't hear from you, I'll accept it because you do reap what you sow. Whatever you decide, I'll understand.*

*Love,*
*Mother*

Without thinking, Noelle moved to the phone. Dialing effortlessly, amazed to find she still remembered the number, she listened to the long-distance ring. Four rings. She was about to hang up when the woman's voice answered. It did sound sort of like her mother—but older. Naturally Mattie was older, five years had passed. Noelle hung up.

"That was stupid," she scolded herself. "If you're going to call, you ought to talk." She dialed again.

The woman answered again. Noelle gripped the phone with both hands. "Mom? This is Noelle. I got your letter." Noelle listened to her mother gasp, then burst into tears.

"I'm so glad you called. It's been so long. I was worried when I saw the story in the paper. What's going on there?"

"Mom, things are kind of rough right now. We have a hearing this afternoon. I just called to say that I got your letter. I'm going to have to call you back when I can talk more."

*If this isn't dysfunction in action, I don't know what is. I sound like I really want to talk to you.* Noelle wanted off the phone and quickly.

"Wait! After all this time, you can't just hang up like that."
*Why not?*

"Mom, I . . ." *Why did I ever fall into this trap? I could have, should have, just tossed the letter. I can't believe I'm so desperate to talk to you, after all these years. And now that I've finally found someone I want to love who is big enough and real enough to love me back, I'm still so hungry for your love and approval.* Noelle stared at the phone in her hand. It's not too late, her mind screamed, drop the damned thing!

"Noelle, I was wrong. I'm sorry. I could have, I should have done more. You needed me. I know that now. I hope it's not too late . . ."

Noelle struggled to breathe past the thickness in her throat. *Why is she doing this to me?*

"Mom, if you're asking for forgiveness, the past is past."

"I have to know that you understand why I did what I did. Louis and I . . . Noelle, there were so many things . . . We need to talk . . ."

She was not ready for this! "I'll have to call you later—the hearing, you know."

"But, it's been five years, Noelle Where have you been? How did you get to Atlanta?"

"I really have to go now."

"Let me get your address and phone number first. You never put them on your letters. I think I understand why." The rustling crackle of shifting paper nearly canceled Mattie's voice.

Oh, no! Noelle cringed. Not the address book! Mattie obviously still kept the huge, sunny yellow vinyl binder full of her socially prominent friends and acquaintances. She wondered how big it was these days. She was glad she decided not to give her Jamal's number, she thought spitefully.

"Noelle," Mattie's voice quivered with a touch of anxiety that Noelle had never heard before, "tell me what's happening there. I want to know all about the situation. The papers say that . . . well. . . . Are you going to be on trial for kidnapping or anything . . . else?

"No mother, I'm not really on trial. Yet."

"But you could be soon?"

Noelle held her head higher and gripped the phone tightly, her voice etched with ice. "Mother, I have no intention of embarrassing you in front of your church or club members."

"Noelle, I didn't mean it that way. I know I could have given you more of a chance in the past, but please believe in me. I believe in you. I could never be embarrassed by the fact that you loved a child too much to abandon her.

"What's the little girl—it is a little girl, right? What's she like?"

Noelle chose to answer the easy question first. "Yes, she's a little girl, and she's the most perfect child I've ever seen. She's pretty and smart and I adore her."

*This is scary,* Noelle thought. *I'm talking to my mother like she's* . . . My mother! Suspicion snaked through her mind. Why does she want to know about Angel?

"Little girls are very special. The way they make you feel when . . . I'm glad you've found someone to make you happy.

I wish I'd spent more time with you." Mattie's wistful voice seemed to snag on something. Could it have been her heart?

Pulling her feet beneath her on the bed, Noelle's hand caressed the heavy comforter. Closing her eyes, she could still see the brightness of Jamal's warm smile. "Yes," she breathed. "It's good to find someone who makes you happy."

Noelle stopped short of telling Mattie about her involvement with Jamal. The last time she'd told her mother about a man, she'd wound up married to Wayne. Mattie hadn't held a gun to her head, and Noelle herself had said, "I do," but obviously her arranged marriage hadn't been a good idea. If she didn't tell her about Jamal, she couldn't jinx their new relationship.

"Love is important Noelle, "and I'm glad you're happy."

The rich tide of Mattie's sincerity flowed across the telephone lines. Noelle tried to fight the snarl of emotions her mother's voice raised. After all this time, to make this kind of connection. It felt good, after all these years to find her mother. This understanding and empathy was so strange. So different. And, she reminded herself sadly, so unexpected.

"You call her Angel. That's lovely."

Only Mattie would call the child's name lovely.

"She is an angel Mother, the name is appropriate. I'm asking my attorneys to help me find a way to keep her."

"Keep her? Adoption?" Mattie drew the words out in wonder.

"I'm hoping."

"That's a big step, but then you've come so far already. And all you've already endured for the child . . . I read . . . You'll make a wonderful mother." Mattie paused thoughtfully. "Do you think maybe I'll make a better grandmother than I did a mother?"

"Maybe you would at that. But the time! I have to get dressed." The sound of Jamal's footsteps crossing the kitchen alerted her to the time. He was there to pick her up. "I have to go but I'll call you later. We'll talk."

"You'll let me know what happens? Promise me, you'll let

me know what happens. I can't lose you now, Noelle. Promise you'll call. Promise."

"I'll call." Noelle slipped the phone back into its cradle. "I promise I'll call."

# Twenty-four

Jamal's hand dipped beneath the surface of the large rectangular table to find Noelle's. She threw him a quick sidelong glance and squeezed his hand under the table. Her slender fingers were icy in his grip. Nerves, he figured. Returning to the stack of folders in front of him, he consulted briefly with Morgan.

Running the gamut of reporters outside the building, and then in the hallway had been no picnic. She recognized some of the local reporters. They were television faces that used to seem friendly and intelligent nightly, at six and eleven. In person, they were blood-thirsty carnivores demanding answers to questions she couldn't answer.

If she hadn't felt persecuted before, she certainly did now. Even with the door to the hearing room closed, she could still hear them stirring hungrily outside. She knew they were asking one another the questions they couldn't ask her.

Pat and her old boss Dennis Avery sat in wooden armchairs behind Noelle. They all turned as Mr. Jackson, the janitor who originally found Angel, stumbled through a row of wooden chairs. He smiled shyly and fumbled his way into a chair near Pat. Noelle guessed they were to be her witnesses. Her heart sank as Minnie Raymond stalked into the hearing room.

Her eyes were alight with divine purpose, and she stoically ignored her coworkers. Minnie was obviously looking forward

to her featured role as key witness. Pausing dramatically at the
open door, she allowed the reporters' hiss and buzz to enter
with her. Head held high, lips pinched together, she looked like
an old-time schoolmarm who'd smelled something bad.

She bore the large black State Employee Handbook like a
bible. Her extreme, high-heeled red leather shoes tapped with
deliberate fury as she found a seat across the room from Noelle's
supportive contingent. Minnie plainly didn't want to be con-
taminated by sordid social contact with them.

Noelle touched the back of Jamal's hand when the Atlanta
Police Department officer strolled in. Completely official, his
helmet, gun, and shield were all in place, gleaming brightly
against the dark blue of his uniform. Her question was evident
on her face, even before she whispered, "Is he here to arrest
me?"

"No, he's here as a witness for you."

"Me? I don't know that man!"

Morgan leaned across Jamal. "I just dug him up this morning.
He was the first officer on the scene. Your boy here did some
pretty fancy detective work, and it panned out."

"What did you do?"

"I think we found Angel's real mother."

"You found her," Noelle paused, mouth open. "She wants
her back, doesn't she, Jamal?"

"It's not that simple, Noelle."

They sat watching as the court reporter began to arrange her
equipment for the hearing. A little gray-haired man came in
with a small tape recorder and several small microphones which
he positioned around the table. Minnie Raymond cleared her
throat, and leaned forward importantly to inspect the nearest
one as the little man departed.

"She wants her back, doesn't she?" *I know I would.*

"Like he said, it's not that simple. There was an accident that
day," Morgan began. Sensing good gossip, Pat eased to the edge
of her chair, leaning forward to hear better.

Jamal picked up the thread of the story. "Apparently a woman and child were crossing Martin Luther King, Jr., Drive near the Westview Cemetery. You know, the street where traffic comes off the highway."

"Hightower, right at the stoplight," Pat inserted.

"Yeah, Hightower," Morgan continued. "They were crossing against the light, and the mother was struck by a car. There were several witnesses, but none of them seems to remember seeing a child after the accident, especially one as young as Angel. We got the woman's name from the accident report."

"Who was she?" Both Pat and Noelle were on the edges of their seats.

Before either man could respond, a tall distinguished man with graying hair the color of new dimes walked sedately to the table. His mouth was a tired slash, primed for frowning as he stood looking down at the people assembled before him.

"I'm Neal Wilson." He rested his gavel on the table before scraping back the chair to seat himself.

"Ms. Parker." He referred to his notes, "Ms. Noelle Parker?" He looked in her direction.

"Yes, sir?"

"You are represented, I see, by counsel." Under the lights the man's skin shone like polished walnut, the bags under his eyes tightened as he directed his gaze to Jamal and Morgan.

"Yes, sir."

A tall man, everything about him seemed unusually elongated. Extending his long arms to the table, he folded his hands before him. Noelle noted that no cuffs were visible at his wrists. He looked around at those assembled before him, and pulled a deep breath in through his nose.

*Why doesn't he just get on with it,* Noelle wondered. And, where the hell was Angel's real mother, anyway?

"As I said, I'm Neal Wilson, and I'm the hearing officer in charge of this case, in the matter of The Georgia Department of Human Services against Noelle Parker." He leaned over to make sure the reporter was getting everything. Satisfied, he settled comfortably into his chair.

"You need to know, I'm not actually a judge. Rather, I'm here more as a referee. I'm going to listen to the evidence and decide whether or not to recommend that Ms. Parker ever regain her job, and whether or not she should face kidnapping charges." He shifted in his seat, still speaking slowly for the reporter. "I'll also qualify and approve the eligibility of witnesses for and against Ms. Parker. Do you understand?"

"Yes, sir."

Mr. Wilson then sat back and listened while the case was made against Noelle. The state's representative was a man she'd never seen before. Jamal whispered that the tall emaciated man with the red face was an outstanding attorney.

"But is he any good?" Pat's whisper carried across the rows of chairs between them. Morgan looked over his shoulder, and mouthed something at Pat, who huffed and flounced in her seat.

"Is he?" Noelle's eyes were worried and watching both Jamal and Morgan

The two men looked at each other and nodded before replying. *Oh Lord,* Noelle's stomach rolled, *they had to think about it—and they agree!*

"We've worked with him before, on other cases," Morgan began to sketch lines on the legal pad before him. "He's a good man."

"We've always worked on the same side, though." Jamal held his grandfather's gold eagle coin loosely between his thumb and forefinger. "Roberts is a good man."

"That's even worse. You respect him. Why couldn't he have just been some unskilled jerk," she begged.

Noelle sat listening for the next two hours as Evan Roberts detailed every conceivable on-the-job error she'd made over the last two years. She figured the only thing he didn't talk about was the roll of tape she'd stuck in her purse last Christmas.

When he started calling witnesses, she felt like going over

to the cop and offering him her wrists for the cuffs. The feeling was becoming second nature these days.

It didn't help that Jamal kept patting her hand and whispering that it was alright, that no damage had been done. For the life of her, Noelle didn't understand why neither Jamal nor Morgan objected to the things Roberts was introducing into evidence. Every damning item felt like a coffin nail. Surely, how she handled her clients had little bearing on anything being done here today.

Evan Roberts made her sound inefficient and incompetent, even to her own ears. He made it sound like she bent the rules to help favored clients. He insisted that this was not the first time she'd violated the law. Hadn't she gone to client homes to document information that they couldn't get to the office on time? Didn't she often work odd hours to get every one of her cases completed on time? Everything he said seemed damning.

Minnie Raymond fairly flew to the chair Neal Wilson indicated when it was her turn to testify. Obviously enchanted with the opportunity to uphold the rights of the Sovereign State of Georgia against the wanton assault of a heathen like Noelle, Minnie valiantly swore to tell the whole truth. Glaring across the table, Minnie told of the first incriminating telephone call Noelle made to CPS.

She discussed, at length, all of the regulations Noelle had abused. It was evident that she took personal offense to the lack of responsibility shown by someone in Noelle's position. She testified that Noelle was an ongoing caseworker and should have been able to better manage her caseload.

Minnie suggested that if Noelle hadn't been so preoccupied with stealing children, perhaps she would have been able to better do her real job. She even hinted that it might not be a bad idea to audit Noelle's caseload—just to check any possible fraudulent use of public funds.

Dennis Avery sat fuming miserably. "She's telling everything else, why doesn't she tell that the call she took from Noelle was never meant for her? She probably never mentioned the call to Whittaker—would swear, 'she forgot' if anybody asked. No way anybody decent can respect a woman like that," he whispered loudly to Pat and anyone else within hearing distance.

"I think she's demon possessed," Pat agreed.

"You're being sarcastic, but Minnie's so mean she'll say anything to make trouble for this girl. She doesn't have any evidence so she's just gonna stoop to innuendo and lies. I never have seen the likes of it. . . ."

He would have willingly gone on longer, but the referee glaringly silenced him with the banging gavel. "Mr. Avery, you will control yourself. While this is not a court of law, I can and will have you removed."

"Yes sir." Contrite, Dennis looked smaller. Minnie Raymond just sat there, nodding her head and looking mysteriously vindicated. She was well-satisfied with her testimony.

"That Minnie," Dennis puffed his chest a little fuller. "She just wants to be—has to be—the SOBIC."

"The what?" Pat's head turned slowly to face him.

"She always has to be the Son of a Bitch In Charge!" Pat nodded in solemn agreement.

At four o'clock, Mr. Wilson called for a recess until ten the next morning. Because of the late hour, there was no need for Jamal and Morgan to do more than request their witnesses be sworn in in the morning. Noelle's body ached. She felt like she'd done several hard days work, and they still had to make it past the reporters.

"Ms. Parker! A moment please!" Noelle turned to face the pretty auburn-haired woman calling from the back of the room.

"Lark Allister." She offered her hand and Noelle accepted in silence. "I'm wondering if we could talk. Alone."

The southern lady voice seemed perfectly right in cadence and tone, but Noelle still didn't trust her. She had seen this lady at work on last night's news, and her ego still felt bruised by the commentary.

"These are my legal representatives and friends, Ms. Allister. I think it's safe to talk in front of them."

Lark looked at the tall, attractive men and wondered how the short, chubby woman fit into the picture. This was Pat Stevens, if she recalled correctly—and Lark was sure she did.

Giving Parker her full attention, and seeing her so close to Harris's uncalculatedly protective form suddenly made Marie Doshon's suggestion much more reasonable. Lark fit Parker and Harris together in her mind, and yes, there was a very good chance that Doshon was right. They were well-suited to each other.

Pondering the effects of yin and yang, Lark decided to play it straight.

"I've had a chance to talk with Minnie Raymond. There's a lot of stuff being said about you right now, and not all of it is good. I'd like to sit down, get your side of things, maybe get some film of you with the little girl . . ."

"Angel?"

"They say she's pretty. Very photogenic, and I missed her the last time. You remember, I got there just after they . . ." and Lark instantly knew she'd made a tactical error.

Noelle's face closed emphatically. "No," she said.

"Perhaps you'd like to take some time to think about it, and we could schedule a time." Lark felt herself backpedaling strategically, and the two smug attorneys were enjoying the show.

"I've done all the thinking I need to do, and the answer is still no."

"I'll just leave my card with you. . . ."

"There is one question I'd like to ask, Ms. Allister," Noelle tore the card into neat bits of confetti and folded them back into the reporter's hand. "Which letter in the word *no* did you not understand?"

"You're making a mistake."

"Not as big as the one you're making," Pat blurted. "My grandmother used to have a saying; you're from Georgia, aren't you?" She waited for Lark's slight nod. "You've probably heard it, then. 'If you lay down with dogs, you get up with fleas.' If you keep listening to Minnie Raymond, I promise you, you're going to need a major flea dip. The door's over there."

Pat pointed.

Lark's mouth tightened. She had never really liked short, chubby women. "Call me if you change your mind." She turned on her Gucci heel.

"How're you holding up, girlfriend?" Pat as always, was by her friend's side.

"I'm going to make it. Just don't leave me." Noelle held her friend's hand tightly.

"I'm right here."

Looking down at her friend, Noelle smiled. Pat's face showed all the tenacity of an attack trained rottweiler. Noelle knew it would take a small army to move her.

Jamal reached for Noelle's elbow and made sure Morgan had Pat firmly in tow before they began to move. When Morgan's arm swung the door open they faced a scene right out of a bad made-for-TV movie. Minnie Raymond stood, well above the crowd, perched on a shaky wooden chair. Her heavily jowled face, the dull yellow color of pancake batter, glistened with the sweat of a dynamic spiritual fervor.

Her bulky black dress swung to the rhythm of her words as she blasted Noelle and any system that would support her obviously criminal behavior. Clearly, this was her show and she would brook intervention from no one.

"Sounds like she's there to stay," Morgan whispered over his shoulder.

"Let's hope so. It'll give us a chance to get out of here quietly."

"I hate sneaking," Noelle whispered. "It feels like an admission of guilt."

"Then just think of it as leave-taking in somewhat tarnished innocence," Pat offered.

Leading his small party along the wall, Jamal nearly gained the stairwell before Minnie spotted them. She pivoted sharply on the rickety chair to follow their progress, pointing them out loudly. When the chair finally hit the floor, spilling her unattractively to the tile, the reporters were already moving at top speed, chasing Noelle down the stairs.

# Twenty-five

Pat talked with her sitter on the phone as Jamal adjusted the lamp on his desk. Morgan was picking through the remains of a ketchup-stained bag, rooting around for cold French fries. Noelle's head drooped from exhaustion. Pat finished on the phone, and the four of them gathered again around the desk in the den.

"Alright, let's take one final look at what we've got for tomorrow." Papers were shuffled. "We've got the police officer. We've got Mr. Jackson . . ."

"What's the police officer for, again?" Pat was yawning.

"He was first on the scene of the accident," Morgan reached around to rub her back.

"Ooh, do my shoulders." She stretched like a well-fed, contented cat, purring beneath his experienced hand.

"He can testify to the woman's death in a vehicular homicide. He also clued us in as to her name. She was Alison Carter. She had her driver's license in her skirt pocket. The policeman used it for identification. Jamal got the bright idea to check the bureau of vital statistics for a marriage license and any birth records naming her as mother."

"I can't believe that a woman accompanied by a child died, and nobody noticed the child." Noelle's eyes were growing red after the long day. "You never did say though," she added hopefully, "where's the father, or is he maybe an absent parent?"

"Okay. Assuming we have the right woman, I found a marriage license showing Hamilton Carter as the husband. He was a soldier and was stationed at Fort McPherson . . ."

"Here? In East Point?" Pat woke up quickly, shaking off Morgan's hand.

"Wait a minute," Noelle interjected. "What do you mean, 'he *was* a soldier'? What is he now?"

"Deceased. He was lost in action in the Near East. I checked on relatives. Couldn't track down anyone except Alison's grandmother. The woman is eighty years old and in a nursing home down in South Georgia. I still have a query out on some of the father's distant cousins on the West Coast."

"That means Angel's legally an orphan, right?" Pat pulled a manila envelope from her purse. "I didn't want to be premature with this, but in light of this news, you might want to fill these out. I'll take them back for you."

"What's that?" Morgan's straw found the last drop of his soft drink.

"Adoption papers."

"Adoption papers?" Morgan was incredulous. "Permanent? You're not really considering . . ."

Noelle flipped thoughtfully through the forms. "Yes. I'm definitely filing for her."

Drawing a hand across his bearded chin, Morgan dropped his eyes to the papers in her hand. "Noelle, if we can keep you out of jail and clear your name, it'll be a miracle. Adoption, though? I don't know if we can work two miracles."

"Morgan, you're just going to have to try. These have been rough months, and I've learned I care deeply about three people. One of them is Angel. I'm not about to give her up without a fight. And, you need to know it's a fight I plan to win." She turned to face Jamal. "What's her real name?"

"Whose?" He was sleepy, too.

"Angel's."

He pulled a copy across the desk and read, "Monica Renee Carter. She's three years old, four at the end of October."

Morgan began stuffing papers into folders. Jamal wordlessly

followed his lead. Both women sat watching, each lost in her own thoughts.

"Noelle?"

"Yeah?"

"You said there were three people you cared about, and Angel is only one Who else?"

"Pat, you're too nosy."

"You care about you, that's two."

"Shut up, Pat."

"So, does that make Jamal the third person?"

The two men sat silently listening, unconsciously waiting for Noelle's answer. Jamal recovered first.

"You guys had better get some rest, it's after midnight."

"Yeah," Morgan ushered Pat through the side door. "We'll meet you in the lobby at nine sharp. That'll give us time to finalize everything." He regarded Noelle with respectful wariness. "Don't forget your papers, we'll need them to file for custody in the morning."

As the door closed behind their friends, Noelle moved closer to Jamal. His arms folded her safely against his chest and she rested there, pliant and comfortable. Her voice seemed as soft as a caressing southern breeze when she finally answered Pat's question.

"Jamal, I want to be sure you know. You definitely are the third person."

# Twenty-six

Mattie Parker Perry sat demurely on the bench outside the hearing room. Her hands cradled the napkin folded around the pasty cheese Danish she couldn't make herself swallow. The white cotton jacket lay across her lap as she scanned the people in the corridor.

A lot of them were carrying briefcases and boxes of papers. Men and women alike, they all appeared to be involved in something important. A few of them were kind enough, or maybe it was that they were nosy enough to make eye contact with her. One lady actually spoke quietly, and Mattie nearly whispered in response before she found her voice.

"This is a courthouse not a library, and I'm not a child," she reminded herself, sitting straighter. "I hate this courthouse," she mumbled.

More people passed carrying notebooks and recording equipment, and Mattie found herself staring at the walls and over their heads, scrupulously avoiding eye contact. She counted eleven with cameras in hand or slung about their necks. Mattie wondered how many of them were reporters hounding her daughter about this imagined crime.

Which one of them might be that high-toned Lark Allister who asked so many invasive questions on the telephone? Mattie catalogued the passing strangers, preparing to give any one of them a generous piece of her mind.

"Mother?"

Mattie jumped, involuntarily. She hadn't seen her daughter coming. This really wasn't the reunion she'd planned rushing to Cleveland Hopkins Airport this morning. She thought . . . Actually, she didn't know what she expected.

"Mom?"

Noelle stood in the middle of the hall staring at the woman whose features were so clearly stamped on her own face. Standing slowly, as though her knees were made of delicate glass Mattie's hands clutched first at her falling jacket and purse, then reached for her daughter.

Noelle's move to hug her mother was a reflex and conciliatory action. The two women embraced, a little awkwardly, with more warmth than either of them could remember showing in many years. Mattie, in an old familiar gesture, pushed Noelle's hair back from her face.

"You look good Mom. I like the hair." Like Mattie, Noelle found her fingers aching to make contact. Unbidden, they were touching her mother's face and hair, tracing the pattern of the clipped locks. "You never used to wear it so short," she said.

"You really like it?" Mattie patted her own hair, turning her head to give Noelle a full view. The short, graying haircut was very smart. It gave her a flattering and sophisticated look. Noelle and her mother stepped apart, hands and eyes still touching.

"I believe you've picked up a southern accent, dear."

"It's still wrong, isn't it, Mother," Noelle asked wryly.

"The trouble with you Noelle, is that you always jump to conclusions, so defensive. I was just thinking how charmingly beautiful and melodic my daughter's voice is—and how glad I am to hear it again."

"It has been a long time." Noelle found she couldn't look into her mother's eyes, and looked at the floor instead. "Still doing Wednesday lunch with the ladies?"

"Oh, yes," Mattie smiled. "Since you were a little girl."

"Still at the Silver Grille?"

"You've been away a long time. Higbee's is gone now. So is the May Company."

"Not the May Company!" Noelle pouted like a small child. "They had a Hough Bakery!"

"Gone, too, I'm afraid. It's Dillard's now."

"The cinnamon rolls. And the wonderful potato rolls. What about the Spaghetti House, and Captain Frank's on the Ninth Street pier?"

"Still there. Do you only remember your home by its tastes? By the food you grew up eating?" Mattie's eyes were sad, and she wished she had given her daughter better souvenirs of her childhood.

Noelle's eyes again swept the floor. "I guess that did come out of left field, huh? Mom, what're you doing here? I just talked to you yesterday. I didn't want you to . . . I didn't expect you . . . I mean, I'm glad to see you." Noelle's voice trembled with emotion as she closed her mother tightly to her chest. "You look so good to me."

There were a few more lines around her eyes and lips, and of course the hair was different. But mostly Mattie still looked the same. She still had the neat little waistline and the long, shapely legs that had captured Louis Perry. Her eyes were still slightly upturned and her voice was still soft as she quietly murmured her daughter's name over and over.

"That's her mother, right?" Jamal whispered from the corner of his mouth to Pat, as she stood on tiptoe craning her neck and stretching to see better. "Right?"

When Pat still didn't answer, he turned to see her staring and nodding mutely.

"I take it you've never met her before?" Jamal said as Pat continued to stare.

"Noelle mentioned the letter and subsequent phone call she got, but she said nothing about a personal appearance by her mother." Jamal wished he could stop staring, but the startling resemblance was dramatically enhanced by matching tears glistening in their eyes. This could only be Mattie Perry.

"A-hem," Jamal stepped forward.

Noelle's hand reached to firmly grip Jamal's arm as she pulled him closer to her side. "Mom, I'd like you to meet my lawyer. This is Jamal Harris." She felt him stiffen at her side. A quick sidelong glimpse caught the hurt look in his eyes.

"Jamal is also a friend." His face didn't change. "He's a really good friend."

*I'm sorry,* she apologized silently. *Jamal, I don't know what else to call you. I just got my mother back, and you're so precious to me, and still so new. I don't feel right telling my newly recovered mother that you're my lover.*

Lover.

Mattie's attention sharpened to appraise the man who seemed able with a glance to make her daughter's cheek blush and her breathing quicken.

Noelle's eyes found his, and still the words she found were too inadequate by far. *Should I tell her that what you give me is more than the physical? Should I say that you've brought me to a place of stability and support that I only wished for, didn't even dare to dream of, before you? Should I tell her you are the rock that anchors my life? No, none of those things says fully what you are to me, Jamal. You are the man I waited for, the man I've learned to trust, and to believe in, the man who holds more than just my body. My lover.*

Even in her mind, the term was too personal to share. Hurriedly she introduced Pat and Morgan.

"I guess you're surprised to see me." Mattie seemed tentative, hoping for acceptance.

"Yes. Of course I'm surprised. It's good to see you again, but why did you come?"

"I don't know." Mattie fumbled with neat pearls at her neckline as her eyes wandered over her daughter's shoulder. "I suppose I wanted to be with you, because I didn't want you to be alone—this time. I owe you that."

"You don't owe me anything. This is a new life for me, a new set of circumstances."

"But, the past . . ."

". . . is in the past."

"Then I guess it's the past we need to talk about." Mattie sat firmly on the bench, pulling Noelle with her.

"Before he passed, Louis and I did some talking. No, I guess you'd have to call it maturing. We made some decisions. We did some good things—the library council, the Arts Guild, Louis's time on the city council . . .

"Wait a minute Noelle, let me finish. We did some good things together, too. Travel, the homes, and the Lord knows Louis was good to me. But we failed you." Mattie's lips tilted in a worried pout.

"No, don't stop me, let me go on. We did fail you." Mattie's eyes rose to the ceiling in a vain effort to dam her tears.

"We tried to find you after you ran away. Nobody at the hospital had any idea where you went. Louis hired several detectives to trace your letters, but they never came from the same place, and there was never a return address. After five years, I could only guess what you looked like." She pulled a battered sketch from her purse. "This is how I thought you might look."

It was like looking into a smudged, manila and charcoal mirror. Noelle unfolded the drawing along sharply cracked and taped creases.

"Still taking the art classes, huh?" Her mother dropped her eyes to the sketch and nodded slowly.

It was a little scary to see her face so accurately depicted by someone she'd thought had forgotten her, She handed the paper back to Mattie. "Okay Mom. We've covered this. I already forgave you, remember?"

"Yes," Mattie's hand, soft and moist, brushed against Noelle's as she took back her sketch, "but there's more. Your father," Noelle's eyes narrowed suspiciously, and Mattie paused.

"Your stepfather knew he wouldn't be around to apologize. We both knew you deserved more support than you ever got from us." She smiled sadly, "Louis was always good at making money, so he decided to support you in the only way he knew."

"He didn't owe me anything either."

"Stop saying that!" Mattie's outburst surprised them both and her voice dropped guiltily. "We do. We did, and when we looked back over the years . . . anyway, if there's a long court battle you can afford it."

"What?"

"Louis left you a little something. In trust until I found you, or . . . you found me."

"I don't want his money."

"You really don't have a choice. It's not his money anymore, it's yours. He's gone, and it's not as if you can give it back." Mattie smiled as she raised and lowered her shoulders. "Isn't that good news? Don't you want to know how much?" She slipped the long, official envelope into Noelle's hand as Jamal moved away from Morgan and Pat. "Open it when you get a chance."

"Noelle. Mrs. Perry," Jamal's voice sounded stiff, even to his own ears, "I think we'd better get inside, before we draw a crowd."

"Ms. Parker!" The cup of coffee splashed dangerously close to Evan Roberts's sleeve as he and Lark Allister rounded the corner. Moving quickly, the reporter out-distanced the attorney easily. She stopped in front of Noelle.

Unintentionally giving ground, Noelle took a step backward, bumping the bench her mother had sat on.

*I don't need this,* she thought, *not another encounter with this woman.* Neither she nor Jamal had figured out how Allister had found his unlisted phone number, but she had. The woman gave new meaning to the words investigative reporter. She put a hunting hound to shame.

*Maybe I should give her a chance,* Noelle wavered. Maybe Lark really was only interested in telling the whole story like she claimed. She did say that every story has two sides. So, why didn't she tell the whole story last night? She had hinted about the Doshon woman and Jamal. She told about Noelle divorcing Wayne, and if Lark had talked to him, she certainly knew about the Hawkins, Crockett, and Gray fiasco. She didn't tell the rest of it, though.

Last night's newscast flashed across Noelle's mind. The video clips of Jamal shielding her from Lark Allister's aggressive questions, and drawling southern lady voice asking, "Are there any other legal problems you'd like to tell us about?"

Noelle had turned off the television.

*No, she's just a little too comfortable with Minnie Raymond's exaggerationed version of my past for my taste.* No, Noelle decided, she didn't need this.

"Listen," Lark's manicured hand rested on Noelle's arm. "I just wanted to tell you before you went in there, I did my homework on this, and maybe I was out of line before."

"Before?"

"Yes. When I wanted pictures of the child." Lark lifted her head higher. "Actually, when I pried into your life. I talked to your mother." Her eyes found Mattie. "That's her, isn't it?"

Noelle nodded.

"Salty lady." The reporter chuckled as she wiggled her fingers in Mattie's direction. Mattie turned her face away.

"What is this about—really?"

Lark met her eyes briefly, then looked away. "It's an apology, Ms. Parker. I believe I owe you one. I've just been doing my job, you know? Freedom of the press, right to know, and all that. But, the more I learned about you, the more I saw myself in you."

"You mean, you've made some wrong turns in life too?" Noelle's brown eyes searched the ceiling for answers. " 'There but for the grace of God', is that it?"

"No, I'm not gonna go that far," Lark's smile softened at the intended sarcasm, "It's more than that. You could say I got to know you better. I even talked to your ex-husband. What a piece of work!"

"Yes, that's Wayne. A real piece of work."

"You know, I have to look out for what'll make national points for my network, that's my job, and truthfully, your story sounded like it might be a good one. So," she shrugged, "I went after it. Turns out, you didn't do anything all that wrong. Maybe you even did some things I could relate to."

"Does this mean that you intend to stop hounding me and my friends?"

"It means, I'll be watching quietly—quietly—from the wings. I don't believe you have the stuff it takes to be an evil-doer, and you certainly aren't as bad as certain people painted you. I'm even beginning to understand why some folk like you so much. Anyway," the newswoman extended her hand, "I think in your place I might have made a lot of the same choices. Good luck."

Surprised, Noelle grasped the hand and shook it silently. "Oh, there's one more thing." Lark's lips pursed thoughtfully. "I wanna put a little bug in your ear. Evan Roberts is a bit of a rainmaker, but he's a good one. I've seen him throw around a lot of words hoping to hit the target, maybe wash out a few hidden facts. Lot of noise that sounds like thunder, smoke, and fireworks trying to be like lightning. But like the rest of us, he's just a man trying to make a livin'—remember that, an' don't let him scare you."

Lark shouldered past the small, watching group and walked toward the pressroom.

"What was that all about?" Pat blurted.

"She thinks I made the right choices. Some, anyway." Noelle quickly brushed tears from her eyes and scanned the nearly empty hall. "I want to run to the ladies' room . . . You go ahead, I'll be right there."

Mattie nodded, squeezed her daughter's arm, and followed Jamal quietly.

"An apology. I can't believe an apology from her," Noelle mumbled to herself. She shoved the bathroom door with her shoulder.

On its own, the coincidence of the door opening and the flushing gurgle of water would have been unremarkable. Coming face to face with Minnie Raymond as she emerged, tugging her dress into place, from one of the metal stalls changed the circumstances considerably.

"You!"

"Oh, Ms. Raymond," Noelle started to step around her, "excuse me."

"You wish."

"Excuse me?" Noelle had no idea what this aggressively unpleasant madwoman meant.

"There's no excuse for you. None. No excuse for you or for what you did either." As Noelle started to walk away, Minnie strained to get a hand on her arm, fingers clawing to get a grip. "No you can't walk away from me or from what you did. And, I want to tell you what I think of you and your cutesy, clever ways."

"I don't care what you think."

"No, women like you never do. All you care about is getting your own way, looking good, and leaving the dirt for people like me to clean up. But you're going to listen this time."

"You're not making any sense, and I'm not going to stand here and listen to this nonsense." Noelle was moving cautiously.

Minnie's face tightened. Planting her feet solidly on the stained, mud-colored tile floor, she looked ready to throw punches. "Oh yes! You will listen. . . ."

"You're dangerous."

Minnie matched Noelle's backward movement step for step. "Yes, I guess you would feel that way about someone who took their job seriously. People like you get away with murder all the time."

"I . . . I don't know what you're talking about."

"Liar! You do know, but I suppose you think that if you go in there, tell a few lies, blink a few tears out, and try to look pitiful, you'll get off with a tap on the wrist. There's no defense or excuse good enough for what you did. It was irresponsible and unbelievably dangerous. It sets a dangerous precedent, if nothing else. There are regulations and guidelines you could have followed, but you think you're above those. There are places for abandoned children."

"I'm not going to discuss this with you."

"No, you don't have to discuss it with me. There are places for people like you, and you'll have a long time to think about your superiority." Minnie smirked with self-satisfaction.

"My interview with Ms. Allister has been national news for days. There's no place in this country for you to hide. And in there," she flapped her hand vaguely in the direction of the hearing room, "my testimony has already made it clear where you belong. I'm going right back in there and make sure I tell . . ."

"Tell? You're threatening me?" Noelle felt the flush of anger begin in her chest and boil outward. Advancing on Minnie, she backed the shorter woman against the cold, dingy beige tile of the bathroom wall.

"This is a small-minded childish game you're playing. I didn't like that kind of game when I was a child, and I'm not going to let you draw me into it now. You're a cheap, no talent, pathetic excuse for a woman. You need to know that whatever you could possibly tell is of no consequence at this time or any other. You ought to be ashamed of yourself, trying to build a career at the expense of a small child."

Minnie huffed and tried to compose herself. "At the expense of . . . I'm just doing my job! Should a promotion come from my actions, well that's just the reward for doing my job. If you're not guilty of anything, there's no need to bite my head off."

Noelle's eyes narrowed and her low voice shivered with the explosive promise of wrath. "You've got one more time to threaten me or my child, and I'll bite off more than your head!" She turned and walked out quickly.

Minnie couldn't quite control her shaking hands or manage to look innocent as she turned to stare into the mirror.

"Her child," she sniffed at her reflection. "She calls a child she kidnapped 'hers'. She's violent too." Minnie looked over her shoulder to be sure the heavy door was securely closed.

"That took a lot of nerve, threatening me right here in a public place—up in the courthouse. Too bad there were no witnesses. She's crazy. She's just a crazy kidnapper is all . . ."

# *Twenty-seven*

Mattie nervously tried to take in all of the details around her. Hating the commonly institutional room, with its wire-veined windows and heavy, old furniture, she quickly settled herself near Morgan, and the ever-curious Pat. Listening anxiously, she allowed herself to be filled in, and prayed she hadn't communicated her fear to Noelle.

A dark-wooded courtroom was not the best place for a family reunion. Mattie bit her lips to keep from saying it out loud. She had just gotten her daughter back. It would be wrong to lose her now. Unconsciously, she shook her head in denial. It couldn't happen.

Mattie tried to look at Jamal without turning her head. He was certainly good-looking, and with that smooth crooner's voice, he made a striking impression. If he was as good at his job as he was at wearing that Cardin suit, maybe he could get Noelle off after all. Noelle looked at him like she had all the faith in the world in his abilities. Mattie hoped the trust was well placed.

Head held high and breathing deeply, Noelle found her seat at the central table. Jamal leaned close, "what took you so long?"

"I ran into Minnie Raymond, and she promised to eviscerate

me publicly. She called me a kidnapper, a manipulator, and I can't think what all else."

Jamal's hand strayed to his lip, and he leaned closer. "What did you do?"

"I promised to make her think about it."

Morgan slid a hand across his face in an attempt to hide his grin, but it was in his eyes as he glanced at his partner. "Too bad this isn't a criminal trial."

"What!" Noelle's eyes went wide.

"Yeah, then we could declare her a defense witness and make her stay out of the courtroom until it was her turn to testify—just to keep her unbiased, you know."

"Mo, it would kill her. She'd be the first woman in Georgia to unquestionably die of unreleased self importance." Jamal coughed into his fisted hand, trying to hide his own grin.

They both turned as Minnie entered the room. Minnie paused deliberately and stared directly into the icy steel of Noelle's eyes. Her skin grew sallow as she remembered Noelle's promise.

Noelle watched Minnie make her way to a seat on the opposite side of the room.

"I'm glad you're here because I need your strength for this. It's good to have someone strong to rely on. For a change." Noelle's hand brushed Jamal's sleeve. Her breath gently caressed his cheek.

Smiling, Jamal touched her wrist briefly, sending a shower of tingling sparks racing toward her heart. "It's good to be trusted."

Noelle lowered thick lashes in silent prayer. *Thank you Lord, I think he's forgiven me for introducing him as "just" my lawyer.* Her heart clinched at the thought of having hurt him with her carefully chosen words.

Remembering the envelope her mother forced into her hands, Noelle pulled it from her purse. Slipping a finger under the gummed flap, she pulled it open. Sliding the enclosed letter free, she unfolded it. Eyes moving across typed lines, she gasped at the words before her.

Jamal leaned closer, touching her wrist. "What is it?"

Noelle smiled, then bit her lip. Folding the paper, she slipped it back into the envelope. "Call it a down payment on a dream," she said.

He touched her wrist again and she let it remind her of other touches. Knowing Jamal didn't need the distraction, Noelle took a deep breath, and kept the news to herself. There would be time to share it later, perhaps in bed. She felt herself blush warmly, and dropped her eyes to avoid the questioning looks Pat was telegraphing across the room.

Eighty-three thousand dollars. Mattie called it "a little something". Noelle took another deep breath and tried to imagine the kind of facility she could make a start on. The board of directors. Who? Noelle's mind scrambled, dropping people into the slots she now knew she could create. Lark Allister might have some good ideas on where to start, and she certainly owed the favor.

Noelle pulled the envelope from her purse and freed the page, turning it, she read again. Eighty-three thousand dollars, plus accrued interest.

"At this time, with all concerned parties in place, we will resume the hearing of . . ."

Eighty-three thousand dollars plus almost five years interest came to . . .

*I can't count that high.* Noelle barely heard what the man across the table was saying. Damn, she thought, who could without paper and pencil, or a calculator. All those zeros.

Her lip tucked itself automatically between her teeth as Noelle mentally reviewed the budget she and Pat had created for their dream advocacy agency. Eighty-three thousand dollars put a significant dent in the money they might need, and left some over for frills. Silently, fitting the envelope safely into her purse, she blessed Louis Perry's generous apology.

Surely, there were places to find matching funds. Maybe corporate sponsors. If she spent some time in the library, who knows what she might find? And staff—surely the Atlanta University Center might have some recommendations.

Closing her fingers tightly across her purse, Noelle reluctantly returned her attention to the hearing. The hearing officer was moving on to defense testimony. Pat moved to the witness chair, closer to the running tape recorder at the large table, and was sworn in.

She listened as Pat testified. Pat was specific in her choice of words as she detailed the care Noelle had given to Angel and her own children. Facing Minnie Raymond, Pat contradicted everything Minnie had said about Noelle's job performance. Minnie's puckered expression didn't stop her, and neither did the attorneys.

Noelle turned to see how Mattie was taking the testimony. She watched her mother pluck a tissue from the pocket of her purse and dab daintily at the corner of her eyes. She took a deep breath and pushed the tissue back into the little white leather bag.

Pat was still talking.

"It is not my intention to justify anything Ms. Parker did. However, you need to know that she is a conscientious, capable, and skilled individual. In her five-year tenure with this agency, she has consistently proven that she is capable of making judicious and careful judgments. If she judged that child to be less than safe in the company of the Child Protective Services Unit, then . . ."

"Objection!" Evan Roberts dropped his pen to the tabletop, and Noelle flinched. "Evan Roberts is a rainmaker," Lark Allister had said, and he seemed determined to prove her right as he thundered on.

"This isn't a trial. Mrs. Stevens isn't an attorney, and certainly her opinion here is only that—an opinion. There is no need for her to pose a closing statement . . ."

Roberts stopped abruptly as the door to the hearing room

banged sharply open. Noelle turned. The trim middle-aged woman simply stood in the doorway looking into the room.

The clutch of reporters were in a rage of curiosity and constant buzzing motion. Standing on toes and chairs, craning their collective necks, they were desperately trying to make sense of the situation. The little girl in the red plaid pinafore topped dress was almost lost in the intensity of the moment.

"What's happening in there?"

"Who is she?"

"Is she here to testify?"

Ignoring the clamoring reporters, Noelle and Mrs. Dixon found each other at the same time. Noelle was on her feet and moving when Angel saw her.

"Mommy!"

Noelle stopped in her tracks, arms flung wide, stunned by the child's outcry. Each time the child used the term of trust and endearment, her heart nearly stopped. Angel escaped Mrs. Dixon's grasp to run easily across the room, stopping only when she reached Noelle.

Like a quick little monkey, she shimmied her way up Noelle's body, resting only when her arms were tightly twined about her neck. "Mommy," she whispered.

"Who's the lady with the little girl?"

" 'Mommy?' Did the kid call Parker 'Mommy'?"

"Ms. Parker, look over here!"

Determined to ignore the insanity, Noelle angrily turned her back on the screaming reporters and their wildly flashing cameras. A protective hand shielded the child's face from prying minicams. The tall woman's back and shoulders made a determined, camera frustrating shield against the high-held, electronic lighting of their cameras.

A uniformed guard tried to close the door against the determined invading communications force. One last wrist, wielding a microphone, squeezed through the crack just before the door clicked closed.

"I'm sorry." Mrs. Dixon was puffing, trying to catch her

breath, Her brown skin was flushed and moist with the unexpected excitement of her entrance.

"I guess I wasn't thinking," she said. "I wanted to help, and Angel really wanted to see you. She misses you, you know, and I knew you'd be here today. It seemed like a good idea at the time." Her hand fluttered gently, touching Noelle's arm lightly. Her eyes were pleading for understanding.

"It's okay, Mrs. Dixon."

"I'd say that's my judgment," the hearing officer stated emphatically. "This intrusion is definitely *not* okay. Ms. Parker, please take your seat." He frowned at Mrs. Dixon. "Who are you, and why are you here?" He didn't look at all pleased to having had his hearing invaded by a woman, a little girl, and an insistent media.

"This is Angel," Noelle indicated the child, "and this is Mrs. Dixon, her foster mother." Noelle felt like Dorothy facing the Wizard. Her knees felt weak and pretty much nonsupportive. Neal Wilson couldn't have cared less.

"That child shouldn't be here!" Minnie Raymond stood adamantly at the head of the table—near the door. "Her well-being is threatened simply by being exposed to all of this." Minnie's arm swooped wildly to include the roomful of people. "It's wrong to have her here and just another instance of Ms. Parker's self-indulgent poor judgment."

"I had no idea Mrs. Dixon was coming, much less that she intended to bring Angel with her!" Noelle held the child closer.

"A likely story." The corners of Minnie's mouth grew tighter in their determined downturn.

Both Jamal and Morgan were on their feet shouting a number of objections to Minnie's tirade. Evan Roberts sat quietly, observing.

"Shut up!" Neal Wilson's gavel banged lustily. Angel couldn't have cared less as she toyed with Noelle's trembling hand.

"Sit down. Everyone." Wilson was glaring now. "You people are trying my patience. Delete that woman's statement, and let's try to restore some decorum to these proceedings. Where's the child's mother?" He looked fiercely at Mrs. Dixon. "Is that you? Are you the child's mother? Oh. That's right, you're the foster mother."

Mrs. Dixon's hands folded themselves into her lap and began to pleat the skirt of her lavender-printed polyester dress. Her mouth dropped open, then she thought better of it and pressed her lips tightly together. She nodded the affirmative.

Neal Wilson looked disgusted.

Jamal was on his feet and moving toward the hearing officer. He held the file he and Morgan had compiled.

"Mr. Wilson, we've done some checking, and we can prove conclusively that both this child's parents are deceased. We can also prove that as a result of the loss of her parents, the child was abandoned and not stolen." His eyes flicked toward Noelle and the little girl. Neither of them flinched. Evan Roberts leaned back expansively, trying to look bored.

"This child, Monica Renee Carter, is effectively an orphan and has no other relatives. She is consequently a ward of the State of Georgia." Jamal rifled the pages quickly, finding the doctor's report. He held it centered in front of his body like a shield.

"This report verifies that the child has not been harmed physically by contact with Ms. Parker. Indeed, this report indicates she flourished while residing with Ms. Parker. Further, a DFACS-approved psychologist states that contact with Ms. Parker has proven beneficial.

"Because the child was abandoned and available resources were determined unsuitable for a child this age by Ms. Parker, a responsible agent of DFACS, her actions must be deemed appropriate." He placed the report in front of Neal Wilson.

"Uh-uh. No." Minnie was on her feet, hands raised to the heavens, "I object. There is no way. No, this is wrong, wrong, wrong . . ."

"Woman, sit your weary tail down. I've had all of you I can take." Standing straddle-legged, hands clenched at his side,

Dennis Avery, Noelle's former boss, looked like he was ready to go a few rounds with the obstreperous Minnie.

"Frankly," the hearing officer growled between grinding teeth, "I've had as much of all of you as I can take." He turned to the security guard. "Clear this room. I want everybody except Ms. Parker, Mrs. Dixon, and counsel out of here."

"The little girl too?"

"She can stay." Angel stirred happily on Noelle's lap. "Everybody else—out!"

"I'm right outside the door if you need me, baby." Mattie squeezed her daughter's shoulder protectively.

*We've come a long way,* Noelle thought as she watched her mother's back. The dark uniformed security guard forced Pat out, bodily.

"And instruct that mouthy woman," Wilson consulted his notes, "Raymond. Instruct her to keep her mouth shut out there. I plan to make some referrals pending my decisions here today and we don't need her holding any impromptu press conferences."

Standing, the hearing officer turned to his secretary. "Get George Stone on the phone for me."

Watching the hearing officer's exit, Morgan began to grumble under his breath. "George Stone's a Superior Court judge. They don't handle disciplinary hearings. Why would he need to talk with him? And why now? It's not as though he can help Wilson make up his mind. And we're supposed to hang out here and wait while he makes his calls?"

Jamal checked his watch, shoved his hands into his pockets, and leaned back in his chair. "Apparently," was all he said.

# Twenty-eight

"Evan, can I see you for just a minute before we resume?"

Roberts, even after the recess, looked tired. The early morning drive into the city through heavy I-285 traffic had taken its toll on his patience, dug heavy furrows in his brow, and eroded the minimal rest four hours sleep provided. But, he cherished his reputation for professionalism more than the fatigue he was currently nursing. "Certainly Jamal." The prosecutor elbowed a door open. "In here okay?"

"Sure." Jamal followed the state's attorney into the empty office. He flicked a wall switch and blinked as the overhead fluorescents flared to life.

Roberts pulled two dark wooden railbacked chairs forward, indicating one for Jamal. He seated himself with exaggerated care, taking the time to finger the already sharp creases in his pleated trousers. "How can I help you?"

Sitting across from him, Jamal hesitated to speak. "I wanted to talk to you about this case; its ultimate disposition."

Evan Roberts fingered his tie and smiled politely. He was a polite man. Polite prosecutors worried Jamal.

"Really." Roberts said the word in a voice that might have feigned surprise, but was instead fully businesslike.

"Yes. Where, exactly do we stand?"

"We've finally gotten confirmation on the extent of the kidnapping charges, "We, that is the state, are going to prosecute her, and it is going under the heading of kidnapping."

"That's a felony."

"Yes, it is."

"I had a feeling that might be the plan, though it seems excessive," Jamal temporized. "After the court order, what took you so long?"

"I don't know. Ultimately though, it doesn't really matter, does it? I've asked for an early court date—hopefully early October."

Jamal sat forward on the edge of his chair. "What about special considerations?

"Such as?" Evan leaned back in his own chair. "Oh, like the *Good Samaritan Act?*" He shook his head negatively. "That won't work. Her good intentions were curtailed by self-interest. She's as good as confessed to taking the child for her own purposes."

Jamal held his temper. "That's crap and you know it. It won't play in this case. The kid was alone: No mommy, no daddy, no caretaker, no anybody. My client acted in demonstrable good faith, and that's all the *Good Samaritan Act* requires."

"Your client, eh?" The prosecutor fought a brief battle with his lips, and the sly grin won. "Is that how you usually refer to her?"

His fingers were beyond his control as they fisted tightly. Jamal shoved the hand into the pocket of his jacket. "I thought you were a better man than that, Roberts. Above cheap cracks and gossip, and obviously I was wrong. Let's try to maintain a level of professionalism. We're talking about a case here, and yes, in this case Ms. Parker is my client."

Roberts raised an eyebrow and suppressed a chuckle. "Good faith or not, she did it. She took the child, she kept the child, and who's to say whether she would have ever given her up if Ms. Raymond had not come forth the way she did. Your client's going to pay in full."

"That isn't the way things are done," Jamal objected.

"Well Jamal, maybe that's part of the problem. We intend to send a message with this case."

"Message? You want to destroy a woman's life just to send a message." There was no question in his voice. He read the calculation in his opponent's eyes.

Drumming his fingers on the table before them, Roberts looked thoughtful. "I know we disagree on the deterrent value of punishment, however . . ." He shrugged.

"We more than disagree, Evan."

"In this case, we're dealing with a first-time offender."

"Offender?"

"That's right, offender. That is how I'm treating Ms. Parker. It has been my experience that if you come down hardest on the first-time offender, there's very little chance of recidivism."

"Because she'll be locked up! Come on Roberts! Recidivism? That's a ridiculously overblown, useless conclusion."

"Well, I guess that means you've got your work cut out for you. You know what our evidence is, and you know our witnesses."

Jamal grimaced inwardly. Of course he knew. Minnie Raymond, Caren Whittaker, Pat Stevens, and Noelle herself. Disclosure laws required the prosecution to allow the defense team examination access to everything they had. It was supposed to ensure fair enforcement of the law. It was one of the rules, and Jamal knew Evan Roberts always played by the rules. It was one of the things that made him dangerous.

"This is wrong."

"Wrong? We live in a democracy Counselor, and you are fully entitled to think this is wrong. However, the people ultimately decide what the laws should be."

Barely controlled anger flooded Jamal's body with a force that astounded him. What was it about this case that had a power to change otherwise decent people? To give them a vision of things just out of reach, attainable only by destroying someone else? Evan Roberts was somehow different now. Still a good lawyer, but slippery—always in the next room before you got there, holding something back. Roberts's smug, knowing, half-smile told of his confidence, and Jamal wondered what he was hiding this time.

Fixing his eyes on the flag just behind Roberts's head, Jamal took a deep breath and let his anger lead him. He personally disliked the state flag with its Confederate overlay, but knew this was not the time to be distracted.

"Your inference," he said, "is that what Noelle Parker did is a greater crime than service. As counsel for the office of the district attorney, you represent the people, yet you treat this act of kindness as less than an act of good citizenship?"

"Yes," the prosecutor drawled pleasantly, "and the people approve of this punishment for this crime. So, no matter what the outcome of this hearing, we are going forward."

Roberts was enjoying the moment, already hearing how the story would sound over drinks as he recounted it later at his club. "And, for the record, we're also considering the addition of charges against Ms.—uh, the friend."

Disgust made his mouth taste coppery, like dirty pennies, and Jamal glared silently, refusing to supply Pat's name. Refusing to help in any way.

Snapping his fingers to help his memory, Evan found the name he was looking for. "Stephens, that's her name. Helped out every step of the way, by her own admission. She's an accessory.'

"Then, what does that make me?"

Evan smiled at what he first took for a joke. "Damned lucky. Couldn't quite make things stick this time, ol' boy; and don't think I didn't try. You're Teflon in this case—only because you and your partner did things by the book."

The prosecutor leaned back so far his chair squeaked in protest. Standing, Jamal looked down at his lanky adversary. "The people" had nothing to do with this case and now they both knew it. It was strictly a matter of media coverage, and one more notch in Roberts's win column.

"Too bad your client didn't consult with you first. You make a good argument." Roberts grinned widely. You are a good lawyer—know your stuff, I'll give you that too. Y'ever think of politics?"

"I think of them all the time," Jamal said softly. "Too dirty a game, and yet it goes on."

"Yeah. Well, some of us need the work."

Only last night Jamal recalled, he and Morgan discussed the reliability of the rumors. The word was Evan Roberts had political aspirations, that he had his eye on the state Senate. Last night, the rumors had only been that—tales told around the water cooler. Now Jamal believed. The proof was in the bright glint of Roberts's hungry eyes, and the hard line he was taking for the wrong reasons. The state's attorney intended to use Noelle to build his career.

"I intend to make you work every step of the way."

The prosecutor's smile spread wider. "From you, I expect no less, sir. See you in court."

Jamal barely heard the words as the door closed behind him.

The gavel banged sharply, and all in attendance jumped at its smart report. Neal Wilson wanted to be sure his hearing was at full attention before he began. He had no intention of repeating anything he was about to say.

"It cannot be overlooked or disregarded that Ms. Parker did violate a number of state regulations. In fact, it is my opinion that she came within a hairbreadth of violating a few federal regulations as well, but that's not my jurisdiction, and will be handled in another forum. My recommendation is that Ms. Parker face an official reprimand—no further action pending."

The quiet in the room was first marked by Evan Roberts's sharp exhalation, and the snap of his breaking pencil. Jamal Harris's sharp exhalation ran a close second.

Shifting in his seat, Wilson gathered his notes, tapping their edges together. "Ms. Parker, you are therefore cleared of all state agency charges. You'll receive my written decision within ten days as mandated by county regulations."

Neal Wilson balanced his gavel along his fingers. "Finally, Ms. Parker, you may still have to face criminal charges regarding kidnapping, though that is out of my jurisdiction."

Noelle leaned close to Jamal, whispering, "Does that mean I'm fired?"

He paused for a moment. Incongruously her nearness and her perfume caught him off guard. The scent reminded him of satiny skin and summer rain. Forcing himself to be businesslike, Jamal whispered back. "Pretty much."

She groaned softly beside him.

# Twenty-nine

A brisk wind blew across the broad gray expanse of city sidewalk, hurrying golden leaves like coins of tribute across the toes of her stiletto pumps. It was a Monday of perfect autumn. The crisp days and colorful foliage that New England had known weeks before had finally slipped south to Georgia, and Atlanta was all the brighter for it.

The sharp sound of her stiletto heels beat a rapid tattoo that sounded like drummed victory to Minnie Raymond. The handsome brown-skinned, tan uniformed officer at her side was already waiting when she pulled her Escort into the underground parking lot. He'd frowned slightly, but asked no questions when she said she'd prefer to use the outside entrance. He'd simply offered his arm, and escorted her forward.

Minnie liked being escorted. Especially with the golden dome of the State Capitol building glowing in the background. Her heels clicked importantly up the stairs at the building's Capitol Square entrance. She particularly liked being escorted through the media throng with news cameras rolling, focusing on the drama of her announcements and the splendor of her dedication, while perched on the arm of a handsome man in uniform.

Traveling this fine fall morning with the entourage her cause had gathered, she took pleasure in sweeping through the tall and majestic Georgia State Courthouse doors. With her self-appointed special assistant, Harold Michaels scrambling before her, running point, Minnie knew she looked good. She had waited nearly four full months for this day.

Minnie spent her months of solitary evenings in preparation for this day. Even as she'd written her letters, made her calls, and cajoled and coerced her church members and coworkers to follow her lead, she'd believed as only a true believer can that this day would come. Both movement and testimony had been practiced and choreographed before mirrors in her home, and she knew she was ready.

Cruising past reporters through the tiled and marbled corridors, she lifted her hands in a vague conciliatory gesture of patient forbearance, fending off their questions. She had no time to cater to the imprudent curiosity of noisy rabble.

Soon enough, she estimated, Harold would field the calls that would bring about an orchestrated press conference where Minnie herself would stand under hot television lights and announce the triumph of justice. And Lark Allister, that fair-weather reporter, would miss it.

*Serves her right,* Minnie thought. *I'm just like the Little Red Hen. I did all this on my own, and I'm going to enjoy it, on my own.*

The thrill of anticipation that ran through her body was nearly orgasmic.

Minnie planned to handle the calls from the State Director and maybe even the Governor, herself. She could almost hear herself accepting the inevitable praise. But what she really wanted was a promotion and the inestimably valuable currency of political support. Not to mention the office and staff she would claim as her own.

Harold pushed open wire-veined glass doors and stood willingly aside to allow Minnie and her escorting officer to pass, then hurried to reach the next door before them. Harold was a brilliant sycophant, even if he was only hitching a ride on her coattails, but Minnie understood. After all, it took one to know one.

Touching her cheek to reassure herself that yes, her carefully applied makeup was still intact, Minnie smiled for the cameras.

In the second-floor courtroom, Evan Roberts held out his hands to her. "Ms. Raymond! Glad you made it," he said, pumping her hand in greeting. "You know Miss Whittaker?"

Caren Whittaker pushed her glasses higher on her nose, and kept her hand stiffly at her side. Minnie sniffed and looked off into the distance. Noting the coolness between the two women, Roberts released Minnie's hand and began to unload his briefcase, pausing only to speak quietly to his young assistant.

"Where will the jurors be questioned? I'm looking forward to the selection process. Is that where they'll be seated?" Minnie wanted to be sure of her audience.

"Yes, ordinarily the jury would occupy those seats."

"What do you mean 'ordinarily'? Mr. Roberts, this is a trial, and there have to be jurors—right?"

"This procedure has already been handed over to the judge, Ms. Raymond. He'll be the only party involved in hearing this case."

"That seems inappropriate to me. More people should be involved. After all, the consequences do affect public policy and the welfare of a child."

"That may be Ms. Raymond, but the decision has already been made."

"Mine is not to reason why," she shrugged. "Well, it only gets worse." Minnie leaned forward, a hand touching his sleeve. "I hear she wants to adopt the child. Oh, yes she does." Minnie nodded.

"Ms. Raymond, I hardly think . . ."

"I agree wholeheartedly. It's absolutely unthinkable, totally unacceptable to consider this woman as a caretaker. She has no character, none at all. Besides, I ask you, why would anyone want to adopt anyway?"

Evan Roberts body froze as he looked back at his witness. "What? Well, some people want children and . . ."

"Yes, but . . . that is, I'm simply saying that I disagree with adoption, period. The whole idea, even in theory, is ridiculous."

"You work in Child Protective Services . . . ?"

"I mean, why take on someone else's problem? Someone else's throwaway child? After all, isn't that what orphanages are for?" She leaned forward, a conspiratorial gleam in her eyes, her voice reflecting her distaste. "You never know what you're getting into with those kinds of children."

Roberts's mouth hung open in disbelief as he faced the dark abyss of the woman's ignorance. Minnie Raymond was not saying that she didn't care for children—though she really didn't seem to. She was saying that she looked at parentless children as so much trash, suitable only for dumping into state-maintained warehouses. Would her next words be a plea for state-sponsored euthanasia? And would she expect him to support her?

Jamal Harris called prosecution of this case wrong. A warm spurt of watery indecision washed through Evan's bowels. Images of his own six-year-old twins flashed through his mind. Without parents, would they fall victim to someone like Minnie Raymond? Like this little girl and Noelle Parker? Indecision cramped his stomach again.

What of his role in this? What if he was wrong? He looked back at his witness and wished she was somebody, anybody, else.

Minnie spouted politically correct dogma, but in her heart she couldn't have cared less about children on a bet. Evan closed his mouth, and hoped his face had not given away his thoughts. Right now, he didn't like Minnie Raymond very much. Fumbling with a button on his jacket, he moved silently away.

Lynn Carson noticed her boss and his shaky movements as he distanced himself from the black-suited woman. "Is that her?" she asked. Evan Roberts nodded.

"You don't look like you're that sure of her now. I mean you were so convinced she'd clinch this thing for you." Lynn too the moment to straighten her own jacket. "You did subpoena her, didn't you?"

Evan lifted a sheaf of papers from his briefcase. That was one of the things he hated about his assistant. She was too intuitive, too observant. "Subpoena? Hell, she volunteered." He looked away as his stomach continued to reproach him.

Minnie crossed her legs before adjusting the brooch at her throat as she scanned the vast courtroom. So, there would be no jury to witness the triumph of justice It seemed a waste. It was bad enough that television cameras had been banned from the courtroom—now, no jury. What a letdown.

Smoothing her black gabardine jacket and skirt, she glued her eyes to the flag and ignored Caren Whittaker while she congratulated herself on her good sense in selecting such a no-nonsense outfit. It was somber and dignified, striking the correct note of sobriety in the darkly paneled courtroom, unlike the frothy little white woolen suit Noelle Parker wore.

Minnie rolled her eyes at the woman's stiff back. How like her, white in October! Nobody with any fashion sense wore white after Labor Day. That stuck-up mother of hers should have taught her better.

Across the room, Jamal Harris seated himself next to his client. Minnie watched as Noelle's hand found his beneath the surface of the wooden table. She blinked to clear her vision then sat forward, squinting to see better. Was the brazen little tramp sitting there with her leg pressed against his? Up in the courthouse? Obviously there was something unprofessional but very intense going on between them.

The slender fingers twined through his, then held, seeking . . . what? Her eyes were soft, fixed on his in a trusting connection that excluded everyone else in the room. It was obvious that the young woman's heart lay in his keeping. Minnie was reminded of an old song that asked, who needs a heart, when a heart can be broken?

Certainly not her. Minnie felt her expression sour at the mere thought of it. Love, hearts, and pain. Didn't they all go together?

All that wasted emotion, and useless heat and sweaty passion, and look where it had gotten her—here. Minnie raised her eyes to the ceiling in disgust.

"All rise!" Air movement signaled the opening of the door at the front of the courtroom. The bailiff entered, making his formal announcement. Minnie tried to deny the energy surge she enjoyed, and sat taller in her place behind the rail. It was only a matter of time now.

The room seemed to draw itself to immediate attention as the elegant older man strode briskly through the door. He was tall, with an athletic grace that spoke of hours on tennis courts and golf courses. Curly, close cropped, salt-and-pepper hair accented his mahogany skin, giving him a distinctive old-money look. He carried a handful of folders under the arm of his dark, beautifully tailored suit, and mounted the bench as though born to it.

"Dear God, Jamal. Is he the judge? He looks like he was sent from Central Casting." Where, Noelle wondered, were his robes? Not that he needed proof of authority, his imposing physical attitude was armor enough.

In spite of her resolve to stand strong, no matter the consequences, Noelle jumped at the sharp bang of the judge's gavel. Her head lifted and she sat stiffer than before.

"Stay calm Noelle. The man is fair. He's well-respected, and . . ."

"And he's got the power to have me locked up right now. Right?"

"Noelle, that's not a factor," Morgan broke in. "You're not going to be locked up."

"Because I'm innocent, or because they stopped making jails?"

Morgan recognized the signs of anxiety. His practiced attorney's eye roved over Noelle's face, her neatly sophisticated creamy white woolen suit, and the capably feminine hands she folded too quickly together. He knew she was showing the strain of this impending hearing, the last step they all hoped, in a drama banking on her love.

"Basically, we're going to prove, to the state's satisfaction that you did not kidnap Angel, that you simply acted as a Good Samaritan, and in good faith to protect her," Morgan encouraged.

"And that I'm a good and stable citizen? I'm ready to have it come to an end, that's all," she whispered back.

"We all are." His big hand covered hers, and his eyes met Jamal's.

George Stone was good at what he did, and he did it using his good-hearted Baptist upbringing and expert knowledge of the law as his two major tools. The Honorable George Stone had presided over this court for more than fifteen years, and in all that time he had learned one solid lesson: Never say you've seen it all. He banged the gavel again.

"In light of the sensitivity of this case, I want the room cleared of all but the principle witnesses, and the attorneys."

"Clear the courtroom? He can't do that!"

Mattie turned at the sound of Pat's breathily hissed words. She already knew there would be panic in her brown eyes. Mattie had come to know a lot about Pat in the few days she'd been a guest in her home. At Pat's insistence, Mattie had flown to Atlanta for what they both hoped would be the last hearing.

"He can't do that," she repeated. "She'll be alone in there."

Mattie patted the younger woman's arm, and pressed her elbow with the other hand. Steering Pat from the courtroom to what she thought of as *her* bench. Mattie's calm determination quieted her.

"He's the judge, Pat. Besides, Noelle is not alone." Mattie Parker Perry seemed sure of her facts as she lowered herself to the bench. "Jamal is in there with her."

"Noelle's always had a special strength, a resiliency of sorts." Mattie blinked thoughtfully, remembering the times that the steel in her daughter's soul had sustained her. "Maybe it comes from being an only child."

"Or, maybe it's the courage of her conviction." Pat smiled slowly into Mattie's eyes. "She loves that little girl, you know."

"I know that. I also know she loves that tall, good-looking man in there, too."

"Oh Mattie, I'm not sure we're supposed to know that—yet."

"It's okay—just don't tell her we figured it out." Mattie winked and folded her fingers over Pat's. Scarcely breathing, both women flinched at the final sound of the locking courtroom door.

Noelle, with Jamal's help, was on her own.

# *Thirty*

The heavy chamber door opened and quietly closed, and Noelle turned to see the late entrant. Dennis Avery walked easily through the room, seating himself in the empty row. His genteel nod was directed at Noelle.

"Dennis Avery?"

Jamal nodded. "He's an interested party. We're calling him as a witness."

"We are?"

"Character only, and only if we need him," Morgan whispered.

"Why Dennis and not Pat?"

Pat's involvement with this case is tainted by her relationship with you."

"And that's a bad thing?" Noelle's confusion was so complete she nearly missed the judge's request. Then, Evan Roberts was talking, stabbing the air with rigidly pointed fingers. He used his hands like extensions of his voice.

"Your Honor, I am the prosecutor. As you know, I represent the state of Georgia. This woman . . ." he pointed at Noelle, and she tried not to slide beneath the table. His hand extended across the courtroom, and he held one finger straight. He tried to catch her eye.

"This woman has been accused."

Noelle willed herself still, refused to blink. Evan watched her face, and tried to hold his own still as his stomach cramped again. Hoping he would make it without embarrassing himself, he turned to face the judge.

"Enough drama, Mr. Roberts. Make your point," Judge Stone said patiently.

"Your Honor, there was a real crime committed."

"So you've said."

Roberts sighed aggrievedly. His perky assistant reached forward to give him a note which he briefly studied then returned with a curt nod. "Your Honor," Roberts pointed again, "the state calls Caren Whittaker.

Caren pressed honey-colored hair from her face, stepped brightly forward, and laid her hand on the Bible before her. She made her oath, and sat waiting.

Evan Roberts approached her holding a blue-flagged folder before him. "For the record Ms. Whittaker, tell us who you are."

She cleared her throat, and leaned forward trying to look into everyone's eyes at once. "My name is Caren Whittaker, and I'm a principle caseworker in the area of Child Protective Services, for the state of Georgia, in Fulton County." She took a deep breath, and pushed her glasses high on her nose.

Evan lifted the folder. "Can you tell me what this is?"

"Of course," Caren said. "After we received the call from Noelle Parker, the agency started proceedings to take custody of the child. Subsequently, we followed up with an investigation of Ms. Parker, herself." She pointed and took another deep breath. "All that information is in that folder. I can give you the form numbers of the individual reports if you like."

"That won't be necessary." Taking his time, Roberts sifted through all the notes, regardless of relevance, playing for time. When he reached the last note, he thanked Caren and returned to his table. Judge Stone propped his elbow on the podium and dropped his chin into his hand. Noelle thought he looked bored

Morgan and Jamal exchanged looks. Jamal nodded and walked toward Caren.

"Ms. Whittaker, I'd like to talk about the contents of thi

file." His voice was clear and strong, and he wore the authoritative look Noelle remembered from their first meeting. "Taken either out of context, or quite literally, what does this file say about Noelle Parker . . ."

"Objection! Calls for speculation . . ."

"Withdrawn," Jamal said politely. Turning back to his witness he paused, then rephrased his question. "Ms. Whittaker, why do you think we're here today?"

"Objection!" Roberts was on his feet, jabbing his finger in the air. Lynn Carson remained at the table paging desperately through the dog-eared book before her.

"I'll allow the question," George Stone said slowly.

"Your Honor! Relevance?"

"I said I'd allow it." The judge leaned forward to peer at Caren. "Please answer the question."

Caren's blue eyes blinked thoughtfully behind her wire-framed glasses. "My understanding is that we're here, that I'm here, to present evidence in a case that will decide whether or not Ms. Parker is guilty of kidnapping a minor child in the absence of her—that is the minor child's—parents."

Jamal lifted the file in his left hand. His right hand, in his pocket, found his good luck gold eagle. "Can you give the court a definition of the term *custody?* "

"Objection!"

George Stone sighed and furrowed his brow. "Mr. Roberts, didn't you introduce Ms. Whittaker as a qualified, nee, *expert* witness in this field?"

"Withdrawn." Duly chastised, Evan slumped back into his seat. Minnie leaned forward, tapping his shoulder. Her voice came as a breathy hiss in his ear.

"I thought *I* was the expert witness!" Evan squeezed his eyes shut and pinched the bridge of his nose as he tried to ignore her. His stomach cramped again as the acid of doubt flowed liberally. His assistant patted his arm in silent sympathy.

"Please answer the question Ms. Whittaker." Judge Stone made a quick note, then settled back to listen.

"A definition for custody," Jamal reminded.

"Well sure, under current Child Protective Services regulations custody is regarded as the care and protection of a minor child."

"Can you provide us with a definition for the term *kidnapping?*"

"Kidnapping is the unlawful seizure or detention of a person, in this case a child," Caren stated emphatically.

"Can you define the term *hostage?*"

"Objection!" Roberts remained seated.

Judge Stone's eyes measured the two attorneys. "I'll allow it."

"Ms. Parker is not accused of being a terrorist, and Ms. Whittaker's skill in memorizing definitions has not been called into question. What is the relevance, your honor?" Roberts was standing now.

"Mr. Harris," the Judge asked.

"Your honor, Ms. Parker is indirectly accused by the state's witness of taking the child hostage. The term hostage has been strongly linked with that of kidnapper throughout this case by both the media and DFACS personnel. In fact, as recently as this morning's news." He took the newspaper Morgan handed him and held it aloft, displaying the banner headline. "The terms, though not synonymous, are being used interchangeably." He turned to face Evan Roberts. "Since we have defined the one, is it not logical to define the other?"

Though his lips did not turn, Noelle felt his smile. "I'll allow it," Judge Stone said.

Evan Roberts sat wordlessly.

"Ms. Whittaker, can you define hostage?"

Caren nodded eagerly. Like a good student, she recited th definition from memory. "A hostage is a person held as securit that promises will be kept or terms met by a third party."

Jamal walked closer, his dark eyes intent. "Based on thos definitions, the contents of this file," he lifted the folder agai "and bearing in mind your status as an accredited and expert witness," he drawled, "is Ms. Parker a kidnapper?"

"Objection! Object, you fool!" Minnie's words rang clearly through the courtroom even as Roberts rose to his feet.

"I want to answer," Caren said loudly. The definitions she had rattled off were part of some long ago training, but she still measured her cases by their dictates. "No. She's not a kidnapper."

"Is Ms. Parker a hostage taker?"

"Absolutely not!" Turning to the judge, she began to shout over Evan Roberts's objections.

"In all honesty, Noelle tried to call me. My home answering machine was out of order and I only got bits and pieces of her calls, but they were there. Her call to my office was intercepted, and she did the only humane thing for the little girl. She took her home with her."

"Everything we found on Ms. Parker was open and above-board. It's all documented in that file. The child was clean and well cared for—right down to the home we removed her from."

"Object!" Minnie nudged Roberts from behind. "That hussy was cohabiting with that man when we took the child! She was shacked up like it didn't even matter!"

"Your honor, the defendant's place of residence is not in question at this time, and we are prepared to present documentation verifying that the child was unharmed while outside of parental control." Jamal's voice trembled with his effort at control.

"Sustained. Please control your witness, Mr. Roberts."

Evan turned in his seat to place a restraining hand atop Minnie's. They argued in heated whispers before Minnie slunk low in her seat, still muttering.

Caren ignored the outburst, and continued speaking. "There are no relatives available, and I think I should remind you of Georgia Common Law. The child's care can be given over to a responsible adult when . . ."

"With him," Minnie cried as she stood and pointed at Noelle. "She was with him!"

Her voice was lost in the cacophony raised by the prosecution table.

"What kind of example is that to present to an impressionable young child?" Minnie's screaming voice carried above the other sounds in the courtroom.

The banging gavel silenced the room.

"There's no need to remind me of the precepts of Georgia Common Law, Ms. Whittaker. And you, Mr. Roberts, will control your witness—you've been warned. If you have no more questions, Mr. Harris?"

"No more, your honor. At this time, I would like to call Noelle Parker to the stand."

Caren Whittaker gave him a wink and a barely hidden "thumbs up" as she left the stand.

Rising slowly, Noelle left the table to be sworn in by the bailiff. Her eyes held Jamal's as she lowered her hand and moved to take her seat. The cream-colored pleats of her suit fell across her knees, and held her attention as he approached the stand.

He'd already briefed her on the kinds of things he and Morgan would ask her. She knew that they would lead her through the events leading up to, and including the day Minnie Raymond took custody of Angel. She even knew what to expect from Evan Roberts, and that at best she could only hope not to sound like an irresponsible fool in front of this man who would decide her fate.

*If I fail now, then I did all that running for nothing,* she scolded herself, hating the echoing pity only she heard. All that work, learning to be strong, she would have done it for nothing. Her vision blurred, leaving her face hot, and her breath coming quickly, just barely avoiding gasps.

Deliberately slowing her breathing, forcing her pulse to slow, Noelle gripped her thoughts, firmly denying her own fear-bred scorn.

She had left Ohio and her life with Wayne for good reason.

and a man like Jamal was only one of them, she reminded herself, looking across the room, directly into his eyes.

Wanting a good life with a good man, on her own terms wasn't foolish, and she knew it. Learning skills that made her education valid wasn't foolish, it was practical. Loving a lost child wasn't foolish, it was natural. None of these things had been foolish when she left her old life behind, and it wasn't now.

Jamal looked at the poised, graceful woman sitting before him. He wondered if anyone else had seen the brief flare of uncertainty cross her face. He wanted to touch her hand, to reassure her that together they would prevail, but that wasn't allowed. Instead, he asked her to describe the circumstances that brought Angel to her.

Her voice was steady, and certain. She forced it to be. George Stone listened silently, making brief notes as she spoke. Certainly, he thought, Neal's assessment of her as conscientious seemed correct. So, why had she thought herself above the law?

"Judge Stone, it is certainly not that I thought myself above the law," Noelle began as though reading his mind. "It was simply that in this case, there were extenuating circumstances that the law did not adequately address."

Evan Roberts rose open-mouthed, thought of his children, and Minnie, the self-appointed vigilante at his side, then sank silently into his seat at a glance from George Stone. His stomach gurgled, and he crossed his legs tightly. Lynn Carson held a warning finger across her lips when she turned to face Minnie.

"Are you saying that you knew better than the law?"

"No sir." Noelle swallowed hard and spoke directly to him. 'Your Honor, what I'm saying is that when you live a lonely life, you are readily able to recognize those left alone. That child was alone before she met me, and she was never alone after she met me. I love that little girl, and I would never have interfered with her custody or her safety."

"Judge Stone, in the five years I was with DFACS, I saw some harsh sights. Knowing that I can never go back to the agency is heartbreaking, except that I have an opportunity to do something better, something more specific for children left in exactly the same sort of situation Angel was left in."

"Oh?" Stone adjusted his position, and leaned forward with interest.

"There is a long-standing need for a proactive sheltering program for children."

"And where do you figure in this?"

Noelle began a skeletal outline of her child advocacy program. She detailed the shelter she planned to build, and the support she'd begun to enlist. She spoke of the legislation she hoped to see enacted, and she never noticed the growing approval in George Stone's eyes.

When Noelle finally paused, she was surprised to find her hands gripping the wooden rail before her. *This is my last chance,* she thought.

"Your Honor, the last thing I have to say is that Angel is different from those abused or unwanted children, even though she is alone. I love that little girl your Honor, and I would give anything to be her mommy. Absolutely anything."

In the back of his mind, George Stone heard the voice of his wife Rosa. She always teased him about crying at sad movies and bringing home strays—dogs, cats, or people. *A big old softy,* she called him. Rosa was right, he sighed.

"I'd like to see you all, with the child, in my chambers, in thirty minutes," the judge intoned. Standing, he barely waited for the bailiff to dismiss the session before sweeping from the room.


He seemed to notice Angel only after everyone was arranged around the large desk. "So," he teased, "you're the problem child."

Angel's bright eyes narrowed as she gauged him. Drawing her body tightly against Noelle's, it was obvious that she ha seen enough strangers to last her for quite a while, and didn't quite trust him.

Judge Stone didn't give up easily. He continued to talk directly to the child until she began to respond. The three lawyers and the assistant shifted anxiously in their seats, wanting to get on with the business of settling their case. The judge stared them into submission, and they grew quiet.

Angel finally began to respond from Noelle's lap. Judge Stone's gentle cajoling earned him a beatific smile. Sensing he'd gained her confidence, he offered his own lap. The little girl immediately hesitated, then looked to Noelle. With a little encouragement, Angel finally managed to climb from Noelle's lap and walk slowly to stand before the judge.

"Would you like to sit with me?"

Angel nodded and ignoring his lap, climbed easily into the chair beside him. She squirmed and twisted until she made herself fit into a corner near him. He let her take her time. When she finally looked up with a timid smile, the judge nodded and began speaking again in a gentle, friendly tone.

"You didn't tell me your name. Can you tell me your name?"

"Angel." Jamal smiled at the obvious answer. Angel smiled back, happy to have pleased him.

"That's a very nice name, but I thought you had another one. Who is Monica?" The judge's face wore an exaggeratedly quizzical expression.

Angel giggled. "Not me. Not no more." Judge Stone's comically raised eyebrows and O-shaped mouth triggered another series of giggles. Pointing to her firm little chest, the child announced, "my name is Angel." Then she repeated, enunciating slowly, "An-gel," just to be sure he got it.

"Do you know how old you are?"

"Yes, I do. I'm three years old." She raised three tiny fingers, then added a fourth. "Pretty soon though, I'll be four years old."

"Did you have a birthday?" the judge asked solemnly.

Angel frowned, considering. "I had a cake," she said.

"That makes you four, then." The judge corrected her finger display.

Reaching tentatively upward, Angel gently touched the judge's nose with her fingertip. Noelle smiled as she watched. She already knew this game.

"What's your name," the child asked playfully.

"George."

Angel giggled again, repeating the name several times. "I have a book about a monkey named George. *Curious George.*"

"Well," the judge laughed out loud, "that's not exactly me."

"How old are you?"

The judge laughed again. "I'm pretty old. You don't have that many fingers. I want to ask you a question, Angel. Where's mommy?" Angel pointed happily to Noelle and seemed delighted by the notion.

"Is that a new mommy?" Judge Stone's tone was still light, but the adults in the room understood where the interchange led. Angel was nodding yes and ready for the next question. "What happened to your other mommy?"

"My other mommy went to sleep. She went away in the 'mergency car and she didn't come back. I got a new mommy now!" She seemed proud of the awed looks her statement had drawn from the adults around her.

"Are you getting all this? Make sure you get it all," Stone admonished the court reporter at his side. The woman nodded, and fingers flying, bent again to her small machine.

Angel had more to say. "Do you know my new mommy? I love Noelle." She wiggled further back into the chair. Her voice was clear and generous. "She's a good mommy." Tickled by her revelations, Angel was smiling warmly again. Then she continued, her voice lowered as though telling a secret, ". . . she loves me too."

George Stone grinned, "I'll just bet she does."

"But that lady" . . . Angel furrowed her brow, and pulled the corners of her mouth down into an extreme frown. She shook her head negatively.

"What lady, sweetie?" Judge Stone was confused by the child's change of tone and expression.

Angel pointed her finger at him to make her point. Still shaking her head, she puffed out her cheeks and puckered her tiny mouth. "You know, the bad lady who took me away," she insisted. Lowering her head, the child epitomized sadness. "She did not like me. Didn't like my mommy either. She didn't like us, at all."

Morgan bowed his head behind his hand, and tried not to look emotionally involved. Judge Stone suspected the hand covered a smile from the big man. "Your honor, I believe she means Ms. Raymond."

"So noted, Counselor."

"Your honor! Really, I must object. This is all highly irregular." Evan Roberts spread his hands in supplication.

Angel puffed out her cheeks in a sincere imitation of adult frustration. She was looking directly at Evan Roberts. "Do you have a little girl like me?" Angel suddenly asked.

"Your Honor, really."

"Answer the question please."

Evan's lips tightened into a single tight bloodless line at the indignity of being cross-examined by a four-year-old. "Yes, honey. I have a little girl and a little boy. They're six years old."

"You love them, huh?"

Roberts rolled his eyes heavenward as the judge nodded encouragingly.

"Yes, dear. I love them."

"I love my mommy too. That's why I cried and cried when the bad lady came to get me. She made me live in another house, and I miss my mommy a lot. Would you miss your little girl and boy if the bad lady took them away?"

He didn't have to think of the answer. He'd miss his kids as much as he'd miss a kidney or a lung. More. Sheepishly, he examined the leather-trimmed desk before him.

"Yes honey," he finally answered. "I would miss them, very much."

Judge Stone studied the child again. He took a deep breath, and nodded with slow comprehension. "Sweetie?" Angel looked up at him. "Would you like me to fix it so the bad, er, I mean the lady can't come and get you again?"

Angel's face lit up. "Can you do that? Can you make it so I stay with my new mommy?"

"Baby," he grinned, "I'm a judge, I can do anything."

Angel's eyes were huge. "Like a genie or a fairy?"

Judge Stone laughed out loud. "Not exactly, but close." He shifted to pat his jacket pockets until he found a small piece of candy. Angel accepted it eagerly, thanking him prettily. He helped her from the chair and watched her take the candy back to Noelle. "I've heard enough. I want the room cleared, with the exception of you three gentlemen, please."

# Thirty-one

The empty courtroom echoed with the tapping of their heels as the women returned. The motionless flag, solemn benches, and the heavy wooden bar seemed to mock them with their mute symbolic justice.

Feeling abandoned, Noelle pressed her hand against her nervous stomach, and wished she knew exactly what was going on in the other room. She turned to look at Mrs. Dixon, who warily returned her glance, then looked quickly away. Whatever was going on, she didn't want to speculate. Sitting between them, Angel patted both women's knees.

"It's okay," she assured them. "George is very nice, and he said he would fix everything."

Ten minutes later, the men returned. Seated at their respective tables, they watched Judge Stone return to the bench. Seating himself, he shuffled through his notes. "Ms. Parker would you please stand."

Nervously she found her feet, feeling only little comfort when Jamal and Morgan rose to stand on either side of her.

"Investigation of this case does show, in spite of all the irregularities, that there appears to be no damage done to the welfare of the child. Under the circumstances, it appears that Noelle Parker's actions have in fact had a favorable effect on the well-being of the child. We've already covered that ground."

George Stone turned to face Noelle fully. "I understand you plan to file an adoption petition regarding this young lady." He smiled as Angel teasingly waved at him.

"Yes sir."

"I am favorably impressed with your impact on this child. Particularly in light of her precocity, and her peculiar situation. I am also impressed with your determination to stand by her without regard for yourself. Ms. Parker, you do realize that there are those who would call your actions laughably foolish?"

Eyes downcast, Noelle nodded silently.

"Do you have the paperwork with you?"

"Yes sir."

Morgan pulled signed copies from the folder before him, and passed them to Noelle. As she handed them to the bailiff, she held her breath and looked at Morgan. His hand brushed across his bearded cheek.

"Does the state have any objections to the submission of this instrument?"

"None, your Honor." Evan Roberts could feel the heated glare without turning in his seat. He carefully avoided imagining Minnie Raymond's piercing stare and mumbled words. He refused to think of the many reasons she would give for not adopting the smiling child who had found herself a new mother.

For the first time that afternoon, his stomach seemed to ease itself beneath his belt buckle. Maybe he would be able to face his own children again, after all.

They all watched as Judge Stone read, carefully turning pages. Finally, he paused, patted his jacket, then looked around absently. "Got a pen I can borrow?"

Looking at his partner, Morgan's brow furrowed in confusion. Jamal recovered first, walking to the bench and extending the pen he'd been fiddling with. Judge Stone turned a final page, and signed the documents.

"This is irregular and still needs a notary, but we'll take care of that." Judge Stone signed with a flourish, folded the pages, and passed them to the court reporter. He gave Noelle a short, two-eyed wink. "Monica—excuse me—Angel will be going home with you today. The bond you share is obvious. She's a very fortunate little girl to have found you."

Noelle felt herself grinning crazily. Jamal's strong hand was the only thing that kept her anchored to the ground. She felt giddy and light-headed, but sat quietly.

Judge Stone's voice echoed in her ears, seeming to come from a long way away. "You will, of course be monitored over the next six months. If all goes well, and I expect it will, the adoption will be official twelve months from today." He rose to shake Noelle's hand, "I wish you and your daughter well."

"My daughter. Did you hear? My daughter!"

Neither Pat nor Mattie knew whether the scream they heard was from joy or grief. It didn't matter, as they forced the door open—directly into the uniformed back of the security guard. Minnie Raymond and Dennis Avery were dead on their heels.

Still clutching Angel, Noelle launched herself into Jamal's arms. "Thank you. I guess I really did need you after all," she half laughed and half cried into the bend of his neck."

"I knew it all along," he grinned.

"Did you?"

"Oh yeah. All along." Jamal felt the weight of his grandfather's gold eagle coin swing lightly in his pocket. Its good luck had held and spread its glory over the woman he loved. Heart still pounding, Jamal heaved a major sigh of relief.

"So what happened, Morgan? After they put us out, what happened?"

"Calm down, Pat!" Morgan had his hands full trying to explain what had happened while the room had been cleared. Reporters, no longer barred from the room, pressed forward, shouting questions as fast as he could answer them.

Minnie Raymond had heard enough. She could feel her anticipated promotion slipping farther away by the second. "This is a travesty. You can't do that! Surely there's someone we can appeal to? You can't reward someone for breaking the law! That child . . . that woman . . . I tell you this is a travesty and a sin before God."

"Ms. Raymond, a decision has been reached." Evan Roberts said slowly.

"Oh, this can't be! Call that reporter, Ms. Allister. She's got proof that she," Minnie pointed angrily at Noelle across the room, "she's unfit to raise a child. That reporter has proof!"

"We've resolved those charges as of today."

"No!" Minnie's shriek silenced the noisy room as all faces turned toward her.

"Ms. Raymond!" It was George Stone. "Ms. Raymond, according to the Georgia State Employment manual, which we know you respect and adhere to, you are no longer necessary to any hearings here." He looked pointedly at his watch. "Unless you are on official leave, you are due back at your desk. Now."

Minnie looked like she'd swallowed a mouthful of ground glass. Drawing herself up proudly, she gathered her withering dreams of significance. Stalking silently from the hearing room and down the hall, her overly high heeled shoes could be heard scraping and clacking over the tiled floor.

"Is it true the judge consented to adoption of the little girl?" The shouted question caused her back to stiffen as her steps slowed. Reporters and camera operators magically appeared in her path. "Ms. Raymond, will there be any appeals on this case?"

"Appeals," Minnie snorted. "This case has no appeal of any sort." She shoved rudely past the phalanx of reporters and found herself alone. Her throng of supporters had disintegrated. There was no need for her to be escorted into the ignominy of defeat.

"Good job, your highness," Pat cheered from the corner.

"Careful madame," intoned Judge Stone. "You, too, can be banished to your office."

Noelle would never know if her laughter sprang from the sheer joy of the moment, or from the relief she felt at knowing she and Angel would not be separated. Whatever the reason

Noelle loved it! She couldn't help laughing, which of course set everyone else off.

"Everybody's happy," Angel sang, taking Mrs. Dixon's hand.

"This isn't perfect, you know. You did lose your job," Jamal whispered.

"The only thing I lost was the battle. I won the war, and I have a plan. I know where I'm going." Noelle couldn't help her soft laughter any more than she could control the luminous glow of her eyes, and she didn't want to.

Freedom, Jamal knew, was a heady thing.

"Jamal?" The tap on his shoulder turned Jamal to face Evan Roberts and his extended hand.

"I, uh, gave some thought to what you said. You presented a good argument. In the final analysis, I have to agree with your assessment. Ms. Parker is not exactly the textbook version of an offender. Maybe I got a little caught up in the moment on this one. If the situation had been different, if it had been my kids abandoned on the street, I can't think of anyone better to rescue them than Ms. Parker. Seems the law did its job, and the best man won, eh?"

"Thank you, Evan. Until next time?" Jamal graciously gripped the offered hand.

"I know you said politics was a dirty game, but maybe you ought to think about it. There's always room for a good man who knows the law."

"But, then, where would you work?" Jamal grinned, and shook his head. "I think I'm best off where I am. Besides, I like what I do."

"Just remember, the offer's on the table," the prosecutor said before he walked away with his assistant at his heels.

"What do you make of that?"

Looking up into his eyes, Noelle shrugged airily. "Let him go. I'm glad I had the best man on my side The way I figure it, I was looking for a job when I came to DFACS, and now I'm no longer looking. I'm at peace—at rest, and I'm with you. It feels like I've finally come to the place in this world where I was always meant to be, to do the things I was always meant to do.

"You've seen the proposal, the dream scheme. With the money my stepfather left me, I have the means to put my plan into action. That Child Advocacy program we talked about? It's about to become reality. Volunteers are lining up. Caren has even offered to work with us. I've found an affordable space. Pat and I have the proposal finished and I'm presenting it to corporate sponsors next week. The best part though, is the payback."

"Payback?" Jamal frowned. "What payback?"

"Lark Allister. I've already contacted Peyton Communications, and asked for her as our liaison person, though I'm sure she'd prefer to be referred to as a media consultant. They called back this morning. We got her."

"So Lark will do charitable penance." He shook his head. "You know, you're an evil wench. Beautiful, sinfully sexy, but so very . . ."

"Such flattery, sir. Remember, penance is good for the soul." Noelle danced delightedly on her toes to brush a too fleeting kiss at his cheek.

"And Minnie Raymond?"

"Not my problem. I won all the prizes in this game, Jamal. I got a piece of me for myself—don't ask me to explain. I got Angel, and I got you. And maybe in time, I'll get those Kodak moments too." Noelle gave him her radiant, and exclusive smile. She looked around at her supporters. "I'm hungry and I'm free. Lunch is on me!"

"Hey wait," Jamal's hand tightened on her arm. "You're going to be looking for matching funds for that center—remember? You can't afford to splurge treating large groups of people to free meals. Lunch is on me."

"But, you can't do that either," Noelle protested defiantly. "I still owe you legal fees."

"How about if I pay for the lunch and take my fees out in a trade?"

"Trade? Tell me exactly what trade entails," she asked coyly tilting her head to get a better look at him. "I'm not sure it's something I should get involved in."

Her flirting look was doing its job. He had to clear his throat twice before he could answer. "Darlin'," Jamal drawled, turning her away from the celebrating crowd. "I've been thinking a lot lately. I've been thinking about how lonely life was before you. How long I've waited for you—not just someone like you. How lonely it could be without you, and how much I'd miss having you and Angel around. Without you, there's no music, no rainbows, no bluebirds."

"No flowers, no poetry, no romance?" She remembered her stack of BJ—Before Jamal—romance novels.

"Would you take me seriously if I was saying this on one knee?"

"What are you saying?" Her fingers found his lips as she held her breath.

Jamal felt the weight of the Gold Eagle resting heavily in his pocket. Its luck had brought this woman—this woman he'd waited for—into his life and made him strong enough to hold her there. He only wondered if it was strong enough to give him the words that would win her heart for a lifetime. Thinking, too, of his father, Jamal's fears dissolved. His heart knew the words—all of them.

"I'm saying I don't like the idea of living without you." He arched an eyebrow and stepped just a little closer to Noelle, ignoring the flash of cameras, and the jumble of querying voices. Folding her into arms that had waited all day to hold her, Jamal knew the words he had waited to say.

"I'm saying I want some Kodak moments, too. I'm willing to trade my carefree swinging singles lifestyle in for a long-term, contractual, mutually exclusive commitment with a loving woman. Like you?"

Embarrassed and excited by his words, Noelle felt herself hesitate. "That sounds fair. About how long do you think such a contract might last?"

"Oh, a long time." His voice was husky and emotional. "I

told you before, I'm in this with you for the long haul. I intend to collect on this debt if it takes the rest of our lives. So, I figure our contract ought to be good for a minimum of fifty years." He dropped a light kiss to waiting lips, "with an option for another fifty years."

Noelle felt the smile spread as she remembered her long ago lonely wishes for at least fifty years of Kodak moments. "There has to be an expansion clause."

"Absolutely," he agreed cheerfully. "We'll start with Angel, and make her the general manager big sister."

"In charge of at least two siblings?"

"You're a tough negotiator, but a fair one," Jamal whispered.

"I want to hear you say that when she hits puberty."

"I hear that's a tough stage, but we'll handle it together. Always together."

"Is there such a thing as refalling in love? You know I'm kind of new at this happily ever after stuff," Noelle teased.

"But, it's worth a shot, isn't it?"

"Absolutely," Noelle agreed. In the gentle enclosure of his arms, she felt herself falling warmly and securely in love with Jamal all over again. She knew he'd be where ever she needed him to be, and that he'd be man enough to let her stand beside him.

His hands at her shoulders were as firm as the resolve in his voice, and as reassuring as the light shining beneath his hooded lids. The love in his hands had long since slipped the rough mantle of Noelle's troubled past easily, and forever away. His eyes told her only that she completed the equation he'd struggled all his adult life to fulfill.

Her instincts had been right about him from the very beginning. He was not a man to trifle with. Nor was he a man to doub and fear. He was a man to love—for a very long time. Her han closed over his in loving semblance of a handshake.

"It's a deal then."

# *Epilogue*

Pat subtly shifted from foot to foot. The pink satin slippers were pinching her toes like crazy as she stood next to Noelle.

Mattie Parker Perry sat in the center of the pew on the front row dabbing her eyes with a frivolous white lace hankie. Dennis Avery sat stiffly beside her, holding her fingers in his. Sniffing bravely, Mattie held her head high. The tremulous little smile never faded from her lips, and the tears continued to pool in her eyes.

What does she have to cry about, Pat wondered? Mattie has a charming new granddaughter and a handsome new son-in-law who truly loves her daughter. She and her daughter worked their way through a lot of old emotional baggage, only to find each other in the end. From the way Dennis was holding the lady's hand, could be she was holding his attention, too. Maybe Mattie was crying tears of joy.

Pat stood taller, and tried to look attentive. After all, that was what you did if you were matron of honor in your best friend's wedding. It wouldn't do to miss hearing the words and promises she'd agonized over. Noelle's vows were beautiful and well thought out, though it had taken weeks to find the right words, even after she declined Pat's libidinous suggestions.

She insisted on having exactly the right words to convey her feelings to her new husband. Invited guests and anybody else listening were just incidental to her passionate declaration of love and commitment.

And, oh but the woman was stubborn. "The first time, I only said I do, Pat. And then, I proceeded to do everything wrong. This time, I have the right feelings about the right man, and I'm going to have the right words, too."

"What about the right dress?" Pat had laughed, then caught herself when she saw her friend's eyes. The fiercely adamant look on her face more than underlined Noelle's sincerity, and Pat knew better than to argue.

Listening in her tight shoes, Pat admitted the girl had a point. Lighting the unity candle was only the first step on the path of trust her friend was now willing to walk with a man who had bravely sought a woman—a special woman—exactly like her. Noelle's words expressed the triumph of her found love and learned faith over the pain and fear of her past. Pat watched as Noelle, eyes shining, voice clear, placed her hand in Jamal's, and recited her vows.

"I stand not just before God and this company, but before any who would ask, and all who would know to declare my love, my passion, my faith, and my hope—all that I give you willingly. Jamal, you have found ways to open doors I thought forever closed, and helped me to build the strength to learn to look beyond them. With you, I have learned the meaning of helpmate, of walking beside, not walking behind. I look only forward to passing through this life with you.

"In words taken from the Book of Ruth, '. . . wither thou goest, I will go; and where thou lodgest, I will lodge: thy people shall be my people and thy God my God.'

'Where thou diest, will I die, and there will I be buried: the LORD do so to me, and more also, if ought but death part thee and me.' "

Ummm, she just made you want to hum along—sing Halle-lujah, Pat thought, shifting again in the pink satin pumps. The girl had a way with words, but the poetry of the Bible, well that just flat out made you think twice.

Noelle's flawless contralto tones rang out, gracing the church with her confidence. Beautiful in ivory silk and hand-sewn lace, Noelle had earned the right to her happiness—the hard way.

Plucking lightly at the lace and satin ribbon festooning her bouquet, Pat cast a sidelong glance at the groom and his best man. Formal evening wear in basic black flattered them. She took a deep steadying breath. Both handsome men, barbered to perfection, the groom seemed locked in attention to the woman at his side.

Morgan looked great in his tux, standing next to Jamal. So capable, and strong, sexy to a fault, and committed—to her. Catching her eye, Morgan winked and Pat dropped her eyes modestly to her bouquet, smiling demurely into the array of pink and white sweetheart roses and creamy baby's breath. She still privately thought Morgan the more handsome and distinguished of the two men. He looked as proud as she felt when Jamal kissed his radiant bride.

Stealing yet another glance, Pat was struck by the forgotten. She'd have to remind herself, she recalled, to ask him about the big gold coin Jamal had given him last night at the rehearsal dinner. It looked really old and heavy, and rather like the one he held in his hand through the ceremony, now that she thought about it. Maybe it was an Alpha tradition, she mused. Brother to brother, something to do with the black and old-gold colors they so cherished. Jamal said something about the coin bringing as much luck to Morgan as it had to him.

Joining Morgan for the walk back down the candlelit, flower-strewn church aisle, Pat's heart swelled again with triumph as she slipped her hand into his. She silently wished everlasting happiness for her friends. She wished them all the traditional blessings that you wished for anybody jumping the broom. Finally, she wished them no worries.

And when she finished, she only wished one other thing: At her wedding, the shoes were definitely going to be more comfortable.

## *About the Author*

Gail McFarland is a native of Cleveland, Ohio, but now lives in Atlanta, Georgia. She has worked as a teacher, a case worker, and A Peace Corps Volunteer recruiter as well as in a residential shelter for abused women and their children. She is now an aerobic instructor and Fitness Trainer. She has been writing and publishing short fiction since 1990.

I only hope that you've enjoyed my characters as much as I have. Let me know what you think, and what you'd like to see in the future. I can be reached at:

Gail McFarland
P.O. Box 56782
Atlanta, GA 30343

# COMING IN OCTOBER . . .

**SWEET MYSTERY,**         (0-7860-0563-7, $4.99/$6.50)
by Lynn Emery
After her father's death, blues guitarist, Rae Dalacour is lead back to Belle Rose, Louisiana to solve a decades-old mystery. She encounters Simon St. Cyr, a link to the past and a seductive man promising to turn overwhelming desire into sheer bliss.

**WHITE LIES,**         (0-7860-0564-5, $4.99/$6.50)
by Doris Johnson
Artist Willow Vaughn, and landscape architect, Jake Rivers, are both bound for their families. When their roads cross, a love to treasure for a lifetime is conceived. But when secrets between the two families surface, their love risks being a casuality of family rivalry.

**FORGET ME NOT,**         (0-7860-0565-3, $4.99/$6.50)
by Adrianne Byrd
Detective Jaclyn Mason vows to find her partner's killer. She turns to his best friend, FBI Special Agent Brad Williams when she discovers she is being framed for the murder. For years, they have mutually shared a secret crush which, when ignited, promises to turn to love. Surrounded by deadly lies, they must find it in their hearts to trust in their love.

**FIRM COMMITMENTS,**         (0-7860-0564-5, $4.99/$6.50)
by Geri Guillaume
Executive of a successful computer software company, Cydney Kelly, is enraged when the company is sold to Daryl Burke-Carter. Her negative preconception of him is reversed by undeniable attraction. When their budding relationship is the gossip of the small company, their every move is watched. What's more, Daryl is suspected of grave business violations. Cydney must save her reputation, the future of the company and her newfound love.

# LOOK FOR THESE ARABESQUE ROMANCES

WHISPERED PROMISES            (0-7860-0307-3, $4.99)
by Brenda Jackson

AGAINST ALL ODDS              (0-7860-0308-1, $4.99)
by Gwynn Forster

ALL FOR LOVE                  (0-7860-0309-X, $4.99)
by Raynetta Manees

ONLY HERS                     (0-7860-0255-7, $4.99)
by Francis Ray

HOME SWEET HOME               (0-7860-0276-X, $4.99)
by Rochelle Alers

*Available wherever paperbacks are sold, or order direct from the publisher. Send cover price plus 50¢ per copy for mailing and handling to Kensington Publishing Corp., Consumer Orders, or call (toll free) 888-345-BOOK, to place your order using Mastercard or Visa. Residents of New York and Tennessee must include sales tax. DO NOT SEND CASH.*

# ROMANCES ABOUT AFRICAN-AMERICANS!
## YOU'LL FALL IN LOVE
## WITH ARABESQUE BOOKS FROM PINNACLE

SERENADE                                         (0024, $4.99)
by Sandra Kitt

Alexandra Morrow was too young and naive when she first fell
in love with musician, Parker Harrison—and vowed never to be
so vulnerable again. Now Parker is back and although she tries
to resist him, he strolls back into her life as smoothly as the jazz
rhapsodies for which he is known. Though not the dreamy innocent she was before, Alexndra finds her defenses quickly crum-
bling and her mind, body and soul slowly opening up to her one
and only love, who shows her that dreams do come true.

FOREVER YOURS                                    (0025, $4.50)
by Francis Ray

Victoria Chandler must find a husband quickly or her grandpar-
ents will call in the loans that support her chain of lingerie bou-
tiques. She arranges a mock marriage to tall, dark and handsome
ranch owner Kane Taggart. The marriage will only last one year,
and her business will be secure, and Kane will be able to walk
away with no strings attached. The only problem is that Kane
has other plans for Victoria. He'll cast a spell that will make her
his forever after.

A SWEET REFRAIN                                  (0041, $4.99)
by Margie Walker

Fifteen years before, jazz musician Nathaniel Padell walked out
on Jenine to seek fame and fortune in New York City. But now
the handsome widower is back with a baby girl in tow. Jenine is
still irresistibly attracted to Nat and enchanted by his daughter.
Yet even as love is rekindled, an unexpected danger threatens
Nat's child. Now, Jenine must fight for Nat before someone stops
the music forever!

*Available wherever paperbacks are sold, or order direct from the
Publisher. Send cover price plus 50¢ per copy for mailing and
handling to Kensington Publishing Corp., Consumer Orders,
or call (toll free) 888-345-BOOK, to place your order using
Mastercard or Visa. Residents of New York and Tennessee
must include sales tax. DO NOT SEND CASH.*